PETER SHIRAEFF

*

FLATTERY'S FOAL

TRANSLATED FROM THE RUSSIAN BY
ALFRED FREMANTLE

NEW YORK · ALFRED · A · KNOPF

1938

TO

MY BROTHER

SERGEYI

PART ONE

PRONUNCIATION OF PROPER NAMES

Bourmin, Aristarkh Sergyeevitch	Bōōr-mēn', Är-ēs-tärkh' Ser-gēē-yĕ'vitch
Chesmensky, Count Orloff	Chĕs-mĕn'skē, Or-lov'
Devyatkin, Semyon Andreyevitch	Dĕv-yat'kēn, Sĕm-yôn' Än-drä-yĕv'itch
Gobyetchya	Gōō-byĕtch'ya
Goubaryeff, Nikolai Petrovitch	Gōō-bä'ryĕv, Nē'kō-lī Pyĕ-trō'vitch
Grishin, Yegor	Grē'shēn, Yĕgg'ôr
Grouzdyeff, Mickhal Mikhalitch	Grōōz-dyêv', Mē-khal' Mē-khäl'itch
Khokhryakoff, Stepan Fyodorovitch	Kôk-rē-ä'kov, Stä-pän' Fē-yôd-ôr'ô-vitch
Klymchouk	Klēm-chook'
Kortsoff, Griska	Kōrt-sov', Grē'skä
Koultyapy	Kōōl-tē-ä'pē
Kourotchin, Semyon Andreyevitch	Kōōr-ôt'chin, Sĕm-yôn' Än-drä-yĕv'itch
Loukoff, Nikita Loukitch	Lōō'kôv, Nē-kē'ta Lōō'kitch
Loutoshkin, Olimp Ivanovitch	Lōō-tôsh'kin, O-lēmp' Ē-vän-ô'vitch
Ouvarovna, Agrafena	Oōv-är'ôv-na, Ä-grä-fā'na
Penkoff	Pān-kōv'
Petoukh, Pyotr Petrovitch	Pyĕ-tōōkh', Pē-ôtr' Pyĕ-trō'vitch
Prokhoritch, Semyon Ivanovitch	Prô-kôn'itch, Sĕm-yôn' Ē-vän-ô'vitch
Rakitin, Ivan Petrovitch	Rä-kē'tin, Ē-vän' Pyĕ-trō'vitch
Sinitsin, Vasil Kapitonitch	Sē-nē'tsin, Vä-sēl' Kä-pē-tän'itch
Sossunoff, Vassily Alexandrovitch	Sôs-ōōn'ov, Väs-ĭll'ē Äl-ĕx-än'drō-vitch
Syomka	Sē-um'kä
Ternovsky, Alexandr Egoritch	Tärn-ôv'skē, Äl-ĕx-än'dr Yĕgg-ôr'itch

ä as in *art*; ā as in *pain*; ē as in *need*; ĕ as in *then*; ĭ as in *pin*; ī as in *hide*; ō as in *goal*; ô as in *sailor*; ōō as in *gloom*.

C H A P T E R · I

Olimp Loutoshkin, trainer and driver of trotting horses, sat in his dining-room over a half-emptied glass of tea; his face wore the tense expression of a man who has lost his last ruble and, the first blundering efforts to retrieve his fortunes having failed, yields himself up to grim and hopeless resignation.

Before him lay a sheaf of bills, from saddler, veterinary, and farrier, and a marked race-card for last Sunday; his right arm rested on the table, his fingers clutched a note from the glamorous Saphir, playfully reminding him that tomorrow was her birthday.

The note had been brought by the groom, Philipp, together with the blunt announcement: "Met the farrier again—shouted at me—swears he'll sue you."

Loutoshkin flung his head back, screwing up his eyes; his keen and comely face set harsh and grim. He had left off thinking where he could get money. Such thoughts, which robbed him of his sleep, condensed each morning into a dismal sediment; whence ever and

3

anon welled like a poison-bubble the memory of the fund he had raised from his companions for the sick driver Grishin. At such times Loutoshkin would glance covertly at the race-card, as an obedient hound looks at a bone which has master has forbidden him to touch.

Six hundred and seventy rubles, collected for Grishin, lay in the drawer of his bedside table; today's races promised a good haul if there was high play at the pari-mutuel.

"Suppose I stake it all on Woodpigeon in the first race? That mare can't lose!" Loutoshkin winced. "But if by any chance . . ."

His left eyebrow mounted quizzically; Loutoshkin got up, strode to the tall mirror, and gazed long at his face, which was distorted by a sneer.

"So you're a rascal!" he announced, and repeated the word as though he were painting it in big, bold characters: "Rr-aa-sc-al!"

"But, after all, am I a rascal?" flashed un unbidden thought. "A rascal if I lose, but if I win—a smart fellow and an honest man! Sheer cant and claptrap! And besides, we're all of us rascals. Keeping the grooms without wages for two months, isn't that rascality? Rightly considered, all these notions of rascality and honesty are relative. . . ."

Loutoshkin's thoughts bolted with him down the perilous path of "the revaluation of all values." His brain reeled with audacious maxims, conned in the

4

class-room, out of Schopenhauer, Hartmann, Nietz-sche. . . .

It was six o'clock in the morning. The door creaked, and the groom, Philipp, with unwashed, puffy face and leaden eyes, entered the dining-room.

"Shall I get the mare ready?" said he, and smothering a hiccup, turned from Loutoshkin, like a dog that fears a whipping.

Loutoshkin fastened his eyes on him, rapped the table, and said in a quiet crescendo: "If you—turn up at the stable—drunk again—I'll send you to the devil! Understand?"

Philipp's round beet-red face seemed on the brink of tears. He shivered, as if a cold blast had struck him, and said hoarsely: "What, Alim Ivanitch? I've not touched a drop! . . . May I be damned if . . ."

"Get out, you son of a bitch!" said Loutoshkin. Thrusting his stop-watch into his coat pocket, he followed the groom into the stable-yard.

"Did she get through her feed?"

Philipp spat scornfully.

"Feed? She'd eat the manger if you'd let her! She's half-starved! If you ask me, Alim Ivanitch, you'll get no work out of her; mopish, ribs like Venetian blinds, and . . ."

"But I *don't* ask you," snapped Loutoshkin, and ignoring the salutation of the two lads who were cleaning the harness, he strode on through the stable to the

5

loose-box at the far end, followed by Philipp.

Her rueful head thrust in a corner, the grey mare did not even look round at the intruders. She seemed still more lean and melancholy than when they had brought her yesterday. Loutoshkin's heart sank. "Philipp's not far wrong—thin as a rake and—"

"Get her ready!" he said gruffly as he left the box.

Philipp and the two stable-lads prepared the grey mare for harnessing. Loutoshkin stood by and rapped out occasional commands:

"Lower that bandage!"

"Ankle-guards!"

"Check!"

Piece by piece her harness was put on, as a bride is apparelled for the bridegroom, and the mare sloughed off her melancholy. She revived visibly, and her soft moist eyes lit up. Her ears, twitching like a bedevilled pair of compasses, would shoot erect at every sound, and at every movement of the grooms. A faint thrill darted through her delicate forelegs. Through the barred doors of their boxes the other horses peered anxiously at their new companion, and some knocked their hoofs against the wooden floor.

Loutoshkin was pleased that the mare was so quiet and yet so sensitive; he saw at once that she was teachable and also "game." Like all drivers, he could not abide stolid horses, however fast. When he drove such cattle, he felt like a good trencherman forced to ap-

6

pease his appetite with stale, unpalatable fare.

As he watched Flattery, he recalled the words of the sick Grishin, on whose recommendation the owner had placed her in Loutoshkin's charge: "Keep a close eye on her; she'll be a top-notcher."

In half an hour they were on the track. The vast expanse of the hippodrome, shaped like an oval dish, gleamed and shimmered in the morning sun. The track, sprinkled with yellow sand, was handsomely set off by the lush turf and flower-beds which it encircled. Sulkies flickered to and fro; this was the usual hour for training. Loutoshkin raised his dangling legs and shortened the reins a little. Flattery plied her watchful ears, and shuffled her feet like a ballet-dancer, whenever a sulky met or passed her; and each time Loutoshkin soothed her with a word. The driver Sinitsin, with a high-stepping black stallion in the shafts, now overtook them and, with a swift glance at the lean, shaggy mare, called out contemptuously:

"From the knacker's?"

Loutoshkin answered nothing, but the reins just quivered in his hands, as if he would have struck Flattery.

Sinitsin never missed a chance of gibing at him. The semi-illiterate ex-hackneyman could never forgive Loutoshkin for his education, nor forget that the latter "had been to college" and was the only one of the drivers who went to plays and concerts. "Your lordship!"

he would sneer, alluding to Loutoshkin's birth. This touched Olimp Loutoshkin on the raw; he was the bastard son of the titled landowner Varyagin, who had kept a decayed stud-farm in the Ryazan province. This eccentric harboured a strange passion for the ancient world; all his stallions bore the high-sounding names of gods, and his mares those of goddesses: Jupiter, Poseidon, Black Zeus, Astarte, Grey Venus, Chestnut Venus, and the like. When the dairymaid Marfa, widow of his coachman Ivan Loutoshkin, bore him a son, he christened the boy Olimp and brought him up in his own house. All the incongruities of Loutoshkin's life, since first he saw the light in a cattle-shed through the joint offices of a patrician and a dairymaid, were as if forecast and predetermined by the coupling of that plain peasant surname with the proud prænomen culled from a classical dictionary. Varyagin died in the same year that Olimp, having passed out of the scientific high school, entered the Institute of Mines and began to employ his leisure in regenerating the neglected stud-farm— soon to be driven out by the lawful heirs, who appeared, as if from nowhere, in the form of two dilapidated spinsters. Henceforth his passion for horses ruled Loutoshkin's fate; from a mining student he transformed himself into a driver. . . .

After "turning the mare up," Loutoshkin prepared for a brisk trot over the whole mile track. He pressed his stop-watch into his palm and drew the reins taut.

As if she had expected this, Flattery picked herself up, shook her head as though impatient to be free, and, changing her gait, struck out with indomitable spirit. Still fearing disappointment, Loutoshkin reined her in and watched her action closely; but seeing its buoyancy and the powerful lash of her hind feet, he surrendered himself half-consciously to his growing enthusiasm and, forgetting doubts and cares and all that he had left behind, exulted in his union with the horse, and with a movement so adroit that a strange eye would hardly notice it, gave her her head and sat revelling in her speed. Having trotted the first quarter, he turned back to the start, and with a click of his stop-watch, "cut her loose." Flattery took the first quarter at so startling a speed, almost uncanny in a novice, that Loutoshkin did not trust the watch and dared not look at it again till they rounded into the straight at the half-mile. There was no mistake; Grishin was right: the mare was a "top-notcher."

Loutoshkin quivered; his feet, propped against the bar of the sulky, slid down limp and helpless; sweat poured from his forehead; he heard his heart pounding, a lump gathered in his throat. He checked the mare, slowing her down to a jog-trot. Almost immediately a horse drew level with him—Sinitsin's magnificent black stallion. For some time the horses trotted abreast, neck and neck, while Sinitsin watched the mare intently; then he asked:

9

"Where did you get her?"

"At the knacker's!" snapped Loutoshkin as he turned out of the track.

Philipp and the two stable-lads met him at the gate. Usually Loutoshkin would leave the sulky here and hand the horse over to the grooms, but this time he drove straight up to the stable. Philipp, scenting something in the wind and burning to hear of Flattery's performance, nevertheless rose to the occasion. He asked no questions, but waving the two lads aside, began to unharness the mare.

Stripped of her smart accoutrements, Flattery hung her head and fell into her dumps again. Philipp deftly scraped the sweat from her with a wooden knife of his own invention, dried her with straw, and threw a rug over her. Meanwhile the stable-lads took off her bandages. Philipp handed the halter to one of the lads for the customary cooling walk.

"Wait!" said Loutoshkin.

"Rub her down?" asked Philipp. Without waiting for an answer, he bellowed at the lad: "What the devil are you gaping at? Give me the lotion."

Philipp rolled up his sleeves and began, with unwonted zeal, to knead the joints and tendons of the unresisting mare with a composition of sugar of lead, tincture of opium, and water. Loutoshkin followed him round her, giving orders:

10

"Start higher up! That's the style! Rub harder! Down to the fetlock! Right!"

"Band-ages, so her legs won't swell!" said Philipp. "And look here, keep your wits about you. No wool-gathering when you take her out. I know you, you young oafs! . . . Better walk her round the yard, she ain't safe with you in the street."

"Very good, Philipp Akimitch."

"Shorten your rein, you squinting star-gazer!"

The lad took out the mare. Philipp rinsed his hands in a bucket, wiped them on his breeches, and glanced sidelong at Loutoshkin.

In his eyes, sodden from drunkenness, smouldered a single question: "How's the mare shaping?" The un-uttered words had hammered in his brain ever since Loutoshkin had driven into the stable-yard instead of handing over horse and sulky at the gate. The question was as vital to the groom as to the driver. Indeed, in his heart Philipp considered the groom the more impor-tant.

"A horse's work depends on his condition, and his condition on the groom!" he was fond of saying, but he ascribed his drunkenness to the lack of good horses in Loutoshkin's stable.

"If I had Champion in my stable now—damn me if I'd touch another drop! . . ."

Philipp's round face bespoke such tortured curiosity,

1 1

his wide mouth stood so eloquently open, and a bead of sweat at the end of his bulbous nose trembled so irresistibly that a laugh burst from Loutoshkin. But he said nothing and left the stable, toying with his whip. Silently Philipp slunk after him, like a dog.

At the door of his house Loutoshkin, heedless of Philipp, let fall the words: "Ought to make it in two twenty soon!"

Philipp took off his greasy cap and crossed himself.

CHAPTER · II

LOUTOSHKIN ENTERED THE DINING-ROOM, flung his cap and whip on the table, and paced briskly to and fro.

Hope stirred in him, the unavowed, long-slumbering hope of some success that should cut the Gordian knot of chits, I O Us, and unpaid bills, and sweep him to the front rank of crack drivers. On the great days of the races he had seen the triumphs of his rivals with an excruciating sense of impotence and spleen. His stable, matched with theirs, was a beggarly row of shacks, with a job-lot of second-raters, owned by a tribe of petty turfites. If you gave those horses to the famous American driver William Kayton himself, his bright star would go out, phut!—like a strong lamp with no oil. In his vexation Loutoshkin was often minded to cry out to the delirious crowd of clappers—and the jubilant victorious driver—and the grinning millionaire owner —some shattering home truth, such as "Rich and poor cannot run together," or "Full bellies laugh at empty

13

ones"—that truth which he first grasped on that momentous day when he was told he had no father, no name, no right to live.

"My dear young man, you mother was a dairymaid! . . . You a student! You an heir! Your place is in the stable!"

How often afterwards, when he met some purse-proud owner, was he reminded of that day, of the bitter-sweet, wizened faces, framed in lace bonnets, exhaling eau-de-Cologne and valerian drops, and the pudgy little hand which proffered him a fifty-ruble note: "Take that, my dear young man, for your travelling expenses. God be with you!"

This memory seared and tortured him; and many a rich owner wondered why, in the midst of a business deal, the driver Loutoshkin brusquely cut short the conversation, paled, and named such a fantastic price for training as would have roused even William Kayton's envy, and when the plutocrat expressed amazement, rejoined haughtily: "Though I am only a trainer, that's my price. . . . And I want no more discussions with you, understand!"

With that he would walk off; walk off to some upstart owner and, despising this petty bourgeois in his heart, agree with him for some pittance, and dispute the contests with his old "job-lot," rarely to gain a prize and taste the sweets of victory. . . .

The grey Flattery had come suddenly, like a fairy

14

gift. That she was a first-class animal Loutoshkin had no doubt. Now a new problem haunted him: how could he keep Flattery in his stable? Her present owner was a merchant from Zamoskvoryetchye, the commercial quarter on south side of the River Moskva. He knew the type too well. For them a horse was so much merchandise. They cared nothing for sport; their world was like a coin, two-faced and always spinning, heads and tails, buying to sell, selling to buy. If he went there and then to Flattery's owner, dwelt on her points and pedigree, and foretold a brilliant career for her, that squat, gooseberry-eyed grain-dealer would glean from all his discourse but one word: profit. Tomorrow he would start looking for a purchaser, and as Loutoshkin was not accounted a crack driver, Flattery's new master might at any time remove her.

Standing at his open window, Loutoshkin gazed long at the mare, whom the stable-lad was tending. In her light rug Flattery walked meekly up and down, craning her neck to crop the fresh green tufts, and all unmindful of the doubts and problems of the man who watched her from the little house facing her stable. Tiring of this prosy promenade, she lunged playfully at the lad, whisked off his cap, and tossed it on the ground.

Loutoshkin smiled. He called out to the lad:

"Send Philipp here!"

Sitting down at the table, he dashed off a telegram to the stud-owner Aristarkh Sergyeevitch Bourmin:

MARE FOR SALE BY FIREDRAKE OUT OF PEPPER-
BRANDY REPLY IMMEDIATELY LOUTOSHKIN

Bourmin was a rabid devotee of the Orloff trotter
and would never let a mare of that breed pass into other
hands. This Loutoshkin knew, and he was sure that
Bourmin would agree to his condition: that Flattery
should be left with him to train and drive.

Philipp entered the room.

"Got any money?" asked Loutoshkin. "Send this
telegram—express. And keep your mouth shut."

"Do you take me for a duffer, Alim Ivanitch?" said
Philipp, at once piqued and gratified. "I was born and
bred to this job."

Loutoshkin drummed his fingers on the table and
said hesitantly:

"By the bye, Philya, look in on Semyon Prokhoritch,
try touching him for fifty—eh?"

Philipp sniffed inauspiciously. He stood with averted
head, meticulously folding the telegram. Then he
spoke out:

"No go!"

Loutoshkin's eyes wandered to the marked race-card
on the table. Philipp stole a glance at it.

"What about Volodka?" said Loutoshkin still more
tentatively.

"He'll be betting himself. Before a racc his own
father couldn't squeeze a cent out of him. Not to save

16

his life he couldn't. You've more chance with Semyon
Prokhoritch . . . though I don't think he'll shell out.
Won't hurt me to go, of course, but in my opinion—
nothing doing!"

"Do go, Philya. . . . Tell him by tomorrow—*tomorrow* I'll pay him."

"How much shall I say, then?" sighed Philipp.

"Fifty. . . . No, say a hundred. I'll pay him back
tomorrow, without fail."

A rustling sound issued from the bedroom, followed
by the ash-grey head of his wife Elizabeta. Its querulous
voice whined:

"Going out, are you? Leave me some money, please.
You must know I haven't a penny!"

"I've no money," snapped Loutoshkin, taking up his
cap and whip.

Elizabeta Vitalyevna glared viperishly at her husband. He watched her twitching lips and, guessing the
words that were about to burst from them, smiled
grimly; then when the woman made no sound, but
flounced into his bedroom, slamming the door behind
her, he strode noiselessly to the door, stooped, and
listened. Thus bent, motionless, holding his breath, he
paused for a brief moment. . . . Suddenly his whip
shook in his hand, and viciously, like the tail of an angry
cat, the lash began to sweep the floor. . . . A blow of
Loutoshkin's fist, and the door flew open.

"What did you say? Repeat those words!" he exclaimed hoarsely, advancing on his wife, who stood by the bed with her back to him. "Now then! You won't, won't you? 'Boor! Muzhik!' That was it, wasn't it?" Loutoshkin's pale, distorted face was terrible.

His wife turned round and, eying the whip twitching in his hand, murmured: "Don't hit me! *Don't!*"

For some time they stood face to face. Elizabeta Vitalyevna stared, crouching and fascinated, at the whip.

"Don't hit me!" she said, still more softly; suddenly she broke down, sat on the unmade bed, and started sobbing.

Loutoshkin jerked open the drawer of the bedside table and, snatching up the notes and coins collected for the sick Grishin, hurried from the room.

AT the top of the Bashilovka, the racing centre and its main thoroughfare, the panting Philipp overtook Loutoshkin.

"Telegram's gone, Alim Ivanitch; here's the receipt. As for the other business . . ."

"You've got nothing?"

"Not a cent—wouldn't even listen to me."

"Got any money of your own?"

"*Me* got money? Eleven rubles, that's all."

"Out with it!"

Philip scratched his head and fumbled.

"Well now, I was going to put it on Samurai—I'd have made five rubles! . . ."

"*All* right! You won't lose anything! Take it at once to Elizabeta Vitalyevna; tell her I'm dining out. . . . You've not seen Yashka?"

"Yes, I have. He's gone to Mitritch's."

Mitritch's third-class eating-house, not far from the fashionable Yar restaurant, was the favourite haunt of drivers; here, early and late, they bridged the gaps of work with arguments on horses, drivers, stables, studs; recounted fabulous exploits the track, traced out the pedigrees of trotters, and sipped glass upon glass of tea, that staple beverage of drivers. The keeper of the house, the genial, moon-faced Mitritch, always coatless, with a check waistcoat in the winter, and in summer an embroidered Ukraine smock, would have graced the chair of professor of hippology; he backed his fancy every race-day and was never known to lose.

On the entry of Loutoshkin, who would drive Samurai that day, Mitritch came forward deferentially.

"I wish you luck, Olimp Ivanitch!" he said, as he grasped his hand.

Loutoshkin, scanning the table for Yashka Gouskoff, returned the greeting absently, but Mitritch stuck like a burr.

"Trotting today, Olimp Ivanitch? A dead-sure thing for you, your stallion's in fine fettle! Short odds, I'm afraid; I shan't get two to one against you. . . ."

Gouskoff was drinking tea in the far corner. Loutoshkin sat down by him and ordered cognac and lemonade. Waiting till Mitritch had gone, he looked at the handsome gypsy face and whispered: "Business!"

Yashka's glittering eyes flashed over the adjoining tables. He moved closer. Loutoshkin filled the two goblets.

Mitritch's face, watching them from behind the bar, suddenly clouded. The quiet conversation at the secluded table, between two drivers in the selfsame race, had set him thinking; presently he smiled; an agreeable thrill ran up his spine, the embroidered smock seemed all at once too tight.

The key-word, luminous and pregnant, stamped itself upon his brain: "A deal!"

But after it came sobering thoughts, a train of weighty, and seemingly incontestable, deductions.

Mitritch knew today's program by heart. In the fifth race six horses were competing. Number-one driver was Loutoshkin, behind Samurai—number Three, Yashka, driving Dawn, the sorrel mare. Loutoshkin could not let Samurai lose without risking the discovery of his collusion with Gouskoff. Moreover, Samurai's owner would certainly remove him from Loutoshkin's charge, especially as, in the hands of his former driver, Grishin, the stallion had never lost a race. But without Samurai, Loutoshkin might as well shut his stable; his other horses were a batch of crocks.

"But Loutoshkin's at his wits' end for money!" Mitritch reflected. "He's on his uppers. Philka's been scouring the Bashilovka."

"I can do what I like with Samurai," Loutoshkin was saying in a low voice to Yashka, ". . . leave 'em all gasping. . . . *You'll* be nowhere. Understand?"

"Yes, that's plain enough."

Loutoshkin tossed off his glass and looked searchingly at Gouskoff.

"But my stallion *might not be in trim today*," he resumed. "I'm going to hustle him the first quarter, the field'll be all pumped. After a start like that, Samurai'll want to break. . . . Got me? Now, if you keep your mare in hand . . ."

Gouskoff looked furtively from side to side; almost imperceptibly he nodded.

"Agreed?" said Loutoshkin; only his lips moved.

"Done!" replied Yashka softly.

"Olimp Loutoshkin," pleaded Mitritch, as the latter passed on his way out, "I thought my money was as safe as houses with you. . . ."

His brown eyes darted from Loutoshkin to Gouskoff, seeking an answer to the distracting question: "Loutoshkin or Yashka? Samurai or Dawn?"

Loutoshkin yawned:

"Well, damn it, if I lose, I'll give you your ten rubles back!"

"I can't afford high stakes, Olimp Ivanitch. But I had to back you for a trifle, and I knew your horse would win. I wouldn't put a cent on Yashka. . . ."

Loutoshkin paid for the cognac with Grishin's money. He took out the six hundred and seventy rubles and kept searching in the bundle for a five-ruble note. Mitritch's right eyebrow twitched. He had been sure that Loutoshkin had no money.

Having escorted Loutoshkin to the door, Mitritch went to the table which the two drivers had vacated and sat down, mystified and brooding. . . .

On reaching the hippodrome Loutoshkin sought out the horse-dealer Aron by the one-ruble seats and handed him six hundred rubles.

"On number three, fifth race. Six hundred exactly."

Aron's eyes bulged.

"On Yashka?"

"Yes."

Aron hastily gobbled his saliva and clacked away as if he had swallowed a sewing-machine:

"Six hundred rubles is big money, bless my soul it is. Dawn's never done more than two twenty-three. Samurai'll outclass her, she'll lie down in the first quarter; a fine thing it'd be is she should win, with your horse in the field! Only a fool would think . . ."

"He's not in form," said Loutoshkin sullenly.

"Samurai not in form!" Aron gasped. "Why, only yesterday I saw him with my own eyes, prancing along as proud as Punch, like Kaiser Bill through Belgium. . . ."

"Have it your own way!" Loutoshkin cut him short. "We'll talk later. Number three in the fifth."

"How about an each way bet?" Aron suggested, but Loutoshkin only frowned.

As Aron turned towards the totalizator, Loutoshkin stopped him and, rummaging in his pocket, brought out a few more notes.

"Here's another sixty rubles. Put it all on. . . ."

Without looking round, Loutoshkin went to the dressing-room. On the landing a scrap of conversation caught his ear:

". . . Willow Wand, I dare say. She's a dark horse, and . . ."

Loutoshkin staggered, as if struck from behind. He stopped dead. Before him rose the image of a smart filly, a late-comer to the track, who belonged to the obscure owner V. K. Kokoreff. Willow Wand was trotting in this same fifth race. Her owner was driving her.

Turning his head, Loutoshkin saw on the landing two men whose dress and features wrote them down as touts from the south side of Moscow near the horse-market, fellows that could scent out the hidden purposes of drivers and of owners, that knew the horses' points blindfold and their performances by heart, and drew a modest competency from the "tote"; they were coarse, big-voiced, and insolent; their loud cloth caps,

23

bull-necks, and shaven pates packed the cheap seats, and they hissed like hydras at any driver who chanced to disappoint them.

Loutoshkin's first thought was to accost them and ask them about Willow Wand. Something, at least, he would glean from them. A gesture, a flicker of an eye-lid, would suffice.

One of them was tall and tough, with a close-trimmed, flame-red beard; the other, a stocky, red-faced fellow, in an unbuttoned linen coat, stood strad-dling his legs and plucking at his nostrils.

"She's the likely one. We'll back her for fifty. Hope Kokoreff doesn't let us down, though!" said the tall man, in the same nasal tone as the words first inter-cepted by Loutoshkin.

"I'm with you; on number four, then," said the other.

Loutoshkin's brain whirled. . . . Dawn, Samurai—Yashka and the sick Grishin—Saphir's birthday. And above the turmoil, like a sinister electric sign, riding the fret and tumult of the night—two words:

DARK HORSE

The six hundred and seventy rubles, Grishin's money, were in Aron's charge now, and already the bell was ringing from the judges' stand, proclaiming that the races had begun.

CHAPTER · III

As usual of late, Yegor Ivanovitch Grishin lay abed. Over him hung his driver's panoply: his black silk jacket, green cap, goggles, whip—and under the whip, his stop-watch. Lying there alone, he would stare whole days at these trappings that were so familiar, yet he could never remember to tell Avdotya Petrovna to sew up the split seam on the right sleeve of the jacket. . . . Sometimes he would take down his stop-watch from the wall and contemplate the jerky movement of the hands. The hurrying sequence of the seconds, the relentless march of minutes, called up familiar shapes of horses trained and timed with this machine. Starting it, stopping it, Grishin would gauge the speed of spectral trotters over ghostly tracks—over "quarters," "halves," and miles—rounding the bends and covering the stretches; he watched the starts and finishes, picked fields from famous horses, peopled the course with his own person, by turns becoming driver, starter, judge, spectators. . . .

Enter Avdotya Petrovna. "At it again with that stop-watch? Why don't you sleep a bit?"

"I'm trotting, old lady," Grishin would say jocosely, as he clicked his stop-watch, trotting against time to the Devichi cemetery. "I'm not afraid to die, old lady, but it wrings my withers to think they've no hippodrome up there. . . . If I could only get out on the track just once again, how it would ease my heart!"

With a sigh Avdotya Petrovna would take the stop-watch from him, hang it on the wall, and tiptoe out, stealthily wiping her moist eyes.

When she left him, Grishin would draw his wasted hand along the quilt and, clasping and unclasping the fingers, gaze at it. . . . Time was, and not long since, when that now weak and worthless hand could snap a horseshoe like a chicken-bone or stop a spirited horse in mid-career. . . . How many had passed through his hands! Greys, bays, and chestnuts, vicious and mild, quiet and fractious, they had submitted to each movement of his fingers, answered to every tremor of his rein, and borne him speeding round the charmed circle of the hippodrome.

On the wall opposite the bed hung a huge photograph representing a powerful grey stallion. This was the horse with which Yegor Grishin first entered the track and won his first prize—at Moscow—twenty years ago.

As he looked at the horse, Grishin's past life surged through his memory as one unbroken, breathless race,

26

without end or beginning, start or finish. Not many trotters, but the one tireless phantom Trotter, with steel heart and muscles, whirled him for twenty years round the walled circle of a vast, endless hippodrome. Life, hot and clamorous, flashed by, floated behind, and vanished, reapproached again and again, to dwindle in the distance—but evermore beckoned the streaming path of that unrelieved, unending circle.

AFTER the race Loutoshkin visited Grishin.

"Alimoushka! That's good, that's good!" The sick man welcomed him as a child welcomes a present. He would have jumped out of bed, but Loutoshkin restrained him.

"I've just dropped in for a moment; brought you some money."

"Money be damned! Sit down and be sociable! . . . What on earth have you got there? What happened today? Was William driving? Sit down, I tell you! How did Turquoise trot? She was in rattling good company!"

Loutoshkin took the six hundred and seventy rubles from his pocket and laid the money on the bedside table.

"We've raised a little fund . . ." he began, but Grishin pushed the money away testily without looking at it.

"Time enough for that! You and I know what money's worth! Time enough for that later! Tell me about the races. Did you drive Samurai today?"

"Yes."

"What luck?"

"None."

Yegor Ivanovitch shot a glance at Loutoshkin; his forehead wrinkled fretfully. Thrusting his hand under his pillow, he drew out his race-card, opened it at the fifth race, read it, and scanned Loutoshkin's face.

Yegor Ivanovitch plucked at his sandy peasant's beard and began panting like a baited hedgehog. The two drivers sat in silence. Then Loutoshkin looked at Grishin's face and guessed his thoughts; his mouth twitched nervously as he prepared his answer.

"Was it Yashka's race?" said Grishin hoarsely.

Loutoshkin nodded and, turning away, strode up and down, cracking his finger-joints.

"A-ah!" sighed Yegor Ivanovitch.

A long spell of silence followed.

Loutoshkin walked to the bed and gazed into his friend's sullen countenance.

"Yegor!"

"Well?"

"All wrong, you'll tell me?" said Loutoshkin after a long pause, and broke into a spate of words. "But in my opinion it's *all right!* That's what the bastards need!

28

We soak them, but they ask for it! . . . Win and
they'll hiss; lose and they'll hoot you off the track. How
would they like to be in my shoes! For two months I
haven't paid my men—dead broke! Dead sick of trotting for the prize, with double entry dinning in my head
—so much owing to the saddler, so much to the black-
smith, so much to the pawnbroker. Yegor, I'm fed up
to the teeth! All very well for you to talk, with your
stable full of thoroughbreds, but what have I got?"

"And now you'll lose Samurai," said Grishin.

"He can go to the devil! What can I do with Samurai
alone?"

"Look at me," said Grishin gravely, after a pregnant
silence. "In twenty years I've never once run crooked.
Not once, Alim. I've driven fair. But tell me, how
much *cordon rouge* have I drunk in my day? How
much have I treated others to? Oceans of it! . . .
Yashka! Trotting today, dead drunk in the bar tomorrow, what's honour to him? But you've got a reputation
to make, rep-u-tation, Alim. That'll put breed into your
stable."

Giving the race-card a contemptuous tap, Yegor
Ivanovitch said caustically:

"You've lost. And to what horse? Daw-awn!
Neither sire nor squire to her; four legs and a tail, that's
all! . . . Alim, Alim . . ."

Loutoshkin said nothing. He had no remorse for

29

losing Samurai the race. On the contrary, he felt a malicious satisfaction. When after that race he drove out from the paddock with another horse, the seething multitude booed, hissed, and cursed him; for the first time in his life he felt uplifted above all that yelping rabble and, yielding himself to this sensation, brought his horse to a slow walk near the barrier which fenced him from the crowd, and halted, flinging a silent challenge to those clamorous benches. . . . And suddenly the roar abated, and in the ensuing lull a rapturous voice cried from the upper seats: "Bravo, Loutoshkin!" This cry, this single human voice, riding the tigerish uproar of the mob, he stored in his memory as a gift of price, a tribute to his manhood.

Sitting down by Yegor's bed, Loutoshkin told him the story.

Yegor's face brightened. He smiled with sudden relish, and repeated several times:

"Well done! Splendid! That's the physic for 'em!"

Then, with abrupt severity, he asked:

"How's Flattery?"

Loutoshkin took Yegor's shrunken hand in both his own and gripped it.

"Well?"

"Do you know how that mare trots?" exclaimed Loutoshkin, screwing up his eyes. "She's terrific! Two forty-eight at her first trial. I thought the watch was lying. . . ."

Yegor flung off his blanket and, leaping briskly out of bed, seized Loutoshkin by his coat and started shaking it.

"I told you! . . . I *told* you! . . . And what a pedigree, Alim! By Firedrake, great-grandson of Sologoub's Bountiful, that was grandson of Whirlwind and Felucca. She's a jewel, a pearl of price, Alim! Take my word for it, Yegor Grishin's word, you must keep that mare as the apple of your eye, she'll make your name for you. I've thought it all out. Write to Bourmin at once—no, send a telegram—he'll buy her! He'll not miss a chance of an Orloff, he'll give anything for her! He thinks a lot of you, he'll leave her in your stable, nobody else shall touch her. . . . Scribble a telegram at once. . . . Give him the facts—by Firedrake out of Pepperbrandy. . . . A mile in two forty-eight, you said?"

"I couldn't believe it, Yegor, couldn't believe my eyes," Loutoshkin resumed excitedly. "When I saw it, my heart stood still. Did the half easily at a two thirty-seven gait—easily, do you understand?"

He rose and paced the room in agitation.

"Do you know, Yegor, if I had money, I wouldn't let her go, I'd buy her myself?"

Grishin sat down on the bed and pondered; then he puckered his brows, and looked long and intently at Loutoshkin.

"Wild talk, Alim! Such words are not for drivers.

31

Our sort must be fancy-free; if you get tied to a horse, your hands'll fail you. How many have passed through my hands! But I never dallied with the thought of owning one. Look at *him!*" Yegor Ivanovitch raised his eyes to the photograph of the grey stallion opposite the bed. "I might have bought him, but no, I kept my head. And yet I loved him, with a love you don't find nowadays; it's twenty years ago, but I remember. . . ."

Yegor Ivanovitch sighed and sat brooding.

The shrivelled figure, in its loose shirt and sagging drawers, looked mean and pitiful. Strange it seemed that a few months ago this insignificant man, with the homely face of a Ryazan peasant, could vie with the great William in the shrewd and subtle craft of trotting. Loutoshkin, looking at those glassy, nerveless hands, recalled the words of a certain amateur driver who had purchased a horse trained by Grishin: "He's got such a soft mouth, you've only to touch him. There've never been such hands as Grishin's, and there never will be."

Loutoshkin laid his hand on his friend's shoulder and said with sorrowful tenderness:

"Why did you get up, Yegor? Lie down again."

Once more Grishin sighed, moodily.

"Oh, Alimoushka! Yegor Grishin has done with trotting. Played out, brother!"

As he listened to the hard, unsteady breathing of his friend, Loutoshkin groped in his mind for words of

32

comfort, but found none; it wrung his heart to think that he was going straight from Yegor to Saphir's birthday party, and thence to the Yar restaurant.

"What's that money you've brought?" said Yegor peevishly, as he crept under the blanket.

"Want to get you well. . . . We'll send for a good doctor, and who knows if . . ."

"What next?" Yegor flashed at him. "Doctors, eh? . . . I'm past doctors now! Sheer waste of money! . . . I'm done for! I've driven all sorts, for twenty years I've driven. . . . Today the black, tomorrow the bay, the roan, the chestnut . . . I've steered all sorts, and now I'm in the shafts myself, and going in dead earnest. . . . The home stretch, Alim—and heading for the post— the finish!"

TWO days passed.

On the third all drivers received a brief summons from Yegor Ivanovitch Grishin to "do him the honour of taking a glass of vodka with him."

Avdotya Petrovna tried to dissuade Yegor Ivanovitch, but he was inflexible. He drew from under his pillow the money left him by Loutoshkin, counted note after note, and issued his behests:

"Plenty of caviar—best quality, mind . . . balyk too, from the Okhotni market. *Cordon rouge*, two dozen, genuine Five Star. . . . And don't forget the Madeira for Semyon Ivanovitch, he *loves* Madeira . . . rum for Vaska . . ."

"How much more?" said Avdotya Petrovna.

"I know what I'm about," snapped Grishin, and poured out his instructions till the six hundred and seventy rubles had been transformed into mountains of hors d'œuvres and batteries of wine and liquor.

"Driver-fashion—no heel-taps!" he proclaimed from the threshold of his bedroom, smiling ecstatically as he mustered the array of plates and bottles; then he approached and hovered over them, pouncing from time to time upon some oversight. Again and again he asked: "What did Petya say? Did he take the note himself? Said he's coming, eh?"

"He said he's coming," Avdotya Petrovna repeated for the tenth time, with a sigh.

"He's coming, he's coming!" Yegor echoed. "Who should he come to but to Yegor Grishin! He'll throw up everything to come! . . . I remember once at the Yar, I was having a drop with Alim. All of a sudden we heard Petya's voice in the private room next to us—singing. I called the waiter. 'Send Petya here,' says I. 'No go,' says he, 'he won't budge, Yegor Ivanovitch; von Meck's got a party in there, and he's specially invited.' Well, I and Alim scratched off a note: 'Von Meck or no von Meck, we've got a party next door, keeping it up driver-fashion.' Not a minute passed when, lo and behold, in rolls Petya; all the von Mecks and their money-bags could go to blazes! He knows, Petya does, where his songs are wanted! . . . He'd sing till he made us cry, and sometimes he'd start blubbering himself. Once he smashed his guitar, his heart couldn't bear the pain. There's not a man in Moscow can give you 'On the old Kalouga road' like Petya Rassokhin. I've heard many, but none to touch him."

Yegor Ivanovitch sat on a chair and pondered. He dropped his head on his breast and sat long in this position with closed eyes. Then he brushed away a tear, sighed, stood up with manifest effort, and casting a final glance over the table furnished for the guests, asked Avdotya Petrovna to shut the bedroom door and leave him undisturbed.

"They'll soon be here . . . must get ready for 'em . . . lie down for a while. . . ."

Avdotya Petrovna pulled the quilt over him and went out.

Yegor Ivanovitch lay for a long time with closed eyes, just as she had left him. He lay listening to his own body. Heretofore he had had no sense of it, but felt and heard that which dwelt somewhere within him and gave life to his thoughts and feelings. But now for the first time he was aware of his body, and marvelled at its monstrous weight. Especially his legs. . . . They lay under the blanket, like two iron posts, clinched one upon the other, that no force could move—riveted there by some power for all time. . . . And that iron weight, eternal and implacable, crept inch by inch over his whole body, numbing the fingers of his hands, cramping his shoulders, crushing his head into the pillow. Struggling against it, Grishin moved his right arm, which lay above the quilt, and began to raise and lower it, bending it at the elbow; but when he felt the weight upon his temples, he was suddenly afraid and opened his eyes slowly. . . . To his right upon the wall he saw the black jacket, the flaunting bright-green cap, the huge goggles and whip, and under the whip—the stop-watch. The hands were moving.

Forcing his eyes away from the stop-watch, Grishin brought them to rest on the beloved photograph of the grey stallion. And the old campaigner came down from his black frame and stood by the pillow, with bent head, steely, redoubtable, ready to bear his master.

The right arm lifted and fell, lifted and fell, rose for the last time, and sank slowly and reluctantly.

C H A P T E R · I V

ARISTARKH SERGYEEVITCH BOURMIN,
his nose almost on the table, was eying something on the
starched white cloth, and the black rectangle of his
Assyrian beard was twitching. His housekeeper, a close-
corseted spinster with colourless eyes and eyebrows, entered and handed him a telegram. Bourmin thrust it
aside, drew himself slowly erect, and prodded the table
with a questioning forefinger.

Adele Maximovna flushed, stooped to the table, to
the precise spot where the finger in the broad gold
signet-ring was planted, but saw nothing. The finger
rose and fell, touching the selfsame spot.

"What's that, pray?" asked Bourmin in a toneless
voice.

"I can't see anything, sir. Where?" stammered Adele
Maximovna, blowing on the cloth.

"Move my place!"

Globules of sweat gathered on Adele Maximovna's
forehead. Hastily she moved the cover to the opposite

37

side of the table and made a last, distracted effort to see what it was that had offended Aristarkh Sergyee- vitch. But still she could see nothing.

When she had reached the door on her way out of the dining-room, Bourmin coughed. This signified that he desired to speak to her. Adele Maximovna hastened to his side.

"A fly, madam . . ." pronounced Bourmin, and after a decorous interval, proceeded: "A fly—do you realize that?—has settled there and left its—excrement, madam! And you saw fit to lay my place there! Go!"

Moving his chair up to the table, he prepared to break his fast. Before buttering his bread, he explored it from every angle, then he inspected his butter and his knife, and in spreading the butter took scrupulous care that it should lie in an even layer and that every minute cavity in the bread should be filled up. Having poured out some tea, he raised his glass, held it against the light, and scanned it closely. The telegram he opened after breakfast in his study, which was huge and incommodious, like some patriarchal linen-chest. The back of the unpadded chair was shaped like the high, bow-shaped yoke characteristic of Russian horse- drawn vehicles, and its arms were fashioned like two axes. On the yoke was inscribed in stately characters: "More haste less speed." The seat was embossed with a pair of driving-gauntlets, no small impediment to the sitter's comfort. No less uncouth was the enormous book-case, with its distracting set of sliding doors, which, however they slid, so closed the centre of the case that to take down a book from the middle of a shelf called for much patience and dexterity. Conspicuous above the desk hung a richly framed copy of a celebrated old engraving, which depicted Count Orloff on the grey stallion Leopard, progenitor of the Orloff trotters, and under it a photograph of Champion, inset with his famous forebears: Colossus, Colossal, Whirlwind, Carpet-knight, Coquette.

In the controversy then rife among Russian studowners, Aristarkh Bourmin was a die-hard stickler for the Orloff breed and bore in his fossilized heart a glacial hatred for the American trotter and all those who pleaded for the introduction of American stallions into Russia. On his desk lay the stud-book, bound in embossed leather, in which the foals born in his stud were registered. The first of the Bristol-board pages was illumined with a gold vignette—a laurel crown, encircling the words:

THE FAME OF THE FATHERLAND SHALL
NOT BE DARKENED
THE GENIUS OF THE ORLOFF TROTTER
IS IMMORTAL
ARISTARKH BOURMIN

The telegram in his hands was from Loutoshkin. He read it through twice and deliberated. He had known

Loutoshkin for a long time and closely followed his career. He had good grounds for this. As a young man he had been present at a conversation between his father and a friend and was struck by their recital of an argument between the stud-owner Stakhovitch and certain fellow-sportsmen. Stakhovitch had maintained that he could pick out a stallion and a mare, of what colour they pleased, but without a streak of red in their coats, and produce a sorrel foal from them. The bet was made, the foal was born, and to the challenger's amazement, Stakhovitch won his wager.

This story engendered in the young Aristarkh's brain a thought which had teased him ever since: the thought of the ideal driver.

"To cross a crack driver with scions of some other champion and so in due time to evolve a driver of genius"—in some such words the young Aristarkh propounded to himself the problem. Many times he reverted to this thought after the death of his father, when he came into full possession of the stud; and meeting Olimp Loutoshkin at the races, he remembered suddenly that Varyagin, Loutoshkin's father, was a celebrated trainer, and that Marfa, the dairymaid, Loutoshkin's mother, was the wife of the no less remarkable Ivan, Varyagin's coachman, renowned for his rare skill in driving. Loutoshkin did not understand why Bourmin cut short their conversation, looked at him long and mysteriously, and, turning away, began to write hurriedly in a voluminous red book with a morocco-leather binding.

The telegram reminded Bourmin once more of the existence of Olimp Loutoshkin. From the bottom drawer of his writing-table he took out the stud-book in the crimson binding and, gravely turning the leaves, paused at the note which he had made at Moscow when he met Loutoshkin.

"Loutoshkin: by Varyagin out of Marfa; but Marfa?

"Memo. Investigate Ivan Loutoshkin's pedigree without delay," wrote the punctilious hand.

Of Varyagin it was said that he had only to see a foal to put a sire to it, and that after he went blind, he could name a trotting horse by the sound of its hoofs alone. Varlam Varyagin, his grandfather, was famed as a breeder of borzois and racehorses, and his grandmother had broken her neck out wolf-hunting. The Varyagins were neighbours of Bourmin, and their lineage was soon traced. But Marfa's ancestry was more obscure.

"If only Marfa were a horse!" Bourmin reflected, as he smoothed out the momentous message with his palm:

MARE FOR SALE BY FIREDRAKE OUT OF
PEPPERBRANDY . . .

IN the mind of one unschooled in the mysteries of horse-lore, these two names would have called up, at

41

most, the images of two famous trotters—if he had ever seen them. But not for nothing had Aristarkh Bourmin laboured from dusk to dawn, bent double over his books and papers, glossing them with meticulous notes, setting up the family trees of horses, chronicling the peculiarities both of single trotters and of strains and breeds, their power of transmitting this or that quality to their descendants, and much else. Caged in his vast inhospitable den, Bourmin, like an alchemist in search of the miraculous elixir, traced and conjoined the bloods of sire, grandsire, sister, brother, dam, and daughter, in the stubborn and secret hope of lighting on some confluence of bloods that might flash out in the sparkling tide of genius, as the Orloff blood had flashed to light in the heroic Champion. And this long, labyrinthine study had unsealed for him the names of horses, giving them shape and substance, worth and lineage. Firedrake was the son of the famous Whirlwind, sired by Sollogoub's Bountiful, and Bountiful the grandson of Colossal and the great-grandson of the mighty Champion. . . .

"Who knows but the daughter of Firedrake and Pepperbrandy might harbour in her the fire of genius? Does she not, any less than Champion, possess the maximum of hereditary data for the production of a perfect scion?"

Laying his hairy hand upon the telegram, Bourmin threw himself back in his chair and sat in petrified contemplation of the pageant which defiled before him

—stallions and mare, famous great-grandsires, grand-sires, sires, and foals. And as though it were not passing in his thoughts, at the writing-table in his study, but in real life, at some show or parade, he nodded at each horse appraisingly, and his smile showed in the twitching of the great black beard. . . .

He was aroused by the entry of Dasha, the pretty, roguish wife of the cook Dimitri.

"Ain't you going to take your bath today? Mitri's been waiting ever so long!"

Bourmin looked round at her, took up a sheet of paper, and wrote a telegram in answer to Loutoshkin's:

BREED SATISFACTORY TELEGRAPH CONDITION AGE
OWNER PRICE ARISTARKH BOURMIN

"COME HERE!"—he beckoned to Dasha.

Dasha looked round at the door, giggled, and, waggling her plump haunches, sidled up to the table. Bourmin's eyes travelled over her neat, firm contours, and one spike of his arrowy moustache quivered.

"Here is a telegram," he began, pausing between his words and still exploring Dasha's figure with his eyes; "tell Pavel to take it to the station."

Seizing Dasha's hand as she stretched it out for the telegram, he drew it to him and began to stroke her back—just as he stroked the horses in the stable—and went on coaxingly:

"Tell him to ride to the station, girl, to the station, to the sta—tion."

Dasha pretended to shrink from these caresses and kept giggling and glancing at the door. Making no effort to free herself, she said in affected consternation:

"Oh, do let me alone. . . . What are you doing? Oh dear, someone'll see us!"

"Stand still, girl! You've got a good back on you!" grunted Bourmin. "Don't fidget so, keep still! He's to take it to the station, to the station. Now turn sideways, that's right! Does it feel nice when I stro-oke you, like this, down the back? Nice, eh? Tha-at's it, down the back, tha-at's the way! . . ."

"Oh lor', sir, what are you doing? Let me go! I'm ticklish! . . ."

Dasha screamed and, tearing herself from Bourmin's hands, which had suddenly clutched her, cried, with a swift glance at the window:

"Mitri's looking!"

Bourmin broke from her and turned pale. He darted a furtive, terror-stricken glance at each window in turn. Dasha giggled again.

"Were you frightened?"

Thus flushed, her eyes sparkling with guile, her cheeks dimpling archly, she was irresistible. Bourmin looked at her for a long time in silence, licked his chops, and said:

"Come to me after dinner. Go to the bath first."

44

Bourmin changed into a soft brown dressing-gown and slippers and went to the bath-house, as he was wont to do on Monday mornings. Dimitri, the cook, was waiting for him on the doorstep with a blue bowl and towels. Bourmin sent Dimitri in before him.

"Take a sniff at it!"

"Boo-ootiful!" crooned Dimitri, with half-shut eyes, as he issued from the steaming bath-house. "There's no such air in paradise, I'll warrant!"

In the dressing-room be disrobed his master. Neatly and deferentially he folded the linen piece by piece and laid it on a stool, briskly undressed, and when they had both entered the steam-bath naked, slapped his thighs and roared:

"O-oh! It's a blessing of God! *There's* a sweet air! *That'll* put marrow in your joints! Sit down on the bench! There, Sergyeitch! I'll give you a swill down with warm water!"

It was understood that in the bath on Mondays Dimitri should not call his master "sir" but plain "Sergyeitch."

With arms and legs spread out, Bourmin stood helplessly in the middle of the bathroom, sniffing the air distrustfully.

"Well, what are you snorting at? I say it's like paradise, so light and clear!" Dimitri reassured him, and, supporting him by the arm, led him to the bench and sat him down. "Why, you're all of a tremble! Sit down,

45

Sergyeitch; I'll get a drop of warm water in the tub and sling it over you—*that'll* soon stop your shaking!"

Seated on the edge of the bench, Bourmin waited submissively, as he followed Dimitri's movements.

"Oo-ookh, what water! Oo-ookh, o-ho-ho!" Dimitri whooped and guffawed, emptying tub after tub over his body. He turned his streaming countenance upon Bourmin with a laugh like the neigh of a stallion:

"Hi-hihi-hi-hi! . . ."

A small spry fellow, with scanty growth on his face, Dimitri was not at all like a cook in a rich nobleman's house. Bourmin's choice had been prompted by the same reasoning as now urged him to secure Olimp Loutoshkin as his trainer. Dimitri's family tree was clustered with dish-washers and scullions, plain cooks and fancy cooks, and even boasted the names of two genuine chefs. Dimitri himself cooked execrably.

Filling his tub with water, he approached Bourmin. Bourmin tested the water suspiciously with his finger. Ever since that little minx Dasha had begun visiting his study on Mondays after dinner, he had had shrewd misgivings: "Suppose one day there should be boiling water in the tub?"

"Now shut your eyes!" ordered Dimitri, lifting the tub over his master's head; he emptied it and absorbed himself in the mysterious rite of working up a lather. Bourmin sat down, sputtering out the water which had trickled into his mouth.

"A wee bit hotter, Sergyeitch?" asked Dimitri, when he had done his lathering.

Bourmin looked tremulously at the open door of the stove and answered hurriedly:

"No, no, thank you!"

"Oo-ooh, you're a nervous one, Sergyeitch!" Dimitri shook his head. "But steam's the thing to calm you;

> 'Steam is a leech who takes no fee
> And drives your agues into the sea.'

Lie down." He brought the seething basin, flecked with froth, like summer clouds dappling a distant sky.

Bourmin lay meekly, belly upward, on the bench.

"Eykh, that's lovely! A gift of God!" Dimitri took up his parable, kneading his master's belly with a cloth. "The body now, she loves a real rubbing. Every little vein rejoices! A beast, though, say a horse—it's lost on him, don't seem to get the feeling under his tough hide; but a man—he sucks in pleasure with every pimple. . . . Lift your arms, tha-at's it! Under the armpits, that's where the mischief gets! I knew a man had a kind of a vent there, no bigger than a pin-hole; a man like that lives twice as long as you or me, breathes through it, like, as if it was his mouth. . . ."

Bourmin roused himself abruptly and sat up, afoam with lather. Dimitri stopped short and, scratching the inside of his knee, eyed him expectantly.

Bourmin coughed, looked up at him, and said:

47

"Was Marfa's father a coachman?"

"Timofey? He was and all!"

"Timofey, was that his name?"

"Timofey Petrovitch, but they nicknamed him Old Shag. Eykh, he was a coachman!"

"Was he?"

"The best in the province, they don't breed such fellows nowadays. . . . Beard down to his navel. . . . He'd grab hold of a cart by the back wheel and stop it dead—and he'd drink vodka from a bowl, he would!"

"What, from a bowl?"

"Simple enough. He'd pour out half a gallon, crumble a wheaten loaf in it, and lap it up out of a spoon."

Aristarkh Bourmin laughed seldom; his laughs were remembered by his hearers as they remembered grave calamities: some earthquake, fire, or tempest of great hail. And behold, that morning in the bath-house, sitting on the bench, all at once he laughed. The black beard, flaked with foam, jerked up and down, the strong white teeth flashed under his moustache.

"From a bowl, you say?"—he shook with silent laughter. "With bread?"

"God's truth, he did!" said Dimitri, crossing himself. "From a bowl, the old ruffian, with a spoon!"

"You're not lying?"

"Oh no, sir!"

Bourmin looked sternly at Dimitri and exclaimed: "You fool! I've always known you were a fool!"

"Excuse me—Sergyeitch!"—Dimitri corrected himself, remembering that they were in the bath-house, where he must not call his master "sir." "You're in your birthday suit, but it's a gentleman's. I'm a bit drowsy too—makes me forget."

"In the bath and before God all men are equal," said Bourmin stiffly; after a pause he added:

"In the next world, perhaps, you'll be the master, and I'll be the cook."

Dimitri's wet face melted into a complacent smile. He slapped his belly.

"Aha, that'll be grand! Every day I'll give you my orders: chicken broth with vermicelli—I've great notions of that—and tripe with it! Yes and roast goose! I'll grow such a broad mug on me! And my whole skin'll get grainy—white and poultry-like. . . ."

"Tell me about Timofey"—Bourmin cut him short.

"What shall I tell you? Used to take his vodka from a bowl—with a spoon, I say."

"A wooden spoon?"

"Yes, and what a spoon! Big as a pot-ladle it was."

Pressing both hands down on the bench and stretching his brawny legs in front of him, Bourmin sat laughing noiselessly. The lather drying on his hairy body gave it a grey and ancient air, and his beard looked as if it had been rolled in spiders'-webs.

"Thirty years he drove his horses," said Dimitri, taking breath. "When he put on his best togs, velvet cape,

49

plumed hat, and a big watch at his belt, you'd take him
for the Governor-General—and a voi-oice!—as if a beer-
barrel was talking. Once he fell from the box under
the legs of the shaft-horse, a stallion with an ugly
temper. . . . He was just lashing out when old Shag
laid hold of his hocks and flung him on his side, God's
truth he did!

"But the strain broke him in the end, he gave up his
soul to God, peace be upon him! His master had an
argument once with another great gentleman, a count
—Count Pouskyevitch his name was. 'My Timofey,'
says he, 'can stop any troika at full gallop—bring 'em up
on their haunches in a jiffy!' The Count laughed.
'Can't be done,' says he. 'Bet you a thousand rubles it
can!' 'Taken,' says he. So they harnessed three of the
savagest horses they could find, Timofey took the reins,
and they turned into the fallow. He roared at 'em, and
they set off hell for leather—holy fathers, how they
bolted! 'Stop,' shouted the Count. Timofey leaned
back and hauled at 'em—crash! went the foot-rest on
the box, and on they galloped. 'Stop,' cried the Count
again. And again Timofey hauled at 'em, blood running
down his face. Pop! went his leather belt. Bang! went
his shirt-collar and all his buttons. Crack! went his cape
at the back and shoulders. And the blood was gushing
from his ears. He brought the team up standing . . .
but that finished him. He tottered down from the box
and dropped dead—from the *strain*, you see—he'd

burst his guts. Up comes the Count, all shamefaced like, and hands over the thousand rubles. . . ."

For a long time Bourmin gazed at his outstretched legs and pondered.

"Now let me rub your back," said Dimitri.

Bourmin coughed, but said nothing, and turned over on the bench, face downward.

Dimitri plied him with all the tricks of the trained bath-attendant, rubbing, kneading, slapping, stroking, drumming his ribs with the sides of his hands, as if he were chopping cutlets out of him, kneading and slapping him once more, and continually repeating:

"Eykh, that's glorious! Eykh, that's good! Now we're all right! Now we're in fine fettle!" As if he were not the rubber, but the rubbed, he chortled gleefully.

Bourmin lay there, making no sound; his long, supine body, yielding limply to Dimitri's touch, seemed like a corpse on which some outraged peasant was wreaking a belated vengeance.

At last Dimitri had finished; he said, breathing heavily: "You sit down and rest a bit; it's my turn now."

He heated the stove, climbed onto the upper bench, and bleated like a goat: "Ey-eykh, Sergyeitch! What a blessed air! My skin's like silk!"

Dimitri lashed himself with the bath-brush, and Bourmin eyed him quizzically. He never ventured on such flagellations, and the pleasure which Dimitri and the other servants took in them Bourmin explained

51

as "an atavistic partiality for flogging."

Having dressed his master and himself, Dimitri wiped his boiled-beef-like face on a bundle of dirty linen and ceremoniously flung wide the door into the sunlit courtyard, which, after the reeking bath-house, seemed like a new and radiant world.

"God give you good health, sir!"

Bourmin drew from his pocket a twenty-kopeck piece which he had ready and, according to his wont, without looking at Dimitri, dropped the coin, as if into the box at church, into Dimitri's deftly cupped, officious hand.

Nursing cloths and sweet herbs upon their knees, Dasha and Adele Maximovna sat waiting for Bourmin to re-enter the house. They were privileged to use the bath as soon as their master had left it.

CHAPTER · V

Since the day when the grey Flat-tery was bought, and lodged, as it seemed, permanently in Loutoshkin's stable, Philipp came punctually to his morning duties, washed regularly, and, to the surprise of everyone, almost gave up drinking, and bought a new cap, like Mitritch's, with a broad patent-leather visor.

Philipp lived with his sister in two mean, dingy rooms in a suburban street. Nyousha seldom saw her brother. Philipp would arrive late and leave at dawn; only after an uncommonly stiff bout would he spend half a day, or even a whole day, at home.

Such days would begin thus:

"Nyousha!"

"Well, what is it?"

"Nyousha!"

"Well, go on!"

"Nyousha, do you wonder why I drink?"

"You're a drunken sot, of course; that's why."

Philipp would breathe a disconsolate, wheezing sigh and, dangling his legs from the bed (he slept in his boots on such occasions) begin rummaging in his pockets.

"What are you hunting for? Your money's in the till at Mitritch's," said Nyousha angrily. "You won't find yesterday, for all your hunting."

Philipp persisted in his search, and, finding nothing, shrank back into chilled silence. Nyousha brought him a glass of vodka and a plate of sour cabbage.

" 'Drunken sot,' you say"—Philipp revived at the first gulp of vodka—"but you don't understand. It's the cussedness of things that makes me drink."

After another sip and a bite at the cabbage he cleared his throat and delivered himself:

"I drink because life's so contrary"—and seeing that Nyousha had left the room, he pursued her to the kitchen with his discovery.

Hidden by clouds of smoke and bent over a great zinc trough, Nyousha stood at her washing. The stove and the boiling cauldrons on it made the air moist and sultry, almost tropical.

Choosing a stance free of the dirty linen which lay heaped upon the floor, Philipp planted himself and began to tell the story of the bay mare Frolicsome, with whom he had won a prize two years ago. Frolicsome had been sent to Loutoshkin's stable by an obscure amateur, a tyro of the track. The mare hadn't a dog's chance; but at the urgent wish of his pot-hunting owner, Loutoshkin entered her for the cup and told Philipp to drive her. And Philipp won! When they got the word to start, Frolicsome, as expected, fell back to the last place but one. Sinitsin led with Cracus, the favourite, and behind him, in a neck-and-neck struggle for the second place, three horses followed. It so happened that in the heat of the fray the wheels of these three locked, their sulkies fouled, and they had to leave the track, thus yielding to Philipp the second place. But this was not all. Philipp's luck was in; Sinitsin broke one of his reins, and Frolicsome finished first. Her backers won fabulous sums, her owner nearly died of joy; and the recital of that red-letter day soothed Philipp's drunken headaches no less infallibly than the prescribed glass of vodka.

" 'Drunken sot,' says you? . . . Some folks' tongues keep wagging like a horse's tail, but they don't know why, no more than him! You're my own born sister, but you've got no feeling for me! . . . Ever hear how I drove the bay mare Frolicsome, by Leopard out of Frolic? . . ."

Nyousha had heard a hundred times, but according to the proverb: "What matter the toy, if it comforts the boy," she never told him so, but listened patiently till he had finished.

"Vasil Kapitonitch Sinitsin was driving Cracus," Philipp launched out. "There was a stallion for you!

55

Safe as the bank, you could put your shirt on him!
'Well,' says I to myself, 'it's hands that count at our
game! How is it William can get speed out of anything? It's his hands does it.' And I proved it true.
What a race I gave Sinitsin! Made him break a rein,
that's what I did! As I drew level with him at the turn,
I forced the pace, but he couldn't stand it, and I shot
past—'So long, Vasil Kapitonitch, come and have tea
with me tomorrow!' But afterwards—you should have
seen them! All over me, they were—clapping me on
the back, shouting hurrah. . . . And up comes William in the dressing-room. 'Well, Philipp Akimitch,
you showed 'em how to drive! *You* showed 'em'—and
with that he fell on my neck and we kissed each other
—'you've got *hands*, Philipp Akimitch, hands of
gold. . . .'"

Nyousha would hear him out and, emptying the boiling cauldron into the trough, vanish in clouds of acrid
steam.

"It's the cussedness of things . . ." Philipp reiter-
ated, and listlessly resumed his rummaging. On every
"morning after" his thoughts turned to an illusory
three-ruble note, a brand snatched from the burning on
the night before, an emerald paper talisman, whose
magic writing could revive his spirits.

"Go and look for it at Mitritch's!" Nyousha would
say tartly, shooting a preoccupied glance at him over her
shoulder.

"I'll not budge an inch," Philipp protested. "May I break a rein if I haven't just remembered! In my waistcoat pocket it was—must have dropped it, sure enough! . . . God bless me! . . . I wouldn't care if it was a decent sum, but all this fuss to find three rubles! . . . What a nest-egg to be hunting for!"

Nyousha was silent.

Presently Philipp continued: "What's three rubles to us drivers? Nothing. We spit on it, stamp it in the dust. Suppose I go to the races, now, have a red ten-ruble 'un each way on Mimosa, what shall I do with those three rubles? Shan't know where to put them, even. . . . Once before I was stuck for money. . . . Off I went and put two red 'uns on Milord. Eighty-five and a half they paid at the tote—a hundred and seventy-one rubles for my two tickets—over the counter, like a bank."

Nyousha kept silence.

"What a cart-load of washing you've got there!" observed Philipp. He shuffled his feet for some time and at last blurted out: "Can you do a kindness to your own flesh and blood—for the last time? Give me a ruble and a half!"

Philipp knew his sister would not refuse. She never did. For such emergencies she had always a ruble or two put by, in a little lozenge-box, and his request was answered with a sigh and a curt: "There you are, take it; on the chest of drawers."

57

THE grey Flattery had become known, and even dear, to Nyousha, and not only through Philipp's report. It was long now that the two rubles had lain untouched in the little round lozenge-box. Though Philipp still came home sometimes a little merry, he did not stagger to the bed and fling himself down like a log, as formerly, but would sit up to the table like a Christian, ask Nyousha to warm up the samovar, and descant for hours on the wonderful grey mare. Nyousha seldom believed her brother's outpourings, but now she did; and more than once she exclaimed impulsively:

"If only I could get a sight of her!"

"She's a perfect beauty! My word, what a beauty!" Philipp would say, as he rolled his head from side to side and murmured, looking at his watch: "Time for bed now, or I'll oversleep."

Life in the stable began early. By four o'clock Philipp would arrive and begin storming at the stable-lads. They were both heavy sleepers, especially the toad-faced, ninepin-headed Vaska. When Philipp jogged and prodded him, he would turn from side to side, over and over, and howl dismally: "Ha-arf a moment!"

"Pavel, get me the blister!" Philipp would say to his other henchman.

At this word Vaska always sat up with a jerk, as if he had been scalded, wide awake. More than anything in the world he feared that fiery ointment, which was used to cure the ring-bone; ever since Philipp had smeared the stuff on Vaska's face, the latter could never hear the word "blister" without shuddering.

The day's work began with feeding and watering. There were eleven horses in the stable. Accustomed to a strict, unvarying routine, they greeted Philipp's first appearance with a soft neigh of satisfaction, knowing that now they would get water and presently oats and hay. Thrusting their heads against the gratings of the doors, they watched their attendants jealously, with kindling eyes, and champed and snuffled in a low plaintive chorus. The most impatient of them all was the dark bay stallion, Knight Errant. His loose-box was at the end of the row, and he was condemned to see how Vaska and the lanky Pavel passed him by, time and again, with sacks of oats and pails of water. Pressing his distended nostrils to the bars, he would cast a sidelong glance at the stable-lad out of one fiery blue-flecked eye, prick up his ears like the prongs of a tuning-fork, and stand stock still, as if asking: "My turn now?"

The lad would pass him. Knight Errant would arch his comely neck, buck briskly, as if on springs, to the far end of his box, whinny, and, wheeling round, stick his muzzle to the bars and stamp furiously on the floor. This amused the stable-lads, so that they always left him to the last.

After the horses were fed, the stable was at peace, the silence only broken by the measured crunching of

eleven pairs of lusty jaws. Philipp and the two lads had
a light breakfast and afterwards set about grooming the
horses and cleaning out their loose-boxes. Here again
Knight Errant showed his tricks and humours; it always
took two men to tackle him, and sometimes Philipp
had to lend a hand. He feared the tickling of his skin as
he feared fire. Every touch of the cloth or currycomb
set him whinnying, dancing, writhing—hindering his
grooms at every turn. Even the stolid Pavel sometimes
lost patience; he would fling down his brush or currycomb, spit, back two paces from the four-legged Adonis,
and cry out:

"Call yourself a horse? You're a bugger!"

But when it came to his hoofs, no horse was more
obedient than Knight Errant. He lifted his foot of his
own accord and never moved or offered to set it down
till the stable-lad cleaned his sole and frog with hoof-
pick and brush; then he would raise the other foot without waiting to be told. . . .

Till the coming of the grey Flattery, Knight Errant
was the pet of the stable; slices of black bread, thickly
salted, lumps of sugar, and apples, fell to his lot more
often than to the others'. He took the sugar, touching
it only with his lips, with such dainty grace, that once
more Pavel would be overcome, spit, and exclaim:

"Ain't you a bugger? Damn your eyes!"

Flattery's first trial forthwith and irrevocably thrust
the pampered stallion into the background, and the

grey mare took his place as the center of attraction. Her coming cast a glamour over the stable, transfiguring every day and hour as with the roseate promise of a festival; as in the late Lenten season, burgeoning with hopes of spring, when the snow melts, the brooks murmur, and the ice-bound rivers free themselves. Vaska and Pavel cursed and quarrelled over the mare. But Philipp tended her himself; he watered and groomed her and only left her to the lads to exercise.

At five o'clock, when Loutoshkin arrived at the stable, his first question was always:

"How's the mare?"

"Praise be to God!" Philipp would answer jauntily. "She's perking up. In a month, Alim Ivanitch, you won't know her."

Loutoshkin would look Flattery up and down, pass his hand over her knees and hocks, her back and sinews, stroke her broad shoulder, and exclaim:

"That's where the Orloff breed comes out—in the shoulders. Show me an American or a cross-breed that can boast 'em. Broad enough to carry off the prize or to wear the Russian collar. . . . Tell you what, Philipp, from tomorrow you must give her gruel—no more carrots, mind! Got any linseed? Sprinkle a handful of it in the gruel, with a pinch of salt—steam it up well and let her have it lukewarm, see?"

"I know, Olimp Ivanitch. I'm no greenhorn!"

Under their zealous care Flattery soon filled out into

61

her right proportions. When the winter was half through, it was hard to recognize the old hangdog Flattery in the spirited grey mare, with her shapely head, long, sloping withers, rounded ribs, and sturdy knees and trotting-joints. Her melancholy was tempered to a winsome gentleness, which endeared her to her keepers.

Loutoshkin was in no hurry to train the mare. First he wanted to be sure of her condition and secondly— he had his doubts.

Might not Flattery deceive him? Hadn't he known that happen time and again? At the first trial a horse would give a star performance, and then—fade out! Knight Errant, for instance! As a three-year-old he ran superbly for his age, and now it was a year since he had trotted in a race, and it was doubtful if he ever would.

So Loutoshkin put off training the mare from day to day, fearing to risk the shipwreck of his hopes.

In the second half of the winter he began to "work" her. First he tried her in Petrovsky Park. Not only did he sense in her every movement the harmonious interplay of parts, as in a well-adjusted mechanism, but he felt the soul that inspired this harmony. The docile creature seemed to divine the driver's every wish and surrender herself wholly to his will. At the end of February there was a heavy snowfall, driving in the park became impossible, and Loutoshkin took her on to the race-track. The pneumatic tires of the sulky whirred over the swept, icy track, and Flattery was eager to step out. The sharp calks of her shoes bit the ice firmly; the hippodrome was empty; but when Loutoshkin, having "warmed her up" over the first half-lap, was "opening her out" a little on the second, he saw Sinitsin drive onto the track with Samurai.

As the late Grishin had foretold, Samurai's owner, on the very day after Loutoshkin's failure, removed the grey stallion from his stable and placed him in Sinitsin's charge.

Sinitsin overtook Loutoshkin, tossed him a smiling challenge, and "cut the stallion loose." Loutoshkin, forgetting that the mare was not yet ready, that he had not once driven her fast, sent her along after the sprinting Samurai and was soon so close to him that Flattery's nose was pressing on Sinitsin's back.

Sinitsin turned his head and began to urge the stallion forward, but Loutoshkin suddenly reflected:

"What am I doing? Knocking her up at her first trial?"

He reined her in; she shook her head impatiently, eager to show her mettle.

THAT evening when Philipp entered Mitritch's establishment—noisy and stuffy at this time of day—Sinitsin beckoned to him. Drivers, grooms, horse-dealers, petty owners, thronged the tables, drinking tea, slyly sipping vodka, or dispatching omelettes, sausages, or fish and cabbage, piping hot—all the while sweating and disputing, their babel streaked and shot with lurid oaths, rich as the embroidery on the landlord's collar. At Sinitsin's table sat two men: a wealthy horse-dealer from the Mytnaya, on the south side of Moscow beyond the River Moskva—the shrewd and suave Mikhal Mikhalitch Grouzdyeff—and a fair young man with insolent eyes, and fingers loaded with signet-rings. Grouzdyeff held out his hand to Philipp, and in a soft tenor, which ill matched his hard grey eyes, he drawled:

"Welcome, my lad! I haven't seen you for a century!"

Philipp shook hands with them all and sat down; he doffed his squirrel-fur cap and laid it on his knee.

"We hear your master's made a little purchase for Bourmin," began Grouzdyeff. "The mare's pedigree's in her favour; old Aristarkh will give his eyes for an Orloff. But, in our opinion, your master's in too much of a hurry—might have bought the mare for half the price; he's a hot-head, that's what he is! . . . Why the mare's no great shakes—out of condition, came to him half-starved and maybe foundered. *He's in too much of a hurry.* . . ."

Sinitsin's pulpy, sweating face cracked in a broad grin, showing a black row of teeth. Jogging the fair man's knee under the table, he chimed in. "I've got a buyer for your mare, Ivan Alexandrovitch here," he

64

said, jerking his head at his beringed companion. "He'll buy her at once, cash down."

"No, he won't," said Philipp, "the mare's not for sale." He stared into Sinitsin's twinkling eyes, rose, and put on his cap.

"Wait a minute, I mean business," cried Sinitsin, trying to hold him back.

But Philipp thrust his hand away and said: "Look here, Vassily Kapitonitch, I've a good mind to tell you . . ."

"What's bitten the man? I'm serious. Here's a buyer, I tell you. Sit down, and we'll wet the bargain. Ivan Alexandrovitch makes army packs; and packs, you know, need leather straps to 'em. That's where your mare comes in!" Sinitsin would have gone on baiting him, but at this moment something happened that Mitritch's customers did not soon forget.

Philipp swore a round oath, which echoed through the room, tore off his fur cap, and dashed it on the floor. When the general din was hushed, and the attention of all fixed on him, he threw down this challenge to Sinitsin:

"I'll serve you for a year as your stable-lad if the mare don't beat your Magnate in a month. I've said it before witnesses, I'll sign my bond for it. Well?"

Sinitsin sniggered: "Draw it mild, Philya! Get off your high horse! You and your master'll take a toss one of these days." Magnate was the best horse in Sinitsin's stable. "And if you paid me, I wouldn't trust you with my horses—not for a day, let alone a year."

"So you're afraid, Vassily Kapitonitch? Fancy I'll break a rein, eh?" Philipp taunted him.

Sinitsin flushed, took from his waistcoat pocket a note-case with his monogram engraved on it, slipped it under the table, fumbled in it, drew out a five-hundred-ruble note, and smoothed it on his plate. The occupants of the room swarmed in tense silence round the disputants.

Looking not at Philipp, but at Grouzdyeff, Sinitsin said, in a voice which all could hear: "If you or your master want to bet on it, I'm your man! Out with your money! I'm no talker! You'll beat Magnate when crabs take singing-lessons!"

Philipp looked sheepish. His round, womanish shoulders drooped. He looked at the five-hundred-ruble note in Sinitsin's hand and panted in feeble protest: "What's *that*? . . . *That's* not wanted. . . . Money! . . . I never mentioned it. . . . Who said anything about money?"

The onlookers burst into a roar.

Mitritch came up to him, patted him on the shoulder, and, winking slyly at Sinitsin, said: "Drop it, Philipp Akimitch, you'll get no sense out of chaps like that; you know their sort—money on the nail! Drop it, don't you get mixed up with 'em!"

But behind him somebody called out: "Don't give

in to 'em, Philya! Plank down a thousand! Never fear!"

Philipp's confusion would have been complete but for an incident which caused much comment at the time and afterwards.

Often in the evenings there appeared at Mitritch's a figure which, once seen, was not soon forgotten— a tall old man in an old-fashioned frock-coat, with a beard like a tousled mop. His name was Semyon Andreyevitch Devyatkin; he was a grain-dealer from the south side, and no more was known of him. When he arrived, he would choose a table in some quiet corner, pull from his coat-tail pocket his own cup and saucer, after the manner of the Old Believers, and order tea. As he sat there silent, stooping over the table—too low for his great stature—with beetling, shaggy brows, he looked like an ancient eagle-owl, brooding alone on a tree-stump in a forest. Nobody knew why he came, what power drew him here from the south side, from his sober, spotless rooms, garnished with little mats, and lamps burning before Old World icon-cases, to the Bashilovka, that reeking haunt of passion and profanity.

Just as the crestfallen Philipp had pulled his fur cap down over his eyes and slouched towards the door, Semyon Andreyevitch Devyatkin rose and walked stooping to Sinitsin's table: "By your leave, gentlemen!"

Sinitsin, Grouzdyeff, and many others who were

standing round the table turned and faced him.

Brushing his sleeve across his beard, Devyatkin thrust his hand into the pocket of his tightly buttoned waist-coat and drew out a thick bundle from a frayed black case of calico. He unwrapped it on the table. It held bank-notes to various amounts: three-, five-, ten-, twenty-five-ruble notes, neatly secured with slips of paper and elastic bands. Taking a five-hundred-ruble note from under the pile, Devyatkin set it beside Sinit-sin's and motioned with his beard towards Philipp.

"I'll back your mare with ready money."

In the tense and instantaneous silence which ensued, a cluck of satisfaction could be heard from Mitritch, as if some old friend had clapped him suddenly on the back:

"A-aak!"

Everyone saw Sinitsin's stubby-fingered hand shoot out over the table and fall heavily on his five-hundred-ruble note. Somebody hissed. A hubbub followed, each man trying to shout down the rest. Grouzdyeff stood back from the table and cleared his throat. Sinit-sin's reddish face flushed scarlet. He struggled to find words and, working his fingers forward imperceptibly, manœuvred his bank-note towards him. But Devyat-kin loomed over him, tall and stooping, his shaggy grey brows beetling, like some hoary, ominous bird, who had swooped noiselessly upon him.

68

"Cover it, Vassily; what are you frightened of?" cried a shrill, tormented voice.

"Don't be afraid, cover it!" clamoured the supporters. "Magnate's done two fourteen on a sticky track. Cover it, man!"

Mitritch piloted his way through to Devyatkin, and whispered in his ear:

"You're throwing your money away. . . . Do you know the mare? She's in poor condition—honour bright, I tell you. . . ."

Devyatkin eyed him sternly, without answering.

Sinitsin thrust his bank-note in his pocket and staggered back from the table.

"I don't want strangers' money," he said at last, with a forced smile, avoiding the formidable old man's eyes. "I'll take a bet with the mare's owner, but not with you, I'd rather not rob you."

Devyatkin said nothing. He took out the calico note-case and bestowed the rejected stake under the neatly folded bundles, packed them singly in the case, deliberately buttoned his tight waistcoat to the neck, fastened his high frock-coat, and withdrew to his table in the corner.

In a moment Mitritch was at his side.

"I suppose you know something about that mare, sir?" he insinuated.

Devyatkin poured some tea into his saucer, propped

it up on his five fingers, blew on it, plunged his draggled moustache into the amber liquid, and, having sipped his saucerful, replied:

"If I didn't know, do you think I'd risk my money? My dear sir," he added, tapping his left breast, where the frock-coat bulged palpably, "I don't print 'em myself, you know."

CHAPTER · VI

LOUTOSHKIN RATED PHILIPP SOUNDLY ON the morrow, when he heard of the incident at Mitritch's.

Philipp listened meekly. Finally he burst out: "But we'll beat 'em yet, Olimp Ivanitch, sure as God's in heaven, we'll beat 'em! Won't we, now?"

Loutoshkin said nothing, but looked hard at Philipp. Next day he hastened his plans for Flattery and resolved to train her for the cup.

Many horses had passed through his hands, good and bad, fractious and quiet; with every horse he established a peculiar *rapport* determined by a host of details which a layman would not notice. To some he was drawn from the hour he first drove them; on such he lavished all the patient care indispensable for training; others he hated for their sluggishness, perverseness, hard mouths, or other faults. Such horses he drove savagely, breaking them to his will with curb and lash. At once they felt their driver's enmity, which they repaid in kind, engaging in deadly combat with him—flashed fiery eyes at his

7 1

approach, laid back their ears, and swung round menacing hindquarters. More often than not this duel ended in the victory of the driver and his three lieutenants. But the horse was henceforth cowed, no match for first-class trotters. Sometimes, again, Loutoshkin met his master. The recalcitrant black Hetman smashed a dozen sulkies and left his charge as vicious and intractable as when he entered it.

Flattery's training was a delight to him. Each day discovered some new merit in the mare. Her breathing, points, and manners were magnificent. As he watched Flattery in the shafts and in the stable, Loutoshkin checked his observations by his experience with other horses, promptly divined the temper and talents of the mare, and hit on the best way of training her. The artisan had become the artist. By the end of the third week he had Flattery in perfect form. He sent a letter to Bourmin, asking his leave to enter her for the cup forthwith. Bourmin replied by telegram:

COMING TO MOSCOW SOON TAKE NO ACTION UNTIL
MY ARRIVAL ARISTARKH BOURMIN

Time dragged on at Loutoshkin's stable. Vaska and Pavel wrangled ceaselessly over Flattery's prospects and the field she would encounter.

Philipp would listen silent and aloof, or approach the disputants and, looking at Vaska's lantern jaws, affirm:

72

"You can't argufy about horses with a physiognomy like that!"

Vaska would be dumfounded, awed by the out-landish word, which Philipp never would interpret. In the evening, having groomed the horses, Vaska and Pavel would repair in turn to Mitrich's; Pavel to drink a quiet glass of tea, chatting with friends from other stables; Vaska in the secret hope of again witnessing some such dispute as that between Philipp Akimitch and Sinitsin. When he found Devyatkin there, he would sit as near to the table as he could, never taking his eyes off the stooping figure of the shaggy-browed old man.

"Ain't he got money!" he would say, when he got back to the stable. "Whacks out a purse with thousands of rubles in it, bungfull and bursting with 'em. What if he lost it, eh? And I picked it up. . . . I'd stake half on the mare against Sinitsin, wouldn't you, Pashka?"

A week passed, a second, and a third; Bourmin delayed his coming. Loutoshkin could not make up his mind to enter Flattery for the cup without her owner's leave, knowing his wilful and despotic humour. He grew petulant and moody. He would stride to the tall mirror in the dining-room and sneer at the reflexion of his lean, sharp face: "You're no more than a groom— a flunkey!"

After one such fit Loutoshkin could hold out no

longer; he wrote a stinging letter to Bourmin:

". . . I had reckoned on competing for the cup at the beginning of April and have prepared Flattery to do so. Your reply, forbidding me to enter her, and your delay in coming here, have confused my plans and put me in a ridiculous position. The trainer has his plans to make, no less than the owner, with this sole difference, that the trainer is concerned for the successful performance of his horse, while the owner, it seems, is often swayed by other motives. You, Aristarkh Sergyeevitch, cannot be unaware that success on the track depends not only on the speed of the horse, but on the driver's state of mind. A driver is not a coachman or a cabman. In this case, too, he is the trainer of your horse. The trainer builds up the horse's form, moulds the rough clay, creates the trotter. As trainer I must answer for the mare entrusted to me, I am responsible for her success or failure, and I think I have the right to judge whether she should be entered for the cup. . . ."

Precisely a week later came the reply, in a grotesquely long and narrow envelope, stamped with Bourmin's crest and monogram:

My dear Olimp Ivanitch, ran the punctilious characters, *I found your letter highly gratifying, not least because it was instinct with a sense of duty and revealed a conscience keenly alive to the responsibility which a trainer takes for the horse entrusted to him.*

Such sentiments are rare in this age and do you credit. That conscience is a faithful guarantor for the judicious nurture of so subtle and sensitive an organism as the Orloff trotter, the divine, incomparable creation of the inspired Alexei Grigoryevitch, Count Orloff Chesmensky. We are but weak executants of his illustrious designs. Not stinting our material means, not slackening our mental efforts, in sleepless toil, in steadfast purpose, the owner and breeder of Orloffs supports a heavy load of labour and anxiety and seldom tastes an hour of ease or triumph. The great Champion, whose name every true Russian speaks with reverence, was an inexhaustible fount of joy and rapture to his owner, but he plunged him and all Russia into inconsolable anguish on that memorable day in February 1912. What happened on that day? What quenched the light of that resplendent star? What impious hand was raised against the majesty of the Orloffs? What serpent brood struck at the head of that bright genius? Was there a single Russian among all those thousands on the stands who grudged or doubted Champion's victory? There was not, and there could not be. I ask, then, who consented to this outrage? How came this luminary to be eclipsed? From the Members' Enclosure I had leisure to observe that tournament of seven horses, of whom, as you well know, only one was a Russian trotter—to wit, Champion. And I say, and will stand by my assertion: it was the hand of an alien

75

driver that struck this treacherous blow at Champion. The start was prompt. General H led, with Frank Kayton driving him; after him came William Kayton, driving Champion. I saw how Champion, in the second lap, with the effortless, regal grace so proper to him, shot forward and passed General H by half a length, but at the turn the foreigners, father and son, by base conspiracy and perfidy, contrived that General H should recover the lead and carry off the prize. Would not a single glance at that scurvy American colt and our peerless beauty, Champion, convince any man of the perfidy of these two drivers? As I passed through the crowd after the betrayal, I saw on every Russian face the marks of ineffable grief and humiliation. In all that multitude one youth alone rejoiced, the winning driver. When I heard him bragging of his feat, I accosted him: "Young man," I said, "you should be ashamed to rejoice when all Russia is weeping for this outrage!" And the young man, stricken with remorse, under the eyes of scores of onlookers, tore up the voucher which entitled him to a rich reward for his base-bought victory. A magnanimous act, worthy of Alexander of Macedon.

Reverting to my previous observations, let me repeat, my dear Olimp Ivanitch, that I regard you as a trainer with an uncommonly high conception of his responsibility towards the owner of his horse and that our views as to a trainer's obligations are in most fortunate agreement. *This agreement is the surest warrant of success and the most sufficient safeguard against such perfidy as I have recorded in my letter. On my arrival in Moscow we will take the necessary decision as to entering Flattery for the cup.*

Aristarkh Bourmin

Having read this letter, Loutoshkin tore it to pieces in a fury. His first thought was to go at once to the hippodrome and enter Flattery's name. But he reflected that he had not the entry-fee. Next he thought of again writing to Bourmin, and that evening, for the first time since Flattery's appearance, he drank heavily at Mitritch's.

In the morning Philipp handed him a telegram:

ARRIVE MOSCOW LOSKOUTNAYA HOTEL DAY AFTER TOMORROW ARISTARKH BOURMIN

CHAPTER · VII

THE BEST SUITE AT THE HOTEL OVER-
looked the Tverskaya, an arterial road running north-
wards from the Kremlin. Aristarkh Bourmin gazed
at the golden bulbs which topped the Church of St.
Paraskeva and held forth in a squeaky monotone:

"All this was once the home of virgin forest, the
haunt of prowling beasts. Now, conjured by a Tsar's
command, the metropolis of the Empire queens it
here, and wolf and bear have given place to man. . . .
The race of the Bourmins draws sustenance from its
roots in hoary antiquity. . . ."

In the heat of his exposition Bourmin forgot to turn
on the light, and the room was but faintly illumined
by the street-lamps, far below. Framed in the pink-
flushed window, his tall upright figure, in its long coat,
gripped at the waist by a tight silver belt, he looked like
a gingerbread manikin, such as children buy at fairs.
Loutoshkin sat on the couch by the extinguished samovar and waited for a pause in Bourmin's maundering
peroration.

"When are you coming to look at the mare?" he interposed at last.

Bourmin walked to the door and gave a double ring.

"Light," he exclaimed, as the chambermaid entered.

The maid turned the switch and looked in amazement at Bourmin, evidently wondering why the gentleman could not switch on the light himself.

Bourmin seated himself at the table opposite Loutoshkin. His movements were conspicuous for the absence of all curves; he seemed compact of squares, parallelograms, and triangles. As he sat down, he dropped his napkin, and in picking it up, did not stoop, but bisected his body at a right angle from the waist.

"I shall come and look at the mare tomorrow," he rasped, stroking his blue-black beard, "at twelve o'clock. Now I have another matter to discuss with you. How much do you make out of your stable? Two hundred rubles a month? You know something, of course, about my stud—the magnificent blood-stock I have collected there? I offer you the post of principal trainer. The salary will exceed the amount which you drew from your own stable."

This was the last thing Loutoshkin had expected. Bourmin watched his face intently. The forefinger with the broad gold signet-ring crept down the lush black beard.

Loutoshkin's sharp, nervous features resembled those

79

of his father, Varyagin, but his figure must have been his mother's: broad shoulders, stout back, sturdy neck. His remote ancestor Semyon Ermilovitch Mochalkin, one of the three Semyons who were all great drivers, was, by the report of his contemporaries, a puny fellow, but none the less a hero of the trotting-turf, and the favourite driver of Count Orloff Chemensky, who even took him with him into exile, to his house in Dresden.

"I intend to stay two days in Moscow; that will give you time to think over my proposal," added Bourmin after a pause.

Loutoshkin walked abruptly to the window. Bourmin's offer perturbed him. Engrossed by Flattery, he had quite forgotten the finances of his stable during the last few months. They were in bad shape, and Bourmin had obliquely reminded him of this—just as a dark patch of water, suddenly discerned beneath the ice, reminds the incautious skater of his peril. In none of the eleven horses in his stable had he any hope, except in Flattery. And Flattery's owner was Bourmin.

And yet how could he leave Moscow? Tear himself away from the hippodrome, with its thousands of spectators, and bury himself in a country village? And Saphir? The swarthy, roguish-eyed Saphir, sprightly as an elf, true as a stop-watch. . . .

"I can't do it, Aristarkh Sergyeevitch," he burst out, striding to the table. "For years my life has been bound up with Moscow. I can't do it."

Bourmin had expected such an answer.

"A pity," he said.

He took from his wallet seven hundred and fifty rubles and pushed them across the table to Loutoshkin.

"Write out a receipt for your commission on the purchase of the mare."

Loutoshkin wrote it, thanked Bourmin, and as he took his leave, repeated in an apologetic tone:

"I can't possibly do it, Aristarkh Sergyeevitch. I'm highly flattered by your offer and the confidence you show in me, but private considerations compel me to refuse. I'm very much obliged to you. . . ."

Bourmin plucked at his rectangular beard, and again commented:

"A pity."

PRECISELY at twelve o'clock next day a smart cab drove into Loutoshkin's yard. In the cab sat Bourmin.

Vaska was the first to see him. "He's come!" he whooped to all and sundry.

With a trenchant "Get her ready!" to Philipp, Loutoshkin hurried out to meet the visitor.

Philipp wore a sky-blue shirt, brand-new, and his face, twice washed that day with scented soap, shone like a new galosh. Whistling peevishly for Vaska, who was scurrying frantically about the stable, he entered Flattery's box, picked up a wisp of straw from the litter, looked in the manger, found a rag, and brushed it once again over the sleek, speckless coat of the grey mare.

Next he whipped out a pocket-mirror, spat on his palm, and, moistening his fair hair, straightened the parting with the selfsame rag, wiped the patent-leather visor of his cap with it, and waited.

Aristarkh Bourmin, in his speckless dark-blue silver-belted coat, with his Assyrian beard held high and vertical, stalked into the yard. The two lads now stood mute and stiff, their eyes fixed on Loutoshkin, ready to dart forward at a signal from him.

The stable passage was in apple-pie order; the floor swept clean, the harness hanging oiled and polished on the walls, the spare wheels of the sulkies glittering. The air smelt of turpentine and embrocation. The horses peered through their bars, disquieted by the presence of this stranger. Loutoshkin made the rounds with Bourmin, side by side, and told him the name and history of each horse. Bourmin paused only at the boxes of the Orloffs; from the cross-breeds, even the beautiful Knight Errant, he turned scornfully away. As they neared Flattery's box, Loutoshkin motioned Philipp, whose eyes were still upon him, and in a strangely agitated voice announced:

"Pres-ently I'll show you the mare. . . . Philya!"

Philipp and Vaska dived into the loose-box, Bourmin stood aside and plunged his left hand under his belt. In the darkness he could hear a gentle click, as the bit entered Flattery's mouth.

"Come on!" said Loutoshkin to Bourmin, coughing

nervously, and they both went out into the yard.

Loutoshkin was visibly perturbed, anxious for Flattery and for Philipp, though he was sure of both of them. Of all the grooms who had worked under him, there was none like Philipp for showing off a horse. He would make even an indifferent animal step out with a smart, sprightly pace and bring him up short in the accepted style. And yet Loutoshkin was perturbed. He was tempted to go into the box himself, lead out the mare, and halt her for Bourmin's inspection. The man was not merely an owner, he was an expert judge of horseflesh.

"What are you dawdling for?" Loutoshkin shouted.

Almost immediately Philipp came out, with Flattery stepping high and stately. He led her along the wall, turned suddenly, and just as Loutoshkin ordered: "Stop!" brought her up standing, with her feet firmly planted. Bourmin cast a swift glance at the stance of her forelegs and smiled approval. He stepped aside and looked intently at the mare, observing her clean ribs, broad haunches, shapely legs; he came close to her, felt her trotting-joints, and more than once caressed her ample, sloping shoulder. . . .

When the groom had walked her round, Bourmin again examined her, with no less care, and at last pronounced: "The mare's satisfactory."

"But what breed, Aristarkh Sergyeevitch!" exclaimed Loutoshkin.

"The mare's satisfactory," Bourmin repeated. "She has the points of an Orloff. Her mother's half-sister, Pauline, was the aunt of Sturdy. Excellent material for my stud. . . . Unfortunately, many of our native owners," he resumed after a pause, "dazzled by the deceptive speed of foreign trotters, are doing a nefarious work, mingling the noble blood of the Orloffs with the base blood of those Yankee nonentities which are now so much in vogue on all our race-tracks. They are poisoning the public conscience, tempting us to forget the sublime example of incorruptible loyalty to the Orloff trotter, shown to the world a century ago, in the year 1819, by the close friend of Count Orloff Chesmensky, Vassily Ivanovitch Shishkin."

Bourmin turned majestically to Loutoshkin, his hand upraised, the gold-encircled forefinger pointing in attestation heavenward. "Do you know that, on the death of Affable I, at twenty-five years of age, Vassily Ivanovitch ordered him to be buried near the riding-school, in a deep grave, standing, caparisoned in an embroidered saddle-cloth, with hood and harness?"

Bourmin's forefinger sank slowly.

"But what do we see now? Where is our pristine patriotism?"

Bourmin looked austerely at Philipp, who had been listening open-mouthed. "What's your name, man?"

"Philipp, sir."

84

"Tell me, my friend, the American horse is trash—isn't he?"

"Real wash-out, sir!"

"Wash-out! That's the word, *wash-out!*" said Bourmin with relish. "Are you the head groom?"

"I am, sir."

Bourmin took a twenty-five ruble note and handed it to Philipp. "There you are, my friend; divide it among you. And do your best."

Flattery, who had been standing meekly by, as if listening to the conversation, stretched out her lips to Philipp's hand as it closed upon the note. Philipp drew a piece of sugar from his pocket and passed it to Bourmin, who smiled indulgently, proffered it to the mare's satin lips, and, turning to Loutoshkin, said: "I thank you for the purchase of the mare and for her excellent condition. When do you propose to nominate her for a race?"

"Next Sunday."

The faces of Philipp and the two lads lit up. Vaska stealthily approached Philipp and winked at him. Philipp repulsed him with a furious glance and said to Loutoshkin: "On Tuesday, Alim Ivanitch, Taglioni will be running!"

Bourmin frowned. He had long desired to see the far-famed and invincible trotter of Telyegin, the famous horse-breeder. He had come to Moscow with this very purpose. But he wished to keep it dark.

"You've very poor material in your stable," he said dryly as he turned to go; "except Flattery, there's not one decent specimen there. Hadn't you a grey stallion?"

Loutoshkin understood what Bourmin meant; he stammered something about a difference of opinion with the owner, which had forced him to part with Samurai. "With a horse like Flattery in my stable, I don't miss Samurai. With her I can out-trot him any day!" he added firmly.

"The mare's satisfactory," pronounced Bourmin. He stroked his black beard, smiling inscrutably.

THAT evening Philipp went home earlier than usual. He flung ten rubles on the table before Nyousha and proclaimed triumphantly:

"We're off, next Sunday. And here's a present for you."

"Off where?" Nyousha would have asked him, but a glance at her brother explained everything, for her face, not yet old, but seared with heavy toil, had brightened suddenly. Smoothing out her dishevelled hair, she reminded Philipp timidly: "I want to see the race. You won't forget my little ticket?"

"I'll bring you two passes on Saturday. You can sport your new shoes. . . . Eykh, that'll be something like a race!" said Philipp, knitting his brows. "The mare's in high fettle, taut as a spring! Owner's just been to see her, slipped me a twenty-five ruble note. . . . A grand gentleman, with a black beard, and a gold ring on his fist, and a big silver belly-band. We're to enter her for the cup on Sunday; never seen such a horse in his life, he says!"

Nyousha listened rapt and breathless and, as if she were off to the races there and then, began to titivate, patting and preening her hair, straightening her bodice, and glancing at her hands, which were red and raw from slaving at the wash-tub.

CHAPTER · VIII

ON THE 6TH OF JUNE THAT YEAR THE black stallion Taglioni, foaled in Telyegin's stable by the half-American mare Mystery and sired by the American horse Heubingen, defeated his rival Turquoise in the Kolyoubakin Stakes and established a new record: two miles in four minutes and twenty-four seconds.

On the Friday an article appeared in a Moscow newspaper.

"This black stallion," wrote the anonymous hand, "now the premier trotter on the Russian turf, is of moderate stature and exquisite proportions. Taglioni's action is amazingly beautiful and effective. His every movement is so nicely synchronized, so admirably directed towards speed, that it is startling to behold. He keeps unerring time, a quality of the highest value in a trotter of such eminence. It must not be forgotten that Taglioni now holds the record for the mile and a quarter and is the third best trotter in the world, being only

88

excelled by Harvester and Cresceus. The example of this incomparable performer should open the eyes of all those die-hards who are the implacable enemies of cross-breeding. This pot-house patriotism costs our country dear. . . ."

Bourmin, who had gone to the races on Tuesday and seen the victory of the famous trotter, read this account on Friday and forthwith ordered his boxes to be packed. As he paced the room, he tweaked his beard unmercifully, marring its foursquare proportions; he wound strands of hair upon his finger, thrust them in his mouth and chewed at them, then braided them again into hard plaits, which slowly uncoiled as he released them.

Stepping to the window, he surveyed the golden pinnacles of St. Paraskeva and smiled grimly. "Russia's metropolis delivered into the hands of aliens!" Taglioni was almost American, and Samuel Kayton was driving him. "Pfff! The ancient capital, the heart of Russia! . . ."

The chambermaid answered the bell.

"Why don't you bring me my bill?" he snapped at her. "Have you lost all sense of order in Moscow?"

Having dined, he summoned Loutoshkin.

Wholly absorbed in Flattery's approaching début, Loutoshkin arrived agitated and preoccupied and unwittingly fanned Bourmin's wrath by speaking of Taglioni:

"The most astonishing thing about it, Aristarkh

Sergyeevitch, is that Taglioni had only just been brought from Petrograd, on the day before the race! And he finished with a broken shoe, you know! Marvellous!"

Bourmin listened sullenly; he coughed, and said:

"Flattery's to go to my stud-farm. Be good enough to get her ready."

Loutoshkin blenched. He noticed Bourmin's ruffled beard and sour looks. But still he could not quite believe his eyes or ears; he stammered out:

"But she's entered for the cup on Sunday?"

"The mare will not compete," said Bourmin dryly. "I have informed the committee that I am withdrawing her."

Loutoshkin staggered back, his lower jaw twitching.

For a moment he stood motionless, fastening his eyes on Bourmin; then he ground his teeth and growled point-blank at him:

"Don't you dare to do it! Do you hear me? Don't you dare!"

"Sit down," said Bourmin in a toneless voice, seating himself in a plush-covered armchair.

Loutoshkin kicked over the chair offered him and leaned across the table. His hands trembled.

Bourmin coughed. "My dear Olimp Ivanovitch, I value your talents as a trainer—talents which have not yet had a chance to prove themselves. As you so happily phrased it in your letter, 'the trainer moulds the rough clay, creates the trotter.' A most apt simile. It vouches for the maturity of your intelligence. Now it is my wish to afford you . . ."

"Why isn't the mare running?" Loutoshkin interrupted, in a voice tremulous with rage.

Bourmin paused, and proceeded:

"It is my wish to afford you the only possibility of giving scope to your capacities, of whose excellence I have convinced myself by a profound study of the laws of heredity and consanguinity. The success you seek today is a mirage. But in the future, I am firmly assured, the hippodrome of the capital will acclaim you as a master of your craft and the victorious driver of my horses. My establishment—"

"Why isn't the mare running?" demanded Loutoshkin once again.

"My establishment," Bourmin proceeded, in the same level, high-pitched voice, "is stocked only with first-class material. It is your destiny to shape it—'from the rough clay to create the trotter.'" Bourmin raised his forefinger. "Is not that a glorious mission for a trainer? To inscribe his name in golden letters in the annals of . . ."

"I ask you, why isn't the mare running?" shouted Loutoshkin, shaking the table in his fury and upsetting his unfinished glass of tea.

Bourmin scrutinized his face, paused for a moment, and said tersely:

"I have the sole disposal of the mare. She will go to

my stud-farm, where I have my plans for her. You will box her without delay."

He took out his wallet, counted some notes, and passed them to Loutoshkin. "Here is the amount necessary for the transport of the mare. Write me a receipt. You will send your head groom with her."

Loutoshkin fell back from the table and sank heavily down on the divan. Bourmin watched him, stroking his beard the while. His features were impassive. The broad gold ring slid calmly down the beard, crept up, and again descended. Through the door came subdued sounds—footsteps muffled by carpets, ringing of bells, and murmuring of voices. . . .

"The trainer creates the trotter," Loutoshkin began slowly, staring vacantly before him, laughing softly. Then, taking fire again, he rose abruptly and advanced upon Bourmin.

"Aristarkh Sergyccvitch! Is the trainer no more than a groom to you, a hireling? No, he is a man that can forget his father, his mother, the woman he loves—but his horse, never! For every driver there exists one horse, the ideal, you understand me? Till you have that horse —that mare, perhaps—you dream of her, and in each new horse that comes, you fancy you have found your dream. You are deceived. You hate the deceiver. . . . A driver? What is a driver? 'Up he gets,' you think, 'then off and away, trot, sprint, and the prize if he's lucky.' You're wrong! Look here, I'll tell you how it is,

I'll tell you. You say we thresh and ruin our horses, don't you? Well, listen! They bring me a mare, let's say. I begin to work her. I train her for a week, a month, and find her just so-so. Then suddenly, over twenty or thirty yards, she gives me such a burst of speed and shows such action that—I'm staggered. And that's the end of it! The end of both of us! I remember that infernal grey or chestnut back, rippling like the sea, as if it would stream out of its harness . . . every finger remembers that soft thrumming of the reins. I'm fairly done for! I believe in her, heart and soul, begin to see her in my dreams. 'She's found, she's found at last,' I think. I set her apart from the rest, groom her myself, and all the time I'm driving her I'm on tenterhooks—'Now, now,' I say, 'she'll show me that glorious action and that burst of speed.' I keep her a year, a year and a half, in my stable—every day begging—bullying her to show her mettle. But no—she's betrayed me, Aristarkh Sergyeevitch, betrayed me, do you understand? She's worthless, worthless! A man may kill a woman who betrays him. . . . That's how it starts, you see. I won't give in. 'I'll make you do it,' I say, 'you bitch, I'll flog you into it.' There's an excuse for anything in such cases, anything! That's why we punish and spoil our horses, that's why, Aristarkh Sergyeevitch, do you see?" Loutoshkin fell silent, and as if trying to remember why he had said all this, he wiped his forehead.

Then he stretched out both hands to Bourmin.

93

"Aristarkh Sergyeevitch, don't take Flattery away from me. Don't send her to your stud. Please don't."

Bourmin stroked his beard in silence.

"Aristarkh Sergyeevitch! You don't know what that mare's like, what a heart she's got! *She's* no deceiver. Don't take her from me! . . . I'll work for you without a salary. Only let her stay."

Under Bourmin's moustache a smile of satisfaction was just visible. He was thinking of the laws of heredity. He remembered Loutoshkin's remote ancestor Scmyon Mochalkin, servant and friend of Count Orloff Chesmensky.

He spoke: "All that you say, Olimp Ivanovitch, is most significant. Again I offer you the post of principal trainer in my stud, and shall expect you to communicate your reply by telegram not later than the 15th of June. Now take the money for the transport of the mare. And I hope we shall resume this conversation, which, I repeat, is most significant, on my estate."

Loutoshkin took his leave. The drive home from the hotel would be as tedious as a sick man's morning. In the Bashilovka he would find Philipp, Vaska, Pavel, and the grey Flattery waiting for him.

At the Tverskaya Gate he abruptly ordered the cabman to turn back. He gave him Saphir's address.

CHAPTER · IX

ON BOURMIN'S VAST ESTATE HORSE-breeding was the hub of life. Seen from afar by the approaching traveller, bronze horses ramped above the stable gates. To the peasants of the two adjoining villages, the stylish trotters, hitched to light high-wheeled wagonettes, and the American harness without yoke or collar, were a familiar sight. The children did not play "horses" as elsewhere, they played "drivers and trotters," while the grown-ups flavoured their speech with horsy jargon. A walk was termed a "jog," shrewish women were called "vicious," pregnant women said to be "in foal." On the estate itself it was as if there were no human beings. There were stallions, mares, colts, fillies, carts, sulkies, knee-boots and ankle-boots, reins, whips, riding-school and stables—spring-halts, galls and other equine maladies; there was the "vet," there were drivers, grooms, saddlers, farriers and travelling horse-dealers—and overriding all from the big white house on the pond's edge was one man's will, pervading, ruling, setting its seal on everything. With horses the day began and ended, and at night fantastic shapes of horses galloped in men's dreams. Over the hushed household, over the snoring grooms, the drowsy watchman, and the kennelled mastiffs, over the main gate of the stables, reared the black figures of those pawing steeds, a bright light flashing on their flanks of bronze. Only a melancholy hound durst sometimes challenge them, lifting his muzzle in a querulous bay of protest.

Loutoshkin was assigned his own suite of two rooms, with windows opening on the stable. On the day after he arrived Bourmin showed him the stable and the riding-school, ordered the horses out for his inspection, and invited him to dinner. Over the meal Loutoshkin made some attempts at conversation, but was met with silence and raised eyebrows. He learned afterwards from Adele Maximovna that Bourmin never spoke till he had finished eating. That day, as usual, Bourmin began the conversation after the dessert, when coffee had been served. He broke the silence with Loutoshkin's dictum:

"From the rough clay the trainer creates the trotter."

Having spoken, he stirred his coffee, sipped, and looked up at Loutoshkin.

"I am affording you, Olimp Loutoshkin, full scope to express your responsible creative activity. In the stable—you are master."

This phrase Bourmin repeated at the end of their

conversation in the study, where he had conducted Loutoshkin to show him his library, his notes, pedigree-charts, and stud-book.

"Moreover," he added, "I give you authority to incur any reasonable expenditure which may contribute to the improvement of the Orloff trotter."

For Loutoshkin a new life began. Work with the yearlings and two-year-olds required much effort, concentration, and knowledge. He had much to learn; the breaking of colts was an art almost unknown to him. He differed from other trainers, the bulk of whom were illiterate and had scarcely seen a printed page, in that he had read widely and deeply in the abstruse literature of horse-lore. Bourmin's library held an admirable collection of books on all questions bearing on the horse. Bourmin himself, in frequent converse with him, enriched him with much precious information about foreigners' methods, the lay-out of their riding-schools and tracks, their systems of exercise, training, and the like. In a short time Loutoshkin had acquired such confident proficiency as can only be had by the checking and counter-checking of theory and practice. The horse became an open book to him. The colts shaped well under his hand.

Seldom did he find himself at leisure. When he did, he was overwhelmed with boredom, the tedium of blank desolation. As if wakened from a dream, he perceived with sudden terror that all round him there was

97

nothing at all but horses, and words, thoughts, and conferences begotten by them. Some noise, indeed, would reach him from the world without—of war, defeats, and treachery in high places; but such noise died quickly here, as if there were no air to carry it. On its heels came the neighing of horses—stallions, mares, and weanlings; and wagging her hindquarters, horse-like, Dasha would amble past his window on her way to the bathhouse.

But Bourmin stroked his beard and smiled complacently at his wise choice of a trainer, whose guiding hand was everywhere, now in the stable, now in the riding-school, who never went out, and seldom rested, poring whole nights over the stout volumes in the library.

"*Count Alexei Grigoryevitch Orloff-Chesmensky created the incomparable Orloff trotter. It is our task to deliver the Orloff out of the hands of aliens by creating our own past-master of the art*," he wrote and underscored in one of his numerous memorandum-books. The same day he doubled Loutoshkin's salary.

Twice a week Bourmin entered the stable for the early grooming; such visits were premised by a peculiar ceremony in confirmation of the words spoken to Loutoshkin on the morrow of his arrival: "In the stable you are master." As he neared the entrance of the yard, Bourmin would stand patiently till Loutoshkin came to meet him, being advised by the grooms of his approach. Often Loutoshkin delayed his coming, sometimes purposely. Bourmin would meekly await his pleasure.

"May I come in?" he would ask, when the trainer at last showed himself; and stepping aside, he would bid Loutoshkin enter first.

Not often did they pause at Flattery's box, and at such times the conversation petered out. Loutoshkin would say nothing of the mare, Bourmin would put no questions. Only once did he ask for her to be brought out. Flattery was already in foal. Loutoshkin looked sullenly at Bourmin, who was examining the mare, and remained silent.

When Flattery was brought back to the stable, Bourmin stroked his beard with a smile of self-gratulation and declared:

"The foal will be without doubt the pride of the Orloffs. In him the blood of Sollogoub's Bounty and the incomparable Khren unite. . . . But at the end of the winter season we can race the mare."

Loutoshkin made no answer.

Autumn and winter came and at last the fateful February of 1917.

The cook Dimitri, who had gone to the town to buy spices, entered Bourmin's study with his accounts and proclaimed hilariously: "Our Tsar's been and—what do you think?—tee-hee-hee! . . ."

Bourmin glanced up at him incuriously and began to look through the accounts.

"Abdjicated and sloped off to Germany!" resumed Dimitri. "Here's one of them papers from the town tells all about it." He took the crumpled newspaper from his pocket and dropped it on the table.

Bourmin drew himself up, blasted Dimitri with a look, and bellowed: "Out of my sight, you loon!"

When Dimitri had gone out, he took up the newspaper, read it, and tore it into shreds.

That evening Bourmin drove to the town.

ONE starry August night that year Bourmin was taking his half-hour's constitutional in the park. It was pleasant to mark the discreet sounds that stressed the silence—the tap of the night-watchman's staff in the village across the pond, the shrill pipe of the grebe, the low booming of the bittern. Now and again he heard the forlorn, gentle thud of a ripe apple falling; or suddenly, from the tops of the yellowing limes, came a mysterious flutter and a beat of wings—all sounds familiar, immemorial, peaceful. Never and nowhere was his thought so free and fruitful as on these nightly walks in the park before he slept. Was it not here, just where the lawn slopes down to the pond, that Aristarkh Bourmin conceived the masterly design of mating the seventeen-year-old Baroness, daughter of Avenger and Caprice, to the grey Sorcerer, son of Destroyer! The yearling Baron was now the best colt in his stud, and

Bourmin had no doubt of a brilliant future for him.

"Chaos, transformed by the divine fiat into the majestic order of creation, must be our inspiration and example," he mused as he walked homeward. . . . "Even if Flattery's foal should die, the principle would hold, for in the famous Baden, bred by Vyaremsky, the blood of Electioneer is repeated in the fourth generation three times on the male side and once on the female. . . ."

CHAPTER X

"NOT ONE OF OUR MARYEVKA FOLK HAS
ever had a horse to call his own!" said a loud voice by
the kitchen window. Bourmin knew it well.

He heard a responsive sigh.

"What a power of horses he's got there!" the voice
proceeded. "If every family had one, there'd be enough
for two Maryevkas."

"Enough and to spare," a voice concurred. "He's
overrun with 'em!"

Bourmin stopped. One of the speakers was the cook
Dimitri; Bourmin recognized his voice.

"I've always fancied that mare; my word, what a
beauty!" resumed Dimitri in more cautious tones.
"She'll draw well-nigh a ton weight and not turn a hair.
I've had my eye on her for a year. She'll make me the
snuggest farmer in Maryevka!"

"Indeed she will!" the other agreed, and paused, ap-
pearing to reflect.

"But I must tell you, Mitri Egoritch," he demurred,
"that mare's not fit for farm-work. Won't cotton to

coarse feeding either. . . . And then, those racers won't stand still, you know; they're tricksy. . . ."

"Tricksy, are they?" scoffed Dimitri. "Eating their heads off, that's what makes 'em tricksy. I reckon she'll play no tricks when I've got her. Put her to hard work, I will; give her chaff instead of oats. I'll tame her! She'll soon forget her soft life and her high-toned masters!"

What most amazed Bourmin was that his cook had spoken of a farm. It seemed Dimitri had his own farm in Maryevka, one of the villages near Bourmin's estate. Bourmin was astonished and incensed. Dimitri was a cook, a slave of spits and pot-hooks. Every morning for nine years he had submitted to Bourmin through Adele Maximovna a list of the provisions he required for dinner, supper, and next morning's breakfast. For nine years his name had been linked inseparably to a chain of precise concepts: beet soup, bouillon, beef cutlets, soufflé, blancmange, and suchlike; for nine years the fellow had gone with him to the bath-house every Monday, undressed, washed, and dressed him again. Never had Bourmin suspected that his cook had a life outside the life of the kitchen and those Monday ministrations. And suddenly it turns out that he has some sort of farm and interests in Maryevka—prates of owning his own horse! A cook to own a farm! A cook to own a horse! A cook to talk such perilous nonsense!"

"I'll dismiss the fellow!" Bourmin growled, and was

about to descend in wrath upon these babblers when a third man joined them, Stepan, the night-watchman, who had lost an arm at the front last year and been sent home. Stepan was also from Maryevka.

"Stepan, is that you?" Dimitri whispered.

"It's me; who else should it be?"

"When are we going to divide up the old bastard's horses?"

"Soon as the harvest's in, that's what we settled," answered Stepan grimly. He spat audibly and added: "For my part, I'd as lief start this minute!"

Bourmin listened no more. . . . The peace of the old avenue was shattered, stormed by the monster brood of chaos. Everything known, established, and serene was suddenly distorted out of recognition. The very whistle of the grebe was ominous, the night-watchman's heavy tapping measured the brief minutes till the hour should strike.

"REV-O-LU-TION!" For the first time Bourmin spoke the word, which he had never yet pronounced, to which he had long shut his ears, his very consciousness. And the walls of his vast sanctum, hung with pedigree-charts and photographs of the beasts in whom he gloried, confirmed with repeated echoes the abhorred word: "Revolution."

NEXT morning Bourmin drove to the town again; in three days soldiers arrived, sent by the Commissary of the Provisional Government to protect his stables. Bourmin had other studies now; men took the place of horses. Over long lists of names his thick blue pencil hovered, pouncing on those that he deemed suspect. And the more he conned these lists, the fewer were the names that had not his blue cross against them.

In this task his trusty ally was Adele Maximovna. As an old-clothes-man scents out rags, she would sniff round the kitchen, servants' hall, and wash-house, gleaning chance phrases, words, sighs, mutterings, innuendoes, and bear off her booty to her master's den. Up and down the lists crept the blue pencil, setting Bourmin's brand on the open face of revolution, the deep, mannish voice of Adele Maximovna prompting from behind his chair, and each night Aristarkh Bourmin sighed with relief, his account with the revolution almost settled.

"Go now!" he would say to his faithful housekeeper. "Go, and remember: this is no revolution, it's rank brigandage! That fellow's no cook, he's a Jacobin, a Danton! You can go. I thank you."

One evening, when there were only four names left unmarked, those of Adele Maximovna, Loutoshkin, the steward Fyodor Epifanof, and the groom Yakof, reported missing at the front six months before, Bourmin sent for Loutoshkin and addressed him thus: "A hun-

dred years ago the Emperor Alexander I, having hon-
oured the Khrenoffsky stud-farm with a visit, mani-
fested to the Countess Orloff Chesmensky his desire to
possess some stallions bred on her estate. And what
was the sequel? Four stallions were picked out for the
acceptance of His Majesty—but they were all gelded
first. . . ."

Bourmin made a long pause, fastening questioning,
probing eyes upon Loutoshkin. Then he proceeded,
neither raising nor lowering his voice: "The Countess
could not have acted otherwise. The will of her illustrious parent was sacred to her. Count Alexei Grigoryevitch had stipulated in his will that no stallion should
leave his stud entire. He meant to preserve the purity
of the breed which he had fostered."

The forefinger with the broad gold ring rapped significantly on the table.

"By this means the will of the Emperor was frus-
trated. History has justified this act. Emperor and
Count sleep with their fathers, the Count's daughter
is no more, but the Orloff trotter lives. On my stud-
farm I have gathered the pure scions of the untainted
Orloff breed. Does not this lay upon us both the high
and solemn duty of taking all measures in our power to
preserve it? By keeping a vigilant eye upon the stable-
hands you will be in a position to form a correct judgment as to the loyalty of each. Remember that the
most plausible consultation about horses may be a cloak

for anarchy and Jacobin cabals. Here is a list of the men whom I shall ask you to dismiss immediately."

Having cast his eyes over the list, Loutoshkin raised them, stared point-blank at Bourmin, and enounced tersely: "That's useless. There's an end to everything. The Orloff trotter will remain, perhaps. But the owners—their day's done, Aristarkh Sergyeevitch! Nowadays every stable-boy's a Pougatchoff. It's plain to me. . . ."

"Pougatchoff was caught and caged, sir!" Bourmin snapped, and after a moment's thought, ordered peremptorily: "Go!"

When Loutoshkin left the study, a blue cross stood against his name.

Twenty-four hours after this interview the detachment sent to guard the estate was unexpectedly withdrawn, and on the following night Adele Maximovna ran half-dressed into Bourmin's bedroom screaming: "Dan-ton!"

Bourmin's sleep was rent by a fiery chasm. . . . The brood of chaos wantoned surging through his brain . . . "Rev-o-lu-tion!"

In curl-papers and chemise, folding her hands over her flat chest in dumb dismay, Adele Maximovna stared huge-eyed at the study door, stained by the red glare of the flames without. Bourmin sprang from his bed, entered the study at a bound, darted from window to window, and struck the frame of the big french window, which, being unfastened, opened with a jerk. He heard the hissing flame, saw billowing smoke and vengeful crowds, heard roaring, neighing, and the crash of staved-in doors, and, retreating from the window, from the roar and crash and flame, from the hissing Gorgon head of revolution, into the deep recesses of his study, gazed up and down its walls with frenzied, rolling eyes.

They were all here. Marshalled and aligned immutably. The proud and dazzling Champion, his majestic sire Colossal, the shapely Coquette, the dapple-grey, steel-thewed Granite, bred by Baron Tol, and Affable beside him. . . . All, all! From the gilt-edged black frames the lines and circles of the charts stood out; while over the writing-desk rode furiously in the red glare, astride the powerful grey Leopard—Count Orloff Chesmensky.

Bourmin pleaded with outstretched hands.

For the first time in his life he raised his voice in a plaintive, helpless cry: "Oh—Count!"

PART TWO

CHAPTER · I

SOUTHWARD CREPT A COLUMN OF COS-
sacks before the oncoming Red armies. The highroad,
six score yards in width, sprawled languidly across the
fields beneath sallow clouds, which had hung for days in
the sultry, stagnant air. Long before the arrival of the
column the Shatnyevka peasants had begun to drive
their horses and cattle across the river, to hide their oats
and hay, round up stray pigs and poultry, and take the
wheels and shafts out of their wagons. In the short time
since the civil war began they had learned how to deal
with all armed forces, whether White or Red or the
familiar, but no less formidable, Green peasant bands,
so called because they were outlaws, hiding in woods
and hills, claiming the land for the peasants, and harry-
ing Whites and Reds alike.

When he heard of the approach of soldiers, Nikita
Loukoff ran home like a madman, rushed to the cow-
shed, and then burst into his cottage. "Syomka not
home yet?"

"There's a hasty man!" said Nastasya. "The boy's

just about got there, and you expect him home?"

Nikita sat down on the bench and stared glumly at the floor.

Six months ago a party of Reds had commandeered him and his cart. More than a hundred miles he had plodded with the baggage-train, and seeing no prospect of release, he had ridden out of the camp one night, leaving his cart behind him. But half-way home he fell in with a battery of Cossacks, who hitched his horse in double harness to a limber, and Nikita trudged back horseless and cartless to Shatnyevka. To those that asked him whether the Cossacks had given him anything for what they took, he answered: "Ay, they gave me something—a couple of clouts on the ear, good weight."

Nastasya looked at her husband in bewilderment. "What did you want Syomka for?" she asked.

Nikita, instead of answering, shook his head hopelessly. "Sure as fate, they'll meet him on the road. . . . What shall I do now?—sinner that I am! . . . There's soldiers coming from the town," he explained to Nastasya.

Presently he bestirred himself. "See here, wife; I'll run off through the orchard to the Settlement. Maybe I'll find him, but if I don't, and if he comes back alone, you drive the stallion across the river to the Burnt Marsh, leave him a nose-bag with some oats, and let him stay there till I fetch him. If they ask for the master of the house, say he's away fighting—on their side, whoever they are. Take out the front of the cart and roll it down into the pond—wetting won't hurt it. Drive the sow and her litter into the stall and lock it up—and take the oats out of the bin, there's two and a half bushels in it. And don't you unlock the door, your husband's with the army, mind. I'll be off now, maybe I'll find him."

Skirting the beans and cabbage-patches, scrambling over fences, Nikita soon arrived at the deep gully which split the village in two and reached almost to the Settlement, whither Syomka had ridden out on the stallion to buy nails. This ravine was flanked with orchards; the stream that ran through it was overarched with willows and fringed with nettles—of a man's height—and straggling burdocks. A sweet cool air rose from it. But on Nikita ran, the sweat showing in dark patches through his shirt. Three miles more to the Settlement.

His kinsman Gregory was in his barn. He started up from the straw that he was chopping.

"Well met, kinsman! That's odd, now, I was thinking of giving you a call. They say your sow's farrowed; me and the old woman have been wanting one of her pigs this long time back, and . . ."

"Seen Syomka?" Nikita panted.

"I've seen him sure enough. Stopped and had pancakes with us. He'll be nearly home by now, I reckon. Why, you're all in a muck-sweat; what on earth? . . ."

Nikita clasped his head and, without wasting words, ran back to the gully.

SYOMKA had started back from the Settlement with the nails tucked into his shirt. As soon as he reached the boundary of the village, he saw a cloud of dust, and a swarm of men trailing along the highroad, like a giant hedgehog. Fearing to miss the soldiers, he whipped up the bay stallion with the end of the halter. They struck the tail of the baggage-train as it was entering the village. On the rear limber lay two Cossacks, lounging full length and howling out two separate songs. It was plain they were in no mood for harmony. When one set up his howl, his comrade presently gave tongue, and the two tunes, grappling in mid-air, crashed and subsided. A pause, and again the voices would contend: "In his tall grey hat stood he," sang one. "On Volga's foaming bank," struck in the other. It was as though two wrestlers in hob-nailed boots had hit the floor together and were sorting out their legs.

From his high perch on the stallion Syomka looked gravely down at the sweat-begrimed faces of the singers and was about to drive on when one of them jerked up a bristling black shock-head like a gypsy's and, with a glance at Syomka and the bay stallion, nudged his comrade.

"Stop!" he yelled to Syomka, flinging over the lim-

114

ber's edge a pair of legs in puttees and torn boots.

"Eh?" said Syomka with suspicion, as he checked the stallion slightly.

"Stop, I say, I've business with you!"

The bristle-pated fellow sprang from the limber and strode towards him; his comrade, whose feet were swollen, staggered after him and seized the stallion's bridle.

"Down with you!" said the swarthy Cossack.

"Let me go!" whined Syomka, tugging at the rein and digging his bare heels into the stallion's flanks.

"Get down, I tell you!" said the swarthy fellow, and dragged him off the horse.

Syomka was dazed. Afterwards he understood it all.

In a trice the soldiers had their horse out of the shafts and the stallion harnessed in its place. Syomka screamed and clung with both hands to the stallion. The black fellow pulled out a rifle from the limber and snarled at him: "Let go, you tadpole, or I'll shoot you!"

"You shan't have him, you sha-an't! Hey, Papanka! He-e-elp!"

A swinging blow sent Syomka full-length into the road, his shirt open, the nails scattering. Limber and stallion rattled down the road on the heels of the baggage-train. Syomka ran after them, in tears, and bawling for his father, but remembering the nails, turned back, still whimpering, and groped in the thick dust for them. When he had found and counted them, he looked at the mangy nag standing ruefully at the road's edge and uttered a hopeless, piercing shriek, as if his throat were being cut. Suddenly he stopped and again looked at the horse. In his big, tear-brimmed eyes some thought seemed kindling. For a few moments he stood thus, staring at the horse, his mouth agape, as though a cry fought for utterance and could find no passage— one hand clutching the nails collected in his shirt-tail, while the other scratched the inside of his knée. . . . And there stood the foundered nag; its mangy head drooped to the earth, its lower lip sagged, slopping audibly, its wispy tail brushed feebly at the flies that fastened on its sores.

"Oh! Oh! Oh!" howled Syomka, as he saw his father running towards him from the orchard.

"Where's the stallion?" cried Nikita, in a ghastly voice, as he came near.

Syomka replied with a still more piercing howl.

Nikita looked at the broken-down jade and with a savage blow knocked Syomka to the ground. Once more the nails fell from his shirt and were scattered. At sight of them Nikita's wrath redoubled; he gripped Syomka by the hair and bellowed hoarsely: "Saved the nails, did you, you stinkard! I'll give you nai-ails! I'll murder you!"

Pitched headlong in the dust, the boy staggered to his knees, stood up, and again fell sprawling. With one more sounding thwack, his father left him and ran to the village, fury smouldering in his eyes.

HAVING heard Nikita's story, the Chairman of the Soviet scratched his head and sighed: "Your stallion was a good 'un, no denying that. But we can't do nothing—'cos why? The front, you know—there's a civil war on. Go to the Volost, I'll give you a sustifikit as how you've lost him. They'll think of somethin', maybe. . . ."

In the hut Nastasya wailed shrilly, Syomka lay over the stove crying, his face battered and swollen; in the yard, by the lopped and wheelless wagon, stood the melancholy beast, as bald as a flayed carcase. Nikita gazed long at her, grinding his teeth. He struck his boot into her hairless flank. She groaned, turned her head round—she was blind in the left eye—and edged away from him. That evening Nikita walked to the Volost, the central office of the rural district, returned drunk, and made a long search for Syomka, who was hiding from his reach. Neighbours drifted into the yard, examined the mare, sighed, condoled with her master, and drifted out again. Sometimes Nastasya would steal out of the hut and stand long in contemplation of the mare, quietly sobbing and drying her tears upon her apron.

Nikita drank for two days. On the third, at dawn, he left the storeroom, where he had flung himself to sleep, went out to the mare, and scanned her narrowly. A moth-eaten look she had—all scabs and patches. An old horse surely, for her eyes were sunken and her legs gave at the knees and trembled as though they would break under her. Nikita pulled out her tongue and looked at her teeth. She was ten years old if a day.

"What shall I do with you?" he groaned. "A mighty help you'll be to me! Fall down at the sight of work, you will! Take you to the vet, eh, and have the whole village grinning at me? . . . Can't do without a horse, though. Gaffer Mitritch wants three hundred for his gelding—and where's that money coming from?"

Nikita pressed his palm into her sunken flank. She staggered.

"Can't even stand, she can't!"

Syomka crept out of the hut and, seeing his father, darted back in fright.

At noon, with fifteen eggs and two pounds of butter in a knotted scarf, Nikita set out for the veterinary's house at the headquarters of the Volost. He had to pass through the whole village. His head drooped as he dragged, rather than led, the shambling beast. When he met an acquaintance, he would start aside, as if guilty of some crime.

His estranged brother, Vassily, who had been formerly a carrier like himself and had always grudged him the grey stallion, popped out of his gate and shouted, so that the whole street might hear him: "Fine swap you've made, Nikita! How much extra did you pay for her? Regular lioness she is!"

The "lioness," as if to spite Nikita, stumbled and fell

118

on her knees. Nikita shook the halter and, seeing the mare did not stir, booted her muzzle savagely. One by one she raised her tottering legs, groaning, and stood up.

"Keep a tight hold on her or she'll run away!" Vassily screamed at him.

The whole journey was a shameful ordeal for Nikita, as though he were running the gauntlet for some dark and heinous deed.

The veterinary was out. Nikita tied up his horse and sat down on the doorstep. He had long to wait and nothing at all to think about. In the last three days he had thought over everything. The stallion was worth five hundred and fifty; the mare would scarcely fetch five rubles for her hide. He had no money for another horse. . . .

Next to the veterinary's little home lowered the ruins of a goodly house; its front had fallen in, showing its gutted ribs and the charred sockets of the doors; against one wall an aged elm reached black and lifeless arms; one of these almost touched the tottering balcony; and along its cornice crept a piebald cat, stalking a crow that eyed it quizzically from the dead branch. . . .

With straddled legs and downcast head Nikita sat twirling his tattered cap, clawing its threadbare visor, or rubbing his sleeve spasmodically against inveterate stains. He dropped his cap and gloomily surveyed the churchyard, blinked at the crosses gleaming in the sun, gazed after the flights of jackdaws, fixed his eyes on the desolate walls that had once lodged the Ispolkom, the Executive Committee of the Volost, and considered that that house was once the grandest in Shatnyevka—and again and again his thoughts harked back to the sleek and lusty stallion; his gaze shunned the tethered mare; but whether he looked at the wheeling jackdaws, or the dazzling crosses, or the dismal ruins of the once rich and lordly mansion, she caught his eyes persistently. The sight harrowed him, as if it were no horse that stood there, but his whole life, henceforth meaningless, hateful, and of no use to any man. . . .

The old veterinary sauntered past Nikita, carrying a sheaf of newspapers. He took no notice of the mare.

Nikita rose to his feet and waited for the veterinary to come out to him. He stood waiting a long while. At last he walked into the house. The veterinary was reading the newspaper.

"I've come to ask you, Alexandr Egoritch, if . . ."

"What?" snapped the veterinary, still reading his newspaper.

"I've brought you that there—that there sick beast," said Nikita, ashamed to call the worn-out nag a horse.

"Colic, eh?" said the veterinary.

In a hollow voice Nikita told his story; he set the butter and eggs down on the table, took an imperial half-ruble from his pocket, and dropped it sheepishly on the newspaper.

"Only tell me, Alexandr Egoritch, is there any hope for her?" he added, peering into the red, seamed, hoary-whiskered face.

Alexandr Egoritch went to the door, glanced at the mare, and whistled:

"Whew, what a beauty!"

After a rapid survey of the mare he returned to the house to wash his hands. Nikita waited moodily on the doorstep.

"Off her feed?" asked the veterinary, re-emerging.

Nikita had had her three days and not fed her at all.

"Won't look at it," he said.

"A tough job, and no mistake," said Alexandr Egoritch. "Got the mange, and starved to a shadow. If the mange once gets into her system, you can say good-bye to her. I'll give you an ointment; maybe it'll do her good. By rights she ought to be put through the sulphur-chamber—but can a man get anything out of you close-fisted clodhoppers? For three months I've been hammering away at the Soviet here: 'Give me the money for a sulphur-chamber!' . . . Your sort'll never be civilized. Ought to be dumped down among the Zulus." The veterinary spat savagely.

"Well, I'll give you an ointment. Rub all the sore places with it, wash them with this green soap and decoction of tobacco-leaves, and rub them again every other day. You must feed her well too: potatoes, chopped small, with her oats, bran mash, and scraped carrots. Got me? Bring her back in a week."

"Think there's a chance for her?" asked Nikita timidly.

"It's touch and go. I *have* known cures in such cases. I suppose you've got a still; might bring me a bottle."

Nikita's face lit up; that request for a bottle of poteen was the best sign of all.

"If only you can pull her through, sir, I'll give you a bottle of pure liquor, unadulterated, sir."

"In a week, then!" said Alexandr Egoritch, as he went back to the house for the medicine.

At the church gate Nikita crossed himself.

As he led her home, it seemed to him that the mare was already going better, dragging less at the halter than before. He felt he had been heedless in not taking a bottle with him; of course the cure would have been quicker, Alexandr Egoritch would have given him a big pot of ointment, and some physic too, instead of that foolish little jar. . . .

When he turned to the mare to urge her on, his voice had lost its bitterness, and many times he waited patiently to give her breath.

The scurvy changeling returned to Nikita Loukoff's house a rightful member of his family.

CHAPTER · 11

JOY CAME TO NIKITA, AS UNFORESEEN, undreamed-of, as the mischance that had struck him down on that day of heat and fury when he lost the stallion.

The whole family danced attendance on the patient. Nikita smeared and washed her coat, clipped the hair round the sores, and groomed her. Nastasya brewed the bran mash, steamed the rich amber-coloured oats, wrapped the pail in an old petticoat to keep it warm, grated the carrots for her. Syomka scrubbed out the stall several times daily and never missed a chance of pressing a salted crust between her nuzzling lips.

Slowly the mare recovered health and spirits. Her bald patches sprouted fresh, silky hair, her tail and mane grew thicker, her legs straightened, rid of their palsied tremblings and twitchings.

One day at noon, when his father was at dinner, Syomka crashed into the room bursting with his news: "She's started neighing, Papanka! Neighing! Pashka

Nikishin was passing down the street; she heard him and she *neighed!*"

His father set down his spoon, wiped his moustache, and looked at Nastasya. "Alexandr Egoritch promised to call today. Let him look at the creature, he won't know her!"

"That's right, he won't!" Syomka struck in. "He'll never guess it's her, I'll bet. Caught sight of her myself as I came back from threshing. 'Whose mare's that?' I says. I never guessed, I'll take my oath on it. Firm as a rock she stood."

The old veterinary guessed.

When Nikita led the mare out of the shed, the grey eyebrows of Alexandr Egoritch, sharply set off by his leathery red forehead, shot up in amazement, and he stepped aside for a better view of her. Then he approached her briskly, examined her teeth, and looked round at Nikita, who smiled complacently. Syomka grinned broadly as he looked from his father to the veterinary, from the veterinary to the mare.

"Well, what do you say to her, Alexandr Egoritch?" crowed Nikita, seeing that the veterinary said nothing and only flickered his grey, tobacco-stained moustache.

"Tried her in harness?" he asked.

"Once; got a good stride on her."

Alexandr Egoritch lifted the mare's forelock; under the hair was a white crescent.

"Do you know who that mare is?" he asked with

sudden sternness. "She's the aunt of Champion. Out of Firedrake. From Bourmin's stable."

Firedrake meant nothing to Nikita, but he had heard of Champion. Throwing the halter to his son, he came close to Alexandr Egoritch.

"Aunt of Champion?" he whispered.

"It's Flattery. Not a doubt of it! That's her!" said the veterinary to himself, still gazing at the mare. "Flattery sure as eggs is eggs. How they cut her up, the blackguards! Do you know"—he spun round sharply on Nikita—"Bourmin planked down five thousand for that mare. She's got blood in her, man! Breed! Flattery by Firedrake out of Pepperbrandy, scion of Sturdy. Treated her myself in Bourmin's stable for a sprain. Does her off foreleg trouble her? That's right; so it did then. I helped Loutoshkin, the trainer, to put a seton on her."

The veterinary began to massage her off shoulder. She winced.

"That's Flattery right enough. . . . Tell you what, Nikita Loukitch, you're in luck. Stick to her, my boy; she's worth more than a wife to you. Even now she'd fetch a thumping price for breeding. But you keep her. Take her to the coupling stable in the spring, mate her with a blood stallion, and . . ."

Nikita drank in every word. When he had seen the old veterinary to the gate, he felt frightened; frightened to think that Syomka just behind him held such a gold-mine by the neck. "Five thousand for the mare?"

The cramped courtyard with its ramshackle lean-to, the gaping cattle-shed which housed the mare, the gate with its flimsy lock, and the back door with no lock at all—all this, after the veterinary's words, flashed on him with sudden instancy and clamoured for redress.

Syomka would circle round his father, seeking to read his thoughts by sudden glances. One evening after supper he went up to him and touched his sleeve.

"Papanka, Papanka?"

"What is it, boy?"

"Do you remember, Papanka, what a lambasting you gave me when you lost the stallion? Out shot your arm, and I went head over heels. Eykh, and it hurt too! . . . And when I was up again—crack!—and you sent me spinning! And the nails all over the road! And what a mug I grew on me! Big as a pumpkin!"

Nikita looked down absently. His thoughts were busy. When the church clock chimed, he would start up anxiously and listen. "That's not the fire-alarm? God save us in this drought!"

Next morning Alexandr Egoritch was surprised by a visit from Nikita, harassed and crestfallen.

He closed the door behind him, cautiously, like a conspirator.

"I've come to you again, Alexandr Egoritch," he said in a hushed voice. "Come for a bit of advice. You'd better have told me nothing about the mare."

126

"What do you mean?"

"You've only made me more bother."

"What's the matter with the man! Talk sense."

"Believe it or not, I ain't slept a wink, I'm that worried." Nikita looked round at the door and whispered: "They'll have the law of me, I'm thinking."

"Who'll have the law of you? For what?" said the old man testily.

"For the mare. They'll have her, won't they?"

"Why?"

"Judge for yourself, sir. . . . Five thousand she cost, and my stallion weren't worth five hundred. . . ."

"Well, what then?"

"Why, they'll get wind of it and take her away from me."

"Stuff and nonsense, man. Who'll take her away? Who wants her?"

"Who? Why, *them*. Them as always takes, the Government, I mean. Soldiers! Officials!"

"They haven't the right, Nikita."

"That may be, but they've got the power. She's the aunt of Champion, don't forget," he added bitterly.

"All the same, they've no right to touch her," said the veterinary; he was about to give his reasons, when Nikita launched out vehemently:

"That's what I say, Alexandr Egoritch, they've no right at all, being as they took my stallion. And what's more, they left me the mare all scabs and galls and good

127

for nothing. The trouble I took with her! And the feeds I've given her! What with two quarters of oats, and well-nigh a hundredweight of bran, let alone the potatoes and the carrots—and now they'll take her, will they? Every man takes what he can get, but get it honestly, I says. How do I get my bread? By sweat and sorrow. I plough and sow, me and my family reap the crop, thresh it, cart it to the mill; the old woman bakes a cake with the flour—and them jackanapeses want to eat it! . . . Howsomever, you can't compare her with the stallion, she cost a mint of money. . . ."

"But who knows how much she cost?" the old man interrupted.

Nikita was silent.

"Whether she cost five thousand or twenty thousand is none of their business," pursued the veterinary. "Nobody knows about her but ourselves."

Nikita looked round sharply at the door and, striding up to his old counsellor, stooped down and whispered pleadingly:

"That's why I came to you, Alexandr Egoritch. . . . For the love of Christ, keep your mouth shut, don't tell anybody what she cost, just think how I'm placed, sir! . . . You know yourself what sort of folks are on top now. You'll do me this kindness, won't you, sir?"

The old veterinary looked at Nikita with bent brows. In the man's wheedling voice, his abject posture and expression, he discerned the Russian peasant, awed and

128

debased by landlords, bailiffs, police, and soldiers, scared to death now at his own good fortune. . . .

Nikita could not understand why Alexandr Egoritch frowned at him; he crumpled and twirled his cap, waiting intently for an answer to his plea. It fretted him to think that in reckoning up what the mare had cost him he had forgotten thirty pounds of linseed and a sack of beets.

"At least I must tell you, she's blind in the left eye, and my stallion was sound as a bell," he stammered.

"Eykh, Holy Mother Russia!" sighed Alexandr Egoritch, waving an arm in powerless protest. "Get a certificate from the Soviet that your stallion was taken from you, and the mare left you in exchange. I'll give you an affidavit that the mare was half-dead and you nursed her back to health."

Nikita went home comforted, bearing a paper from the veterinary with a big seal on it. He entered the cattle-shed, looked fondly at the mare, and spoke to her:

"Well, you're a caution, you are! Champion's aunt indeed! What did they see in you, my lady, that made 'em come down so handsome? Hm! . . . It's a puzzle to me! A man could buy ten stallions for the price of you!"

Flattery, now tall and sturdy, was quite equal to the rough work Nikita gave her. . . . Only her pale grey colour fretted him. Like most peasants he preferred bay horses; a grey coat shows up every speck.

"No doubt about it, though, the mare's a thorough-bred," he reasoned, as he gauged her stature. "He weighed you up all right. . . . But maybe Alexandr Egoritch was just making fun of me. The tongue's easy to wag. But I'll go bail for it, he's a sound man, none of your random talkers, his word's true. And besides, you're clever, my lass, and you've got the manners of a duchess. . . . I'll warrant your late master's stable smelt as sweet as a lady's bedchamber. We're not such high-fliers as that, but we won't grudge you your bite of oats, make your mind easy!"

Nikita walked all round the mare, stroking her loins and running his fingers through her mane.

"How did you lose your eye, tell me, my beauty?" he asked compassionately, and turned up the lid. The eye was bloodless, and creased like a scrap of crumpled paper.

Flattery pressed her shoulder against Nikita's head with a friendly snuffle.

There was much she could have told him on that autumn day. . . . How her lovely foal sickened and died . . . and how one night a year ago strangers had burst into her box, strangers that smelt ill and strong, like Philipp when he stood close to her in the jolting, creaking box that bore her from one stable to another. The strangers had flung a bridle on her, not her own, with a great, clumsy bit, forcing her lips painfully apart, and hurried her out into the flaring yard, where other strangers surged and shouted. Behind the stable, where the white house towered, a big fire cracked and hissed, and a scorching wind blew out of it. One of those red spots that the wind was carrying fell right between her nostrils with a stabbing pain that made her start and plunge, but a strong hand curbed her, with such a jerk as she had never felt, and the stinging smart of a torn lip was added to her pain.

The strangers brought strange days. No loose-box now, with a grating in the door, through which to watch the men passing with pails of water, sacks of oats, armfuls of sweet-smelling hay. Somehow, somewhere the men she knew had gone. No morning shaft of light pierced the long window, no joyous bell pealed out, there came no oats or hay, no groom to lead her into the broad bright passage, no pouring of water on her legs, no rubbing of her sides and back, no walking of her up and down the yard. Day after day she bore the weight of an unknown rider. Often he struck his iron-shod heels into her, sawed at her mouth, tugged at the reins for no reason she could guess, and when he wanted her to go faster, did not make the well-known clucking noise, as the other men did, but flourished his whip, lashing her belly, neck, and head, so that she had to close her eyes to save them. It gave her great pain to trot, for then the weight on her back would start wriggling from her saddle to her neck, would shoot up and bump down with such force that it seemed her back would break the very next moment. A sore came on her neck, and as soon as she stopped, vicious flies swarmed on it.

When the year grew cold and everything turned white, she was worse fed, and her strength began to fail. Every day it was harder to trot, her legs began to tremble and give way. At last she refused to be mounted. She was beaten unmercifully, but her body scarcely felt the pain. They kicked her on the belly and between the legs, cudgelled her neck and wounded head. It was then that something stuck in her near eye, causing a sudden twinge, and she tossed her head in a wild effort to shake off the torturer. Since that day Flattery could not see what was happening on that side where the horse-fly had settled. But since that day her back was eased of her burden, she began to draw a cart with another horse beside her. The cart was clumsy and heavy and kept knocking her hind feet. Once she had only to move her ears and the man at her back would understand her; when she wanted to dash forward, she would prick up her ears, and the reins slackened till she fell into her stride; when more was asked of her than she could do, she twitched her ears and laid them back, so that the man understood and stopped her, soothing her with gentle, crooning words. But now they did not try to understand her, they whipped her to their pace, and every day the cart grew heavier. . . .

And so it went on endlessly. When the green grass appeared again, her journeys lengthened. Often they left the road and passed through forests and ravines; sometimes there was a wild stampede, the air was full of shrieks and thunders and dull crashes overhead. On one such day Flattery was freed from her cruel masters. Others were now in charge of her. But her strength was ebbing fast, her whole body itched, and her legs shook more feebly every day. . . .

When Nikita first hitched Flattery to the cart, it was long before she could bring herself to stir; at the memory of their pain, her shoulders stiffened. When Nikita spoke to her, she turned and fixed her one eye sadly on him, waiting for the blow. But her new master jumped to her head and, instead of striking her, pulled coaxingly at the bridle. She lifted her feet gingerly and walked slowly to the gate. When they came out on the field, she felt her strength return, pricked up her ears, and pulled impatiently.

Nikita understood and let her trot.

CHAPTER · III

AUTUMN WAS AT HAND. FLATTERY brought the harvest home, she ploughed, she harrowed; and Nikita rejoiced in his lusty helpmeet. He measured her by the low-bred farm-horses he knew, and set her high above them. Whether her cart went full or empty, her gait was always sprightly and effective, not at all like the drowsy lurch of a peasant plough-horse. She needed no sharp word, no jerking of the rein to start her. "She's a good workman," said Nikita, "and don't need no telling." He had only to tie up the load and take the reins, and she slipped into the collar and, tossing her head skittishly, set off at a brisk but steady trot. The distant field seemed nearer now, the road smoother, and work delightful.

Nikita was no nightingale, but sometimes, as he turned home at the village boundary, the lilting cart would fire his blood, and he struck up: "Red poppies peeping from the co-orn! . . ."

His harvest in, he set to work on Flattery's stall. He

smeared the wattled walls with clay and dung, mended the roof, gave it a ceiling and a stamped-clay floor. He was bent on making a new door—no light matter; it needed boards, hinges, and sockets, none of which Nikita had, nor could he easily come by them. Nastasya grumbled, but one day he gave her the slip, drove to the Volost with some sacks of rye, and brought home the material for his door, and a sheet of glass into the bargain. Alexandr Egoritch had dinned into his ears that the mare must have light, so Nikita fitted a small window near the door, just like the window of a cottage.

"Are you gone daft?" said his wife, as she watched him at his task. "We've no window in the house, and you want to put one in the cattle-shed!"

"Stop your clack, old woman!" said Nikita gaily. "When you can call Champion your uncle, I'll put in a dozen windows for you. Horses are dumb creatures. If the mare can't speak her mind, it's our place to know it and make her comfortable."

Syomka shared actively in all these preparations. When the neat new door was up, he contrived to lay hands on a stick of red lead and painted Champion's portrait on the spotless deal. His model was a gingerbread horse bought at a fair—a galloping, high-crested little steed, with its tail up and streaming—and to make his work more lifelike, he finished it off with a string of pellets, dropping from tail to floor.

Nikita eyed the portrait, took the home-made brush from Syomka's hands, plunged it into the red lead solution, and held it for a long time poised, pondering some addition to his son's design. Twice he approached the little red cock-horse, brush in hand, but each time his arm dropped limply, powerless to convey his thoughts. So he left the figure untouched, to the great relief of the jealous portraitist. Nikita handed him back the dripping brush, contenting himself with a single sound, which expressed what the brush could not: "Who-oa!"

Now came the season of long evenings and long nights, of starless skies, black as the mire of the highroad, and the frozen wind hung snared and screaming in the wattle fence.

Oil there was none. Like a swarm of cockroaches about a loaf, the family huddled round the potsherd filled with lard, in which a ragged wick swam listlessly. The close air reeked with a stale acrid smell of soot, cobwebs hung like a black hoar-frost on the walls, and the broken shadows of the three seated figures groped over walls and ceiling, mocking the drab cottage with their mirthless antics.

Syomka would crawl onto the table on his stomach and lie trimming the charred wick for hours, and when he wearied of this pastime, drop his bushy blond head on the table and fall off to sleep.

"Go to bed, Syomka!" scolded Nastasya, patching a sleeve or trouser-seat. "Bless the boy, don't you hear

136

me?" And she dug him in the ribs. A peevish twitch of the shoulder, a petulant sniff, and Syomka would sleep on.

Nikita sat in thought. On these long autumn evenings he had leisure for an exhaustive survey of his homely peasant's budget; every kopeck, every nail, was conned and counted; everything was assigned its place and function, and as there was nothing missing or superfluous, the ordering of his household and the framing of his plans turned out a solid piece of work, stout and secure as a home-spun jacket.

Sometimes he would pass a whole evening with Alexandr Egoritch.

The sere old veterinary, whose ideals had withered in thirty years of service, hated the peasants in his heart for their greed, their crass indifference to all that lay beyond the bounds of their own farmsteads. Nikita struck him by the rare and amazing readiness with which he followed all his advice concerning Flattery's treatment. When the man told him that he had heated the cattle-shed and built a window to it, Alexandr Egoritch was touched. Time was when he had yearned "to sow virtue and wisdom, whose fruit is eternal," as Nekrasoff says; but his hopes had soured long since, clotted into a modest craving for a quiet rubber at preference, a snack of caviar, and a sip of cherry brandy. Of late, however, he would feel sometimes the breath of the forgotten past, when his student's coat with the white piping sat so jauntily upon him and he spent whole nights over a pint of beer, discoursing of Kant and Hegel or singing Nek-rasoff's wistful songs, among his ardent comrades. . . .

Nikita always came in shyly, so sheepishly, indeed, that the veterinary knew that he had not come on busi-ness, but simply to talk and listen—as no man had ever yet listened to Alexandr Egoritch. On the stool by the door, grave and erect, Nikita would sit hour by hour, and withdraw regretfully.

Alexandr Egoritch would talk of many things, but after a while the conversation turned invariably to horses. An old turfman and horse-lover, he poured his reviving passion into the peasant's tingling ears and, catching fire from his ardent listener, talked on more vehemently. These talks with Nikita soon became a necessity to the old stager.

"You're quite a stranger!" he would say, meeting Nikita at the market or the Peasants' Council. "Drop in today, I've dug up a book to show you."

He would show him some wonderful book with pic-tures of all kinds of horses in it. What horses, too! And what a sight of them! Powerful Russian cart-horses, shaggy-legged shire horses from England, beautiful Ardenne chargers, toy-like Shetland ponies.

Alexandr Egoritch would explain each picture, and the unlettered Nikita diligently stored his mind with the names of every breed and their several points and properties.

138

"Here's an album of Orloff trotters!" said Alexandr Egoritch one evening, as he took down a heavy tome in a red binding, with gilt headings on each page. "There you are, my boy; all your mare's relations in it!"

Nikita pushed his chair up to the table, thrust out his neck, and held his breath. It seemed to him hardly possible that this book, so fat and formal, could hold anything that concerned him, Nikita Loukoff, or his mare.

On the first page was a portrait of Count Orloff Chesmensky. Alexandr Egoritch told the full story of how, in the Russo-Turkish War, after the battle of Chesma, Count Orloff captured the family of a Turkish general, and how, after the war, in gratitude for the kindness he had shown them, the Count received from the Sultan of Turkey and the general himself some thoroughbred Arab trotters, among whom was the celebrated grey Smetanka, ancestor of the Orloff trotters.

The veterinary turned the pages, showing trotter after trotter to the amazed Nikita. He stopped at a stalwart iron-grey stallion and swept his hand over the picture.

"And that's Flier, from Shipoff's stable, grandsire of your mare."

Nikita propped his chest on the table and fixed his eyes on the stallion. As the imprint of the carbon covers a blank sheet, the portrait of Flattery's grandsire stamped itself upon his brain with all its lineaments:

firm hoofs, high withers, proudly arching neck. The owner, in an unbuttoned jacket, held the stallion by the bridle; he, too, and the very rails and outbuildings behind were etched into Nikita's memory. He drew the book towards him, not venturing to touch the page, and traced the portrait with a gnarled forefinger, panting with admiration.

Alexandr Egoritch looked at him; he smiled, his patchy moustache quivering, as another picture flashed upon him—the millionaire Aristarkh Bourmin in his vast inhospitable den. . . .

"From Warsaw to Tobolsk, from Archangel to Odessa, throughout the limitless domains of Russia, the whole equine population, upwards of thirty million horses, owes its improvement to the will and genius of a great horse-breeder and faithful servant of his country. On your shoulders lies the burden of rousing the dark and brutish conscience of the people to the sacred duty of promoting this improvement. You are sent to heal, not beasts alone, but the other unenlightened sections of the population." Such was the exhortation of Bourmin—and before him on the table, just as now before Nikita, the stud-book of the Orloff trotters was spread out.

Alexandr Egoritch laid his hand on Nikita's shoulder. Nikita shook his unkempt locks and said with a bewildered smile:

"It's mighty queer, Alexandr Egoritch! He's the

spit of my mare; you've got the rights of it."

"Look here, Nikita," said the veterinary, "you've done your job well, and the mare's sound again. Now listen to me! She's ten years old. She'd one foal in her former stable, and it died. What are you going to do with her when the spring comes?"

"Why, breed from her, of course."

"From what stock, though? Got your eye on some plough-horse, I'll be bound."

"Tell the truth, I have. There's one in the Settlement that . . ."

"I knew it!" Alexandr Egoritch frowned. "Get that out of your head. You take her to the district stud-farm. They've got Favourite there. He's the horse for you, I know him. The foal should be a beauty. . . . Easy enough for the gentry to breed trotters. But now —why shouldn't you try your hand at it?—you, a peasant from Shatnyevka! Well, you must rear the foal, take it to Moscow for the races, and cut a dash with the rest of 'em. . . ."

"A queer business," sighed Nikita, and sat pondering. As he went home that evening, strange thoughts galloped through his brain; thoughts of Moscow, the far-off, unknown Moscow, and a big round field, shut in by a fence—not exactly a field either—it had a long, out-landish name to it—and round and round that field were horses from all over Russia racing like the wind. . . . Thousands of people flocked to it to see whose horse could run the fastest, the band roared out, as if the Tsar were holding a review, and the owner of the best horse got the "cup." The word "cup" bewitched Nikita, and although Alexandr Egoritch had explained that the cup was now a prize in cash, Nikita saw it still as a gemmed and dazzling trophy, richer than all the treasure in the world. . . .

His boots squelched in the miry clay, the wind howled, the rain scourged him, darkness and solitude enfolded him, no road nor habitation was in sight. In the inside pocket of his coat he hugged a picture of his grey mare's famous grandsire.

CHAPTER · IV

TOWARDS THE END OF SEPTEMBER, WHEN the first snow fell and the roads were passable, Nikita took his corn to the collecting-centre at the station.

While he waited his turn, some wagons drove in from the surrounding villages.

The stately, well-groomed Flattery stood out from the rabble of scrubby plough-horses like a proud pine-tree from a thicket of dwarf oaks.

The peasants clustered round Nikita's cart, taking stock of the mare and exchanging comments. They asked her age, whether she had ever foaled, what he had paid for her, and so forth.

"She won't beat my gelding, I'll bet," said a Hop-o'-my-thumb fellow, who skipped about like a drop of mercury in a frying-pan.

Nikita stole a glance at him, and a second glance at the hook-nosed grey gelding tethered at some distance from the other horses.

"Your gelding's a pacer!" struck in several voices.

"Got a style of their own, them pacers . . . come from the Kirghiz." "You can drive a pacer a hundred miles —he'll be fresh as a daisy and spunky as Old Nick!"

Nikita squinted at the grey gelding, coachman-fashion, spat, and said in a stage whisper:

"Quack, quack, jabber, jabber—but you don't know what you're saying!"

"Meaning me?" snapped the manikin, ruffling up to Nikita. "Were you talking about me? Me and my gelding?"

And tearing off his cap, he dashed it in the snow.

"Race you for a bottle of vodka! Race you *now.* . . . I'll just heave in this rye, and we'll start 'em. . . . Man of my word, I am! If you win, I'll stand you a bottle. That's the sort I am! Are you game?"

"You'd lose!" said Nikita solemnly.

"You would, you mean. Back her for a bottle, man!"

"I'm not betting, but you'd lose!" Nikita insisted. He surveyed the ring of gaping faces and announced with dignity: "My mare's the aunt of Champion, she's got blue blood in her and comes from counts and sultans."

The gelding's owner stared wide-eyed at Nikita, and cooled down immediately, like a boiling cauldron when cold water is poured in. He picked up his cap, shook the snow out of it, and drawled dismally: "Tha-ats what you should have said befo-ore! She ain't your mare, nor no fa-arm-horse neither!"

Having dumped his rye and taken his money, Nikita drove off to his wife's brother, who was switchman at the grade crossing.

In these lean years Nikifor Petrovitch had contrived to lay in a stock of such rarities as matches, flints for cigarette-lighters, needles and thread, kerosene, and even pill-boxes and powders. When the slow passenger-train came in, his wife, Agrafena, a fat-rumped woman like a cart-horse, would relieve him, so that he could board the train and bring back his merchandise. Nikifor was no talker, he could greet and part without a word, and conversed with his wife in silence—glanced at the tea-pot, thence at the water-jug—and Agrafena put on the samovar; cocked an eye at the stove—time for breakfast; yawned and scratched his belly—bedtime; and when he screwed up his left eye and smacked his lips with a slow gulp, like a fish coming to the surface, Agrafena threw on her shawl and went to a neighbouring switchman for a fresh supply of home-brewed liquor.

Nikita seldom called on his distant brother-in-law, but when he did, he was invariably regaled with vodka. As soon as Nikita had greeted him and sat down on the bench, Nikifor Petrovitch made the masonic signs with eye and lips. Nikita set down a bottle of his own and bought from Agrafena, besides needles and thread, some powders for diarrhœa, fever, coughs, and other ailments, paying in fresh crisp notes which he had just received at the collecting-centre.

"Freight-train in tonight," said Nikifor abruptly, as they parted. "Stops till morning. Wheat-flour and sugar." He shot a sidelong glance, wolf-like, out of his hard black eyes, first at his brother-in-law, then at the mare.

"For the front, I suppose," sighed Nikita.

"Ain't we as good as them?" Agrafena burst out. "It's the *people* that's in power now; the troops won't miss the stuff; may as well die today as tomorrow."

Nikita sighed again as he climbed into the sledge. His head was buzzing from the vodka he had drunk. Flattery jogged on through snow-clad meadows, and Nikita, lolling back in his rug, thought of the hook-nosed pacer and the little bantam-cock that owned him, and wished that he had taken up the challenge. He saw the race, as if it had really happened, and plumed himself on his victory. He puzzled over Nikifor, setting him down as "a deep card," thought of the foal that was to come, of the Moscow races—and sweeping his eyes over the plain, flat as a tablecloth on every side, returned to his visionary race with the grey gelding.

From behind the forest came the hoarse whistle of an engine; then, through the cutting, crept a long file of freight-cars.

"Wheat-flour and sugar," thought Nikita.

"Hie there! Are you asleep? Out of the way!" shouted a voice, almost on top of him.

146

With a hasty jerk of the reins Nikita swerved. A team of black horses trotted by. They belonged to the Ispolkom; there sat his brother Vassily on the box. Nikita gazed after the sledge; suddenly he started and leaned forward on his knees. The mare pulled at the reins as he gathered them up, the soft snow spurted in his face, the beaten track rushed by under the runners, the warm breeze hummed in his ears, the black team came nearer, flashed past, and was left far behind.

Even as he reached the hill that topped the village, Nikita reflected that he had done rashly in overtaking the President of the Executive Committee, that spiteful hound Penkoff—no friend of the peasants—who had cropped up from God knows where, and swaggered about in summer-time in a blue sailor's jumper with a collar flapping at the back.

Next morning Vassily slouched into Nikita's yard. Nikita was grooming Flattery. Vassily looked at the mare, took in the new door to the cattle-shed and the little window, and said scornfully:

"Regular bourgeois you've turned into!"

He looked again at the mare and let fall a word which Nikita did not soon forget.

"I'll take my oath that mare's *stolen!*"

Nikita strode towards his brother, his eyes smouldering, and said hoarsely: "Let me alone for God's sake! Go!"

Vassily noisily bit off the end of his home-made ciga-

147

rette, spat at the new door, and sauntered to the gate. Here he turned round and, seeing Nastasya coming from the hut, shook his head towards the stall, and hissed:

"Grudges a sack of rye to the Relief Committee—and puts a glass pane in his cattle-shed!"

Nikita stood by Flattery and as he watched his retreating brother, clutched the mare's halter with a tighter grip.

CHAPTER · V

MICHAELMAS CAME, AND WITH IT MIRTH and revels. By ancient wont all weddings in Shatnyevka were held over for the high festival which fell on the 8th of November and closed the yearly round of husbandry on field and threshing-floor.

Outside the churchyard all day long, as at a fair, stood scores of peasants' carts, garnished with gorgeous cottage-woven rugs, embroidered ruches round the wagon-yokes, bells jingling on the harness, parti-coloured rugs and ribbons fluttering from the horses' manes and tails.

At the east end of the church three priests took turns to marry the lads and lasses. They ranged them before the lectern, six pairs at a time (there were not enough marriage-crowns for more), thrust down the ponderous brass crowns over the eyes of brides and bridegrooms, and panted wearily through the prescribed ritual. The church was unheated, cold as a catacomb; from every mouth came puffs of steam; over the priests' warm clothes the velvet chasubles bulged comically; from

under them peeped out mud-spattered cassocks and un-
wieldy boots; the air reeked of sheepskin and home-
brewed liquor; instead of the dazzling chandeliers that
used to light the ceremony, single candles gleamed for-
lornly, and the harmony of the choir gave place to the
frostbitten recitative of the precentor, with the sexton's
pious tenor labouring half a bar behind. The nuptial
rite, without its pristine pomp, was like a plush divan
stripped of its gildings and upholstery.

But outside the church walls, up and down Shatnyevka, tipsy merriment was rife. The lusty voices of
the girls, proof against frost and fog, shrilled nuptial
ditties late into the night, hoarse drunkards bellowing
out the bass; courtyards and doors wafted the fumes of
poteen and the fragrant warmth of pancakes; accor-
dions hailed and replied from every corner; the President of the Volost Executive Committee, Penkoff himself, dubbed by the villagers "Nicholas III," came late
to his office three days running and floundered feverishly over his report, which he had begun before the
festival.

Nikita feasted for two days at the house of his uncle,
who had just given away his daughter, and prepared
to take Nastasya and Syomka to the Settlement to see
his kinsman, who was celebrating a son's marriage. His
preparations began early. He groomed the mare and
combed her tail, plaited some bright red strips of rag
into her tail and mane, lined the sledge with hay, and

over the sacking spread a woollen carpet with a green and scarlet pattern. Once harnessing his horse had been a trifling, workaday task, like putting on his boots. But with the coming of the grey trotter, all was changed. The string which had bound together the torn harness disappeared, hip-strap and breeching were sewn up, and traces mended. The halter, a mere noose of string, was discarded for a strap, and in lieu of the threadbare belly-band a new double girth was fitted, made of raw-hide, lavishly smeared with tar and furnished with steel buckles.

With Syomka's eager help the mare was harnessed. When all was ready, Nikita fetched from the hut a pair of scarlet reins, made of stout braid. He had bought them, without Nastasya's knowledge, from Boubnoff, a decayed merchant. Syomka flushed with delight, and though Flattery stood as quiet as a sheep, he checked her gravely: "Steady, my lass, steady!"

Nastasya came out in a new tanned sheepskin jacket with trimmed sleeves, and a neat kerchief. She perched on the rough straw, proud and uncomfortable, Syomka beside her in his father's cap. Nikita glanced com-placently at the bedizened mare, the sledge, and finally his wife, and then strode forward to the gate. He was about to open it when Grigory, bailiff to the Executive Committee, shuffled into the courtyard.

"Good day, Nikita Loukitch. Compliments of the season to you."

Thrusting his wand under his withered left arm, he wriggled into his trouser pocket and rummaged in it for some time. Still fumbling, he gasped out his message: "There—Nikita Loukitch—I've brought you— a summons."

Nikita eyed him sourly as he took the paper, which was stamped and sealed. He fingered it warily. Unable to read, he asked Grigory: "What's this about?"

Grigory waved his hand dismally. "From the President," he answered, and absorbed himself in the task of rolling a cigarette.

Nikita stood twirling the warrant in his fingers, peered at the stamp, scrutinized the seal, and glanced questioningly at Grigory.

"Wanted at headquarters," said the bailiff. "Got to take the judge to town—or maybe the chief himself."

"Vassily's tongue's been wagging," snapped Nikita. "What's to be done now?"

"First they wanted to send for Mitri Ouklein," said Grigory, thawing a little. "His old woman's just been to the Soviet. But the chief told me to fetch you instead. 'He's got the horse we want,' says he."

Nikita frowned. "It's Vassily's doing, plain enough," he said. "If I go to the Soviet now, to beg off, Penkoff won't listen to me; and if I don't go, he'll lock me up, and fine me into the bargain."

"No doubt of that," concurred Grigory. "Sure as fate, he'll clap you in jail; real Tatar he is." He looked

152

at the mare, all tricked out and beribboned. "Where were you off to?" he asked.

"To my kinsman Prokhor."

"Found a wife for his son, has he?"

"He has."

"Where did he get her? From the Settlement?"

"She's one of us, from Shatnyevka. You know Matvey Loutovinoff. It's his daughter."

"What, Dashka?"

"Dashka it is."

"Aha, she's a strapping wench, and a rare good worker too. Just in her prime, fresh as a strawberry! Well, Nikita Loukitch, I'll make tracks. What shall I say? You'll go to the Soviet?"

"I can't see no way out," said Nikita, wringing his hands. "No help for it; I'll have to go."

While the men talked, Nastasya sat mute and muffled on her perch, as if she had no part in all that went on outside the sledge with its damasked rug and festal trappings. Grave and erect she sat, with pursed lips, looking straight before her, waiting for Nikita to stop talking and open the gate into the village street, full of gay sounds and flags and finery.

Having seen Grigory out, Nikita stumped back to the yard. "Get down, old woman. Your journey's over."

And he turned the mare back to the shed.

IN the Volost there was much and various talk about Penkoff. There were some who swore that he had never been a blue-jacket.

His shaven bullet-head, set off by a bushy black moustache, was the bugbear of the countryside, which he was forever scouring in fierce quest of the counter-revolution.

At the meetings of the Volost and plenary sessions of the Executive Committee he was chary of speech, reserving his pronouncements till the end. Having risen, he would cast his watery eyes over the massed heads before he spoke. His voice was deep and hollow, like the sound of a man's finger scraped across a drum. At first the peasants heard him listlessly, as they heard all the officials. They looked to the speaker's manner, not to his words, to grip them. Each one had brought to the meeting his own views and plans, thought out and pondered through the long winter evenings in his hut, and as their homes and circumstances, and the plans bred of them, were much the same, the meeting often followed the same course; the orator would plead, protest—persuade, it seemed; the peasants listened silently, as though convinced—but when a vote was taken on the motion, every man jack was against it. . . . Penkoff knew his peasants. Once he had set out his facts, the deep voice would crack and shoot up the scale into a vibrant shrill falsetto, like the scream of a giant sea-bird: "To-va-ri-schi! Comrades!"

He would rake the front benches with his rheumy eyes and transfix one upturned face. . . . Now spoke the true Penkoff. Lashing his arms, he castigated the bourgeois, blasted the counter-revolution, pounded the table, gnashed his teeth, spat and stamped out his spittle; his hairless pate flushed crimson, the scar on the crown swelled to the likeness of a hangman's noose. . . .

The peasants dispersed shaking their heads and saying:

"Means business, *he* does! Never was such a man!"

Nikita had a cold reception from Penkoff, who cut him short and snapped:

"Have the horse here by eight. No argument! Be off!"

Next morning, long before eight, Nikita brought Flattery to headquarters.

Seeing the low country sledge, padded with straw, Penkoff barked out an oath and asked suspiciously:

"Got a better sledge than that, haven't you?"

"I have, but the off runner's broken."

"You're *lying!*"

"If you don't believe me, come and see."

"Very well, then, I'll soon find a sledge," said Penkoff, and went up to his office.

In a minute Grigory came out with a note:

"Unharness the mare, we're going to get a sledge."

Together with Boubnoff's handsome sledge, Grigory,

as instructed, commandeered an overcoat, lined and trimmed with fox fur, "for a journey to the town on official business," as the President had phrased it.

The old merchant read the writ several times and puckered his grey brows. "Sharp eyes they've got, and claws too; they'll take the shirt off my back next!"

Penkoff settled himself in the sledge, with a rifle at his elbow. It was twelve miles to the town. He broke his journey at the Crofts.

"You know Maximitch; turn in there!" Penkoff commanded.

As they drove up to the cottage of the prosperous bee-keeper, Nikita said to himself: "Proletarian, is he? Trust him for smelling out the honey, though!"

At Maximitch's Penkoff dispatched an omelet, thickly sprinkled with chopped bacon-fat—washed down with glasses of poteen, and tea with cream and honey in it. When they were ready to drive on, Maximitch brought a pot of honey and stowed it in the sledge at Penkoff's feet.

On this second half of the journey Penkoff tried several times to hurry the mare forward. Flattery responded, but Nikita reined her in and steadied her to the customary coachman's jog. Penkoff snatched the reins from him. Nikita brushed the President's hands away and said, looking grimly at the rifle:

"None of your antics! Let the mare alone! Drop it!"

"Dro-op it, eh?" drawled Penkoff sullenly, and sat

156

speechless through the journey, huddled in the fox fur.

In the town they stayed twenty-four hours. The Committee's black team were before them, having brought the Commissary and the judge.

"Well met!" said Vassily spitefully, as Nikita entered the stable.

The next day put Nikita's cunning to the proof. His sledge and Vassily's were ordered for the same time, and he foresaw that if they drove home together, Penkoff and Vassily would so hustle his mare between them that she would get no breathing-space the whole way home. To delay the mare, Nikita broke the shoe of one of her forefeet, and to all Penkoff's curses answered doggedly:

"When I've shoed her, we'll start. If you're in such a stew, you can go home with the others; I've no mind to spoil the mare, to please your fancy."

"Very well, we'll drive to the Volost; we can talk better there."

"You've no call to threaten me; I'm telling you the truth," said Nikita manfully. He left the town long after Vassily and his passengers.

All the way home Nikita brooded over his ill luck and racked his brains how to save the mare from the vindictive clutches of the President: "Sure as God's in heaven, he'll give me no peace now. He'll break me! Can't give him the slip neither. . . . Life's not what it was—worn thin, like—miss your footing, and it snaps. . . . Eykh, my beauty, my little mother, in an evil hour I brought you to my house, nursed you and pampered you, and now . . ."

The thought that Penkoff had power to rob him of his mare shrouded his heart, as wind before a blizzard shrouds the meadows in a cerement of snow—and in its train came darker thoughts, furtive and sinister. . . . His horny fingers tightened on the reins, a chill clutched at his heart, ran to his feet, crept back to his heart, benumbed his brain. . . . They were driving through the Mushroom Forest, scored with sheer, leafless gullies.

The reins trembled, the mare jibbed, plying her pricked ears on the brink of one of these deep clefts. Nikita pulled her up, as the stock of the rifle touched his foot, and turned round slowly to Penkoff.

Two watery eyes, staring with terror, met him; Nikita saw a hand in a white mitten creep to the barrel of the rifle and draw the butt back from his foot.

"Go on!" said Penkoff hoarsely.

Penkoff, Nikita—and doubtless the grey mare, for her ears twitched uncannily—caught a shrewd glimpse of each other's hearts, scented new peril on this ominous journey through the sunless forest, gashed with stark, desolate ravines.

CHAPTER · VI

Never had the old veterinary seen Nikita look so crestfallen. His voice was hollow and spiritless.

"Can you lame the mare for me?" he said.

"Wha-at?" cried Alexandr Egoritch.

"Can you lame the mare?" Nikita croaked again, staring doggedly at the old man.

"Why lame her? Are you out of your wits?"

"I've got my wits about me, right enough; that's why I came."

"Sit down, man, and talk sense."

"I've had a bellyful of sitting; all last night I sat till daybreak," said Nikita stubbornly. He took off his cap, seated himself, and stared at the floor. Then, shaking a greasy forelock which had dropped over one eye, he told the veterinary all that had happened, from the day when he had overtaken the President on his way from the collecting-centre to that fateful moment in the Mushroom Forest when he had been tempted to . . .

159

"Believe me or believe me not, Alexandr Egoritch, I don't know how God kept my soul from sin! . . . The very thought of it makes my flesh creep! I looked round —not a soul, no witness but the forest. 'Well,' I says to myself, 'he'll wreck my life, may as well bring him down with me.' A likely place, that gully. There he sits, muffled up in his cloak, trapped like—not handy to defend himself. And there was the rifle at my knee, I'd only to stretch my hand out! I stopped the mare, and turned her round, and he just looks at me and says nothing, but I saw that he felt his end was near. . . . Then I came to myself, cold as ice, and my guts curdling! . . ."

His tale ended, Nikita sat long silent, crouched, clasping his cap between his straddled legs, and gazing at the floor. Then he drew himself up, slowly, and heaved a long sigh of relief.

Alexandr Egoritch looked at him with wide round eyes, as if he now saw him for the first time; more than once he groaned strangely and fidgeted on his chair. The familiar face of life was rent, as if the mossy crust of a marsh had cracked, showing the dark water beneath, shot with fantastic, writhing shapes and lurid colours. And now Nikita's request seemed neither strange nor foolish. Had he not come from the Mushroom Forest, from peril of soul and body, to ask but a little thing!

"So I've made up my mind to lame the mare," said

Nikita, looking the veterinary in the eyes. "Give me some harmless drug for her. You'll help me—won't you?"

The veterinary still wavered. He paced the room, kicking the chairs out of his path, shifting his long amber cigarette-holder from one side to the other, looking down his nose, and muttering unintelligibly. Then he sat down, drew the high felt boot from his left leg, and began to scratch at the thick sole of his woollen stocking, reinforced with a white heel.

"You've nursed her through one winter and now you want to spoil the mare!" he said, thrusting his foot back viciously into the boot. . . . "Doesn't her off shoulder trouble her after work? Have you noticed nothing?"

"Nothing yet, Alexandr Egoritch. When I came home from the town, she was as fresh as when she started—ready for her feed too."

"Did you drive slow?"

"Neither slow nor fast. Just steady, like."

"Never tried speeding her?"

"Just once, Alexandr Egoritch, coming back from the station. . . . I was a bit lively, like—had a drop with my brother-in-law. Well, that evening, sure enough, she began to limp on her off foreleg, just as you said she would. But next day it was gone like magic."

"Tell you what, Nikita," said the veterinary briskly. "We won't lame the mare, we'll doctor her. We'll put a seton on her—understand? She suffers from an atrophy of the muscles in the off shoulder—what you call a sprain; that's what we'll treat her for. She'll be safe from all the commissars in Russia. . . . And she's to do no work, mind, while I'm treating her. That'll be for three months or so, it's a serious business. Well, it's for you to settle. Think it over!"

Nikita's mind was soon made up.

"Treat her, then! I'll do as you say, sir. You know your business."

Alexandr Egoritch called on the same day after dinner. Nikita locked the gate and led Flattery out of the stall. The veterinary made him run her a few times up and down the yard, then he examined her off shoulder long and intently.

"Look here," he said, "you see how her near shoulder stands out full and rounded, but her off shoulder slumps. . . . We must ginger up those muscles—set the blood flowing in them. Understand me?"

"No call for me to understand; you've got the rights of it," said Nikita meekly.

Syomka, who had been hovering round them, looked searchingly at the near shoulder, then at the off, struggling to probe the mystery. He could not make out how the veterinary could "set the blood flowing." Was he a wizard?

"Take her back to the stall," said the veterinary,

drawing from his pocket a long crooked needle and a length of twine. In the stall he stroked Flattery compassionately:

"Patience, old lady, patience! There's nothing else for it. Pa-tience!"

Flattery nuzzled against Nikita's shoulder, pricking her ears from time to time when she caught the hiss of sledges from the lane behind the stall.

Alexandr Egoritch threaded the needle.

He looked at Nikita. "No need for a muzzle, eh?"

"None at all, sir! Quiet as a lamb," said Nikita, patting her.

"Shorten her head-rope!"

Dabbing a pungent-smelling liquid out of a small phial on the injured shoulder, and drawing the skin tight with his left hand, he plunged the needle into the flesh. Flattery shuddered and squirmed, seeking to shake off the pain. A big drop of blood ran down her sleek grey coat. Syomka's wide eyes, fixed on that ugly needle, brimmed with tears, and when its whole length was embedded in the mare's shoulder, he burst out blubbering and bolted from the stall in terror.

"Maman-ka-a!"

Having drawn the twine through under the skin, Alexandr Egoritch left it in the wound and knotted the two ends together.

"Well, the job's done!" he said, wiping his needle. "But mind you don't let the mare get loose. Keep her on a short rope—see? She must stay like that for about three weeks—understand? In four days I'll call again. By spring—you can race her, if you like!"

Nikita made no answer, but looked sorrowfully at the mare.

On the fifth day the veterinary came, as he had promised.

Passing his arm over Flattery's shoulder, hot from inflammation, he turned to Nikita. "Now watch me, this is what you have to do. Draw the twine through every three or four days, like this."

He gripped the knot of the twine and pulled it slowly and carefully from side to side, drawing out the discoloured matter from the wound. Flattery quailed and shrank, quivered from head to foot; her one eye struggled to discern what the grey-whiskered, red-faced man was doing with her aching, itching shoulder, and she wondered why Nikita could not free her from that scorching pain and the man that plagued her with it.

"As soon as it starts to heal, you must renew the irritation," said Alexandr Egoritch, as he drew the knot back to its first position, "so as to intensify the inflammatory process and draw off the blood from the infected muscles. . . . Off her feed, eh?"

"Don't fancy nothing. Just a handful of oats this morning—wouldn't touch the hay," said Nikita ruefully.

The old veterinary reassured him: "They never eat

much, with a seton on them. In three or four weeks
we'll take it off; then her appetite'll come back at once
—but for the present . . . How would you feel if they
played a trick like that on you?"

"You may well ask—it'd drive me crazy!" said Nikita
with a sigh. "How does she bear it all? She's a dumb
animal—that's the way of it—can't say nothing, can't
complain."

Syomka, at his father's side, looked daggers at Alexandr Egoritch; his cheeks puffed and his lips twitched
as he muttered at the veterinary: "You ought to have—
one of them things—on you! . . . You nosy devil!
. . . Want a brick at your long snout. . . . Ooh!
Ooh!"

Ever since the mare's shoulder was pierced with the
long, crooked needle, and the thick twine thrust into
the wound, Syomka would run to the stall several times
a day to comfort the grey Flattery in her dumb, lonely
sufferings. Flattery snuffled wistfully, as if she would
tell her pain; she tried to nestle her inflamed, itching
shoulder against Syomka, and refused the thick, salted
pie-crust which he brought her.

"Come now, eat it!" Syomka would coax her. "Mamanka baked it this morning, the pie's *nice*. . . . Look
here!"

He would cut off a piece of the crust and begin to
chew it, champing loudly, clicking his tongue, licking
his lips, to entice the melancholy mare. Then he would

165

put the chewed morsel to her lips. Flattery always turned away.

"What is it, then?" asked Syomka. "Why do you look like that? Does it hurt?"

He filled his cheeks and blew on the hot, swollen shoulder. It twitched convulsively. Flattery shifted her legs and again tried to brush her shoulder against Syomka.

"Wait till spring, lassie, we'll go out to night pasture. Boo-ootiful nights we'll have. We'll build a big bonfire, so as they'll see it from the village, and we'll boil a pot of gruel. We'll ask Vaska Siyegir to come. He's got a box with moosic in it, boo-ootiful moosic!"

One day when Syomka visited Flattery, he found her, not in her usual place, tied close to the iron ring by the manger, but in the middle of the stall with her head outwards, while the torn head-rope dangled from the ring. He was about to tie her up again, when he looked at her off shoulder, and instead of the twine protruding from the wound, saw clots of blood and matter. The twine had gone. Syomka took fright and ran headlong to his father.

"Come quick! She's loose! The string's gone—and she's bleeding!"

Nikita found the twine in the manger. The pain had been too great, Flattery had knawed through the rope and ripped the twine out of the wound.

So the veterinary came again. He examined the

shoulder, shook his head, and said:

"Why couldn't you keep a close eye on her, man?" He took the needle from his pocket. "I'll have to put it through again. Tie her up well this time, and you —run along to your mother for some twine—now then, off with you!"

Syomka stood still, frowning.

"Go on, son!" said Nikita. "Bring it and go away quick, no need for you to be looking!"

When the veterinary gripped the skin near the sore with a deft, resolute movement and drew it firmly taut, Flattery moaned like a human creature and shook her head with the pain of it.

Nikita turned away, grinding his teeth.

"That's over!" grunted the veterinary, and he wiped his hands on the horse's tail.

The twine was in its place again, the knot secure.

A few days before Christmas Alexandr Egoritch removed the seton. Twice during the intervening month Penkoff sent the one-armed Grigory to Nikita with an order to surrender the mare to the Soviet Authority.

On the second occasion Nikita went to the President with this affidavit from the veterinary:

The grey mare belonging to Nikita Loukoff is unfit for driving or any other work, being afflicted with an atrophy of the muscles in the off shoulder; this requires lengthy treatment, to which I am now

167

*submitting her in accordance with her owner's
wishes.*

A. E. Ternovsky

Penkoff read the document and flashed his watery
eyes upon Nikita. "Think you can beat Penkoff, eh?
Do you know what I can do with you for sabotage? For
the present, you can go! I'll keep your affidavit."

"It's my bread you're taking," began Nikita, "you've
no call . . ." but Penkoff's cavernous voice cracked
into a furious falsetto:

"That's what we *shoot* men for! *Sabo-ta-age!*
Spreading the counter-revolution, are you? Trying to
fool Penkoff? Concocting a false document!"

Nikita thrust his cap over his eyes and hurried out,
scared and bewildered. He went straight to Alexandr
Egoritch, who changed his clothes and went to see
Penkoff, without waiting to be summoned.

"What do you want?" snapped Penkoff. "Who sent
for you?"

"I've just spoken to Nikita Loukoff, whose horse I
am treating," the veterinary began dryly, but Penkoff
cut him short:

"Treat it, then! I've other things to bother my head
with! Nobody sent for you; you can stay at home, then!
When your turn comes, I'll send for you, fast enough!"

"I protest that by your conduct towards Citizen
Loukoff you are discrediting me, as an official of the

168

State and a Soviet citizen, in the eyes of the people and the authorities," said the veterinary, "and you compel me to communicate my protest to the Executive Committee."

A gurgling, sardonic snort burst from Penkoff:

"Connumicate, con-num-i-cate! . . . They've had their eye on your gang for a long time."

The veterinary's grey moustaches twitched. He was about to make some answer, when he looked at Penkoff's smirking features; he shrugged his shoulders and departed.

Penkoff now left Nikita undisturbed, vexed him no more with visits from the one-armed Grigory or the spy Vassily. The veterinary, too, he did not touch and seemed to have forgotten. But they both knew that Penkoff was not one to forget, and each in his own fashion waited the issue with alarmed suspense.

One evening after supper, seeing that Nikita was getting ready to call on Alexandr Egoritch, Natasya said testily:

"You'll go out once too often. . . . My heart tells me: that mare'll bring us no good. God save us from sin! Suppose we changed her for Mikishka's gelding!"

Nikita looked at his wife and answered nothing.

Emboldened by his silence and the fact that he sat down on the bench instead of going out, Nastasya began to cite sundry instances of cattle that were cursed, ill-wished, or overlooked. She called to mind a piebald calf, bought five years since from a stranger at the fair; that calf had brought fire, hailstorm at harvest-tide, the death of a child, and the failure of the crops next year. . . .

"Everyone knows Mikishka's gelding, but who knows where that mare came from? Soldiers, you say, but *what* soldiers? Maybe they weren't soldiers at all!"

Syomka, who had climbed up to his bed, popped his head over the stove and said: "One of them had a frightening look; eyes like hot coals, and a mop of stiff, curling hair, pitch-black; not natural, he wasn't. . . ."

Syomka stopped, gulped down his saliva noisily, and said in a quavering voice:

"Mamanka, don't the werewolf change himself into a horse?"

He remembered how the grey mare had torn the thread out of the wound and how she had moaned, like a human thing, when the veterinary took hold of her sore shoulder. He crept down from the bed and nestled close to his mother. Now and then he glanced at the antic shadows clambering about the walls, held his ear, as if hearkening to unhallowed voices, or shivered as though an ague shook him.

"How can you tell them wizards?" said Nastasya, following her thoughts. "Once let 'em cross your threshold and they'll put a spell on house and home."

"What a cackle you keep up, old woman! But your head don't know what your mouth's saying. The mare's known, sure enough—what's more, she's famous! Alexandr Egoritch knew her at once. You're only bewildering the boy—he's gone white as a sheet—and all for nothing. What if Penkoff means mischief? Well, he's jealous. Ain't she Champion's aunt and didn't we pass him on the road? And there's that scoundrel Vaska, egging him on to it. But I tell you straight, old woman, I'll not yield without a fight. I'll not let the mare go—and as for changing her for Mikishka's gelding, get that bee out of your bonnet!"

Syomka did not climb up to his bed over the stove, but lay dozing on the bench and had no wholesome sleep till his father had come back from the veterinary's. Next day, when he went to the stall, he stood gazing with new eyes at the mare, lean, shaggy, and uncouth, her mane matted in elf-locks.

CHAPTER · VII

AFTER THE CHRISTMAS FROSTS CAME sudden thaw; eaves dripped, dung darkened the highways, bustling hordes of sparrows filled the warm air with cheeping cries, as if thousands of unseen hands were striking out sparks from fairy tinder-boxes.

At the station stood a long file of open freight-cars loaded with men and horses—a draft, on its way to fight against Krasnoff, the Tsarist general. It was a holiday, and girls and women of Shatnyevka, having heard of the draft, were flocking to the station. At noon it looked as motley as a fair. By every truck stood groups of laughing soldiers, and girls in holiday dress. The girls were shelling sunflower seeds, parrying the soldiers' chaff with sprightly sallies, and screaming shrilly when some wag charged into the thick of a bright bevy and hugged and kissed as many as he could.

In the centre of the train was a car distinguished from the others by a specially constructed door, with steps lowered from it to the platform. On the door was inscribed in black letters:

STAFF

A huge man in a tall fur cap topping a swarthy pock-marked face came out and stood on the middle step. Looking right and left, and suddenly exclaiming: "Hold 'em!" he leaped down towards the troop of girls that frisked and giggled round the adjoining car. The girls scattered like spray, with shrieks and laughter, and clustered again on the far side of the rails. The huge man picked up the cap, which had fallen from his shaven head, and let out a thunderous guffaw, squaring his shoulders and thrusting out his stomach, tightly clasped by a broad leather belt.

"Comrade Klymchouk!" he roared. "How'd it be if we took a dozen of 'em with us to the front? What do you think? A mouthful of sauce won't spoil our dinners! Hey, you sauceboxes, come to the front with us, we'll kick the Tsar's generals in the pants, and you can darn them. Well, are you coming?"

"You can't fool us, we're not afraid!" cried a snub-nosed girl from the centre of the group, and lightly lifting her fire red skirt with fluttering bright green ribbons, she swung it out with a smart flourish and, stamping in her glistening high galoshes, stalked round the circle, shrieking the words of a popular quatrain:

> *I'm not afeared what Dad may say;*
> *"Do as you're bid," says Daddy, oh!*

173

Said Sashka: "Kiss me under the hay,"
So I—kissed my laddy, oh!

The ringing voices of the girls took up the roundelay.

In a trice the huge man stood beside them, swaying, his arms akimbo. "Step out, one of you!" He looked with challenging eyes from face to face. "I'll show you how a sailor can dance!"

"We've got a sailor of our own, a fine one!" said the snub-nosed hussy.

"Dance with the gentleman, go on!" cried several voices.

"Nicholas II's gone, but we've got Nicholas III!" the girl persisted, still more boldly, shaking off her friends, who clutched at the sleeves of her silk-embroidered jacket.

"Nicholas III, eh? What's he like?" asked the man in the fur cap quizzically, scanning the girls' faces.

Nikita's brother-in-law, Nikifor Petrovitch, who was walking home along the rails, stopped and listened. Then he came nearer, stopped again, and observed, as if to himself: "*He's* no sailor, he's a runaway convict! Makes the name of sailor stink, though!"

But somehow this soliloquy was heard by all. . . . When Nikifor made a show of proceeding on his way, the huge man beckoned to him. "Who are you?"

"Just a plain man, a switchman."

174

"One of us!" "From Shatnyevka!" "Uncle Nikifor!" the girls shouted.

Again the huge man scanned the girls' faces, one by one; he glanced once more at Nikifor Petrovitch and asked the snub-nosed Glyashka: "But why do you call him Nicholas III?"

"His name's Nicholas."

"My mother calls me Nicholas too," said the man.

"We don't know nothing about you, but our Nicholas ransacks our boxes under the eyes of the whole village," Glyashka blurted out, more and more emboldened.

"Glyashka!"

"Are you crazy?"

"Be quiet!"

"Don't you know . . ."

Restraining hands tugged at her jacket, but she, like a swimmer that has once plunged into cold water, struck out resolutely, encouraged by the sympathetic attention of the man in the fur cap.

"You can see that painted bitch of his strutting about in Grounka's shoes! Stripped her box as bare as a bone. Made off with Uncle Andrey's canvas, too. . . . I won't be quiet, and I'm not in the least frightened! . . . Let the men be frightened! . . . What do I care for him!"

The huge man looked narrowly at Glyashka and nodded, as if to encourage her still more.

"Passes himself off as a sailor, but in plain fact he's a gallows-bird!" said Nikifor, this time not to himself but to the man in the fur cap.

And looking the man straight in the eyes, he added: "Makes the name of sailor stink. It's true what the girl says."

As President of the Executive Committee, Penkoff had often to deal with detachments passing through his district. So when a mounted messenger brought a note from Comrade Gobyetchya, Officer Commanding the Draft, requiring him to attend at the station for urgent duty, Penkoff buttoned his khaki tunic to the throat, fastened his belt, buckled on his holster, and shouted to Grigory: "Go to Loukoff, tell him to drive round at once. Jump to it!"

Grigory hummed and hawed, scratched himself under his shirt, and would have explained that the mare had not long had her seton off her and was not fit for driving, but Penkoff, as though reading his thoughts, transfixed him with a glare of such malignity that Grigory hastened to obey.

"Better make no fuss," he advised Nikita. "Draft's come to the station; messenger's just ridden up for him. No knowing what he'll do if you cross him now. You might drive her at a walk, like."

Nikita answered nothing. His face darkened. Grigory looked at him and sighed dismally; before leaving the yard, he said: "No help for it, Nikita Loukitch; you'll have to part with the mare, he'll give you no peace otherwise."

Nikita still kept silence.

Meanwhile, as he waited for the mare, Penkoff read through the note once more and surmised to his secretary: "About oats, I expect—cavalry draft, that'll be it."

"But where can we get them oats?" exclaimed the secretary.

"We'll get 'em, don't you worry!" said Penkoff, grinning; he took the note from the table, read it again, and pushed it under the secretary's nose.

"What about it?" asked the secretary.

"That officer must be a field commissary." Penkoff frowned ominously. "Look at his signature—runs up the page like a steeple-jack!"

The signature was indeed remarkable. The bold red characters climbed purposefully upward, piercing the lines of typescript, and the flourish, instead of resting under the signature, rocketed up to the top of the sheet, thickening at the end and stabbing through the paper.

"We had a clerk in our orderly-room could judge a man by his writing," said the secretary. "Tell you his secret thoughts, he would!"

"There's no secret here," said Penkoff, snatching the paper from him. "It about oats, plain enough."

"I don't say it ain't, Nikolai Egoritch; but that chap

could tell characters from handwriting, if you take my meaning—whether a man was savage, like, or mild—or his family life, say . . ."

Penkoff looked at the slashing signature, began to speak, but checked himself and suddenly grew thoughtful. He walked to the window and stared into the street.

"Once," the secretary went on, "the adjutant showed him a letter. 'Tell me,' says he, 'about the party who wrote that letter—character, I mean, and position.' So he takes the letter, looks at it, pops on his glasses, looks at it again, and says: 'Flighty character, Evlampi Fyodorovitch, and ticklish position. But seeing you're my superior officer, I don't dare say anything; only it's as well to be careful; she's sickening of a funereal disease—better let the M.O. have a look at you.'"

Penkoff cut him short: "I'll have a telephone put through from the Committee's office to the station. Got my report to write, and they want me at the station, damn them!"

"A telephone saves a lot of trouble, of course," agreed the secretary. "And you've got more confidence, like, when you can't see who you're talking to."

"Suppose I don't go," said Penkoff, turning to his secretary.

The secretary muttered inaudibly and buried his nose in the papers on his desk.

Yet once again Penkoff read through the note:

> *To the President of the Volost Executive Committee, Shatnyevka*
>
> *On receipt of this order you are to proceed immediately to the station and report to me for urgent duty.*
>
> *Gobyetchya*
O.C. Draft

"We've got urgent duties of our own," grunted Penkoff, and thrust the order into the side-pocket of his tunic, as he saw Nikita driving up.

Presently they rattled off, in a furore of dogs and poultry. When they came out from the lane at the end of the village, with its one-eyed cottages squinting at the bald hillock, the whole station stood out as plain as the pattern on a saucer. Nikita flourished his whip and cried: "Regular fair they've made of it!"

Penkoff could see this for himself: the long file of crimson freight-cars, the glittering throngs, the single figures, hurrying across the meadow to and from the station. . . . Just at that moment a horseman flashed up in his rear, in a red cap and trousers, mounted on a hook-nosed nag, and drew up with them, peered into Penkoff's face, and bounded away downhill, to the station.

Penkoff recognized the messenger who had brought the order. Unfastening the bright mother-of-pearl button, as big as a five-kopeck piece, he took the order from his side-pocket and began to scrutinize the stamp and seal.

"I've forgotten my tobacco-pouch," he said.

"Want me to turn back?"

Penkoff wavered. He looked down across the meadow at the red ribbon of cars, fingering the order speechlessly. At length he said in a hollow voice: "Hurry up!"

Where they were to hurry to was not clear. Nikita drove downhill, towards the station, but when they came out on the meadow, Penkoff prodded him in the back.

"Where are you off to? Said I'd forgotten my pouch, didn't I? Told you to turn back! . . . Can't you understand plain Russian? I've forgotten my pouch, I say."

Nikita turned round sharply.

But they had not gone far before Penkoff shouted: "Never mind now! Drive to the station! . . . Dare say they'll stand me a cigarette or two."

Penkoff sat bolt upright, clutching the order, staring at the approaching station. Thus rigid, his unbuttoned pocket flapping at his side, he strode through the empty, squalid hall to the platform, crossed the rails, shouldered his way through the chattering groups, and stopped at the truck with the plain deal door and steps beneath it.

The huge man in the fur cap stood on the steps looking at him. His burly figure blocked the door and all but the last two letters of the inscription: FF.

"Comrade Gobyetchya here?" Penkoff asked him, glancing at the order.

"Here," the huge man answered, and dived into the car.

At the tail of the train, in one of the groups of girls and soldiers, a concertina wheezed a Cossack dance-tune, and the dancers whooped and whistled to its melody. Penkoff glanced that way, looked to his rear, straightened his holster, and greeted the soldiers standing by the truck: "After Krasnoff, eh, brothers?"

No answer.

Penkoff paused. . . . "Any tobacco about you?"

One of the soldiers passed him a packet of cigarettes.

Before he could light up, the door of the car opened. The huge man came out, and behind him a handsome, swarthy fellow, with an officer's cloak flung in haste over his shoulders. The huge man came down the steps and stood beside Penkoff. From under the handsome fellow's cloak flashed crimson riding-breeches. He had youthful black moustaches, an imperious mouth, and a harsh, throaty voice.

"Penkoff, President of the Executive Committee?" he rapped out, scanning Penkoff and seating himself on the top step.

"That's me!" answered Penkoff as he fumbled in his pockets. Finding no matches, he looked about him in the hope that somebody would help him out; he held his cigarette in his left hand, close against the order.

The swarthy man plunged his hand into his pocket. Penkoff put the cigarette in his mouth and came towards him.

Instead of matches, the man drew out a sheet of paper, looked at it, and fired at him, point-blank, the charge: "Why do you take bribes?"

As if bludgeoned from above, Penkoff's head sank into his shoulders, and his watery eyes rolled helplessly. He took the cigarette from his mouth and smiled.

Then, with assumed nonchalance, he said: "Ask me a few more! I'll answer 'em! I'm an old bird. Can't catch me with tricks like that!"

Penkoff heard whispering at his back. Looking round, he discerned in the crowd of women some familiar bearded faces.

Coming closer to the steps, he said in a low voice: "Better talk about that in private, comrade. It's a big charge you're making. Matter of State! Let me talk it over with you in the car. . . ."

"Why do you take bribes?" shouted the swarthy man. "And why do you steal?" He glanced at his notes. "In September, on Holy Rood Day, you stole from Andrey Voronin two rolls of canvas and a ham, from Agrafena Ouvarovna a pair of high-heeled shoes, a strip of satinette, and a blue velvet— Where's Agrafena Ouvarovna?" he asked loudly, breaking off his recital.

Thrust by a dozen hands towards the car, a young

woman issued from the crowd. She was in drab working-clothes.

Penkoff glared murderously at her. She fell back.

"Are you Agrafena Ouvarovna?" asked the swarthy man, thrusting out his hand.

"I am," faltered the woman, again moving forward. She quailed under Penkoff's glance.

"Now tell us, Agrafena," Penkoff blustered. "You must answer when you're questioned. Tell us who told you to slander the Soviet authorities—eh?"

From half-shut eyes Agrafena shot a panic-stricken glance at him.

The commander of the draft looked steadily at her. "Did he take your shoes?" he asked.

Agrafena was silent. She glanced at the whispering girls behind her, shunning the eyes of the fierce man in the red riding-breeches.

"Come on, out with it!" he shouted.

As if jogged from behind, Agrafena shuffled a step forward; her mouth opened, but not a word could she squeeze out of it.

"He took them, eh?"

Agrafena stood speechless. Her face changed slowly. Fear and perplexity gave place to dull, dogged indifference. Penkoff cleared his throat and looked defiance at the crowd. Agrafena's face told him that now she would not speak. But suddenly Nikifor strode towards him from the crowd, frowning and resolute. He advanced to the steps where the Commanding Officer was seated, and turned to Agrafena. "Don't be afraid, girl! Tell him the naked truth. The whole village knows it; every man jack will bear you out."

At Agrafena's back the crowd stirred. The hum of voices grew into a clamour: "Tell him, Agrafena!"

"Don't be afraid, speak up!"

"Let him have it!"

"Life's hell with a man like that!"

"Stole a pot of honey from the Khlysti!"

"Got a sweet tooth, he has!"

"What happened to Samokhin's cloth?"

"And where did he get that tunic?"

"Don't you fear, Agrafena, we'll stand for the truth."

Greedily devouring all these cries and marking the successive speakers, Agrafena plucked up courage and, standing at the foot of the steps, cried out:

"Help us, protector of the poor, have pity on us! This man won't let us live! He's cleaned me out, me, Agrafena, as says it; don't I live in the same street with him, the devil? Only make him give me back my shoes —and my holiday velvet! The satinette's no great matter, let it go. . . . Help me, protector of the poor, make him give me back my own!"

"Why did you rob the woman?" roared the officer. "Don't you know what robbery means? You don't? Well, I'll soon teach you. . . . 'From Stepan Konovaloff,' he read from his notes, you took 'a khaki tunic, with mother-of-pearl buttons sewn on it. The tunic had belonged to the man's son Pyotr, killed on the Red front. . . .'"

Scores of sharp eyes flashed on Penkoff's tunic. Penkoff fastened the pocket with the mother-of-pearl button and was about to speak, when the man in the fur cap, leaning his burly shoulder against the car, swung free, as if jerked off by the train, and planted himself a hand's-breadth from Penkoff.

"What fleet were you in?"

"The Baltic."

"Ship?"

"Avrora."

"Rating?"

"Able Seaman."

The huge man smiled, and shot a glance at the Commanding Officer.

"Who was your captain in '17?"

Penkoff was nonplussed.

"Well, tell us," the huge man taunted. "You promised to answer all our questions. . . . Well?"

Here the crowd massing behind Penkoff parted; the dour Nikifor Petrovitch strode to the front and testified: "He's no sailor, he's a thieving jail-bird—bringing shame and ruin on the Soviet authority!" A sudden calm followed; beyond the car, sparrows twittered, melted snow dripped from its roof. . . . With black, stubborn eyes Nikifor scanned the upturned faces and

185

had already taken breath to drive home his damning charge when Penkoff fell on his knees below the steps and raised a suppliant hand to the proud figure in the crimson riding-breeches. The hand still held the un-lighted cigarette, which quivered like a wounded bird. "Comrade . . . I'm guilty. . . . Spare me! . . . Com-rades! . . ."

When the huge man snatched his revolver from him, Penkoff made no resistance. He crept on his knees to the lowest step and uttered a heart-sickening cry: "Com-rades, dear comrades! . . . Wait! For God's sake, wait!"

"Shoot him!" boomed the deep voice above his head.

And again there was a deathly stillness, stressed by the twittering sparrows. Five men with rifles dragged Penkoff from the steps and marched him down the em-bankment. After them swarmed the peasants. The handsome officer rose up tall and erect, stood thus for a full minute, then entered the car, shutting the door behind him.

By the car, at the foot of the steps, two men re-mained: the huge man in the fur cap and Nikifor Petro-vitch.

The huge man stood like a statue, one elbow propped on a high step, and gazed below him, earthward. Over against him stood Nikifor, looking down at the tram-pled snow, sprinkled with stumps of cigarettes and husks of sunflower-seeds.

A ragged volley from the embankment rent the blithe chatter of the sparrows; in a hushed and sobered company they passed over the heads of the two men by the steps of the car with the plain deal door and significant black letters.

Water dripped from the roof.

Again a shot rang out, the last.

"HE'S A GOOD MAN AND TRUE, ALEX-andr Egoritch is, and wishes me no ill, that's certain, but he's got no feeling for the likes of us; for why?—he's spent his whole life among the gentry!" Thus reasoned Nikita as he left the veterinary one night.

With all the eloquence of his reawakened passion for the turf Alexandr Egoritch had exhorted Nikita for a whole hour to choose a trotting stallion for the sire of Flattery's foal. Wonderful, tempting words he spoke; Nikita listened, nodded agreement, thanked him—but set his heart more and more steadily on mating Flattery with a good sturdy, farm-bred stallion. The veterinary pleaded well, but wide of the mark, somehow; he would have led Nikita far afield, out of the tracks of toil and fellowship; deep in his heart Nikita felt that this was no time to live alone with his ambition, fattening on un-shared plenty. Why, if he listened to the veterinary, he'd be the only man in Shatnyevka—in the whole Vo-lost for that matter—that would have a life worth liv-ing.

"You can talk and talk," he thought, as he listened to

the veterinary, "but that colt will be a good 'un, what
with the mare being Champion's kin, and bred on a
stud-farm too. . . . He'll be fast enough, I'll bet! . . .
Ain't we got good hay for you, juicy as fresh mutton?—
Just you fall to, my boy!—And a bite of oats to follow—
only none of them trotting notions, mind!"

One day, when he had finished the spring sowing,
Nikita resolved to drive to the Settlement, with an eye
to Gaffer Mitri's shaggy-footed stallion. Nastasya
beamed on him. "Praise be to God, he's cut his wis-
dom-teeth! Got them fal-lals out of his head!"

Nikita came back jubilant:

"Well, old woman, I'd never have believed it! That
stallion's as big as a steam-engine! Back on him like a
bedstead; legs—scares you to look at 'em, wouldn't get
one of his hoofs into a wash-tub; and his chest!—
wouldn't squeeze through a town gate! . . . Load
him up with a couple of tons and he'll never notice it!"

When he met the veterinary next day at market,
Nikita said nothing to him of his new resolve, but began
to talk of Moscow and the races. Nikita was still
haunted by the vision of Moscow and the mysterious
round field where horses from all Russia trotted for the
"cup."

His mother-wit told him bluntly that it was not for
him to go traipsing after trotters, he must yoke Flattery
to the plough and make good use of her; but such
pedestrian thoughts were repeatedly swept off their feet

by a surge of unavowed desires, called forth by the easy, powerful gait of the grey mare, so prompt to answer every movement of the rein, so plainly pleading: "Just give me my head a moment, I'll show you how I can trot!"

And sometimes Nikita was persuaded. High-perched, his knees drawn up, the reins coiled round his hands, with a chilled heart he flickered along the highroad, flashing between the chequered fields—black fallows and green rye—past boundaries and ravines, testing the mare's unproved speed—and his heart burned again, for far-off Moscow, the trotters—hundreds and hundreds of trotters—and among them, swiftest of them all, a young colt from Shatnyevka, son the the grey Flattery. . . .

"Whoa-oa!"

The obedient mare slowed down into a walk—the fallows and the rye lay still, the earth stood firm, the wind abated.

Nikita dropped the reins and brooded.

WHEN three men came into the yard, Alexandr Egoritch, a young farm-superintendent, sent recently to Shatnyevka from the headquarters of the province, and a young man in a leather jerkin, Nikita trembled. He doffed his cap and looked furtively at Alexandr Egoritch. The veterinary's eyes were sparkling. The man in the yellow jerkin peered curiously about him and then shook Nikita by the hand. The veterinary said:

"We've come to look at your mare, Nikita Loukitch."

Nikita's fear returned. He glanced at the veterinary and could find no words. The man in the jerkin, a lanky fellow, like a flagstaff, smiled at Nikita's terror-stricken face. "Don't be afraid, Comrade Loukoff! I'm an instructor in horse-breeding, and I'm here to help you. Alexandr Egoritch tells me you've got a good mare, an Orloff. We'd like to see her."

"Nothing to see!" muttered Nikita, without moving.

"Come on, man, fetch her out, don't be afraid," said Alexandr Egoritch, leading the way to the cattle-shed.

Nikita followed reluctantly and led Flattery into the yard. The instructor no sooner saw her than he cried out ecstastically:

"There's breed for you! An Orloff, every inch of her!"

He began to walk round the mare, feeling her legs, her ribs, her haunches, and continually exclaiming: "There you are, there's horseflesh with a vengeance! . . . Magnificent specimen! That's the stock to improve our country breeds! . . . A splendid animal! She's a worker, and a trotter too, I'll swear! Isn't that so, Comrade Loukoff?"

"You know best!" said Nikita evasively, and added:

"Her shoulder ain't right, and . . ."

"Shoulder be damned!" cut in the instructor. "It's her breed that counts!"

He whipped from his pocket a thick note-book and began writing in it, firing questions at the veterinary: "Flattery?—By Firedrake out of Pepperbrandy?—From Bourmin's stable? . . . Goo-ood! Age? Ten years?"

Nikita glared at the pencil as it skimmed over the page, and looked sourly at the old veterinary, who had brought in this pestering clothes-prop of a fellow.

"What did I say!" he brooded. "He'll take her— that's what he's after with his pencil-scratching. Eykh! Alexandr Egoritch, how I begged you to keep your mouth shut!"

"Magnificent pedigree," said the instructor as he wrote—"scion of Bounty—Sollogoub's stable, Polkan strain. . . ." He closed his book and again feasted his eyes on Flattery.

Turning to the agricultural adviser, he exclaimed: "That's the stuff to improve our peasant breed with! And you didn't even know of her existence, comrade!"

The expert flushed, but before he could reply, the instructor spun round on Nikita: "You give me a call this evening, I'm staying with your adviser here; you and I must have a chat!"

Nikita thought and thought till evening. He could not rid his mind of that cocksure little pencil, entering his mare limb by limb in the fat note-book, and bitterly he reproached the old veterinary for telling the instructor about Flattery. When he knocked on the expert's door, his heart was troubled.

The instructor sat coatless astride a chair. On the table was a portfolio, crammed with papers. He sat in a haze of tobacco-smoke. He had evidently been talking for some time.

"Both for agriculture and for the Army," he was saying, "an immense supply of horses is required, horses of the highest quality. In view of our bad roads, the vastness of the Republic's territory, and the absence of motor transport, good horses are for us a vital necessity. That's obvious. Tractors—by all means! But the horse cannot be neglected. In these years of imperial and civil war the number of horses has decreased by half, if not by more. That's why I call your attention to the horse. The quality also has deteriorated—understand that? Alarmingly! To preserve the good material that is left, this is your plain duty. . . . But your heads are so full of tractors that you've no room for it. There's an example for you!" The instructor nodded towards Nikita. "All honour to him for tending the mare and keeping her from harm! We owe him thanks and encouragement. And you didn't even know that you had such fine material in Shatnyevka! But tending the mare is only the first step, you must use her to improve the rest, your own Shatnyevka horses. What action have you taken in this matter? Have you advised Loukoff on the choice of a stallion? No. Have you explained to him the importance of blood-stock to the State? No. Have you shown him that this brood-mare of his has a use and meaning for the nation? No. Don't talk to me of veterinaries! What's your veterinary about? A lot he cares for the nation, he's got other fish to fry! Sit down, Comrade Loukoff!" He faced round to Nikita, who stood in the doorway drinking in his words.

"I can stand, comrade."

"Sit down, sit down, we'll be a long time talking. Your veterinary told me you want to breed the mare to a trotting stallion. That's a matter that needs thought, brother."

The instructor dragged himself to the table on his chair, scooped up some coarse tobacco from a tin that had held shoe-polish, and rolled a cigarette. From his shaven face, shrouded in smoke at the first pull, came a voice like a rifle-shot: "Want to get her in foal? Well? After that?"

Nikita was silent. The instructor, too, kept silence for some time. He shrouded himself in smoke and chewed the end of his cigarette, still speechless. At last he answered for Nikita: "After that—nothing! Understand me? Nothing!"

The agricultural adviser looked at the crestfallen Nikita, coughed, and said haltingly: "You'll come and see me tomorrow, Loukoff. . . . I'll give you a document certifying that you're the rightful owner of the mare."

The instructor shot out of his chair and paced the room with yard-long strides. Then he stopped short, swung round like a pair of compasses, and clapped Nikita on the shoulder. "Look here, Loukoff! . . ."

Nikita did not lose a word of the instructor's long and vehement speech. What the old veterinary had never told him he now heard, and his heart was lightened: the Soviet not only would let him keep the mare, but would thank him for having saved her for the nation. . . . They would help him with advice, and with money too, if need be.

Nikita also understood that without such help he could never make a trotter of the foal; he had not the right sort of cart, nor the skill, for training him, nor the food and stabling, maybe, that he needed.

"I *had* thought," said Nikita, "of mating the mare with a peasant stallion. . . . Gaffer Mitri at the Settlement . . ."

"Wait," said the instructor, "we'll soon see about that. You know the old saw: 'You can break the twig, but not the faggot.' Well! This sort of thing must be done co-operatively. Understand? You must found a horse-breeders' association in Shatnyevka—get every man with a decent horse to join it. We'll let you have blood stallions free, and money if you need it. Then things'll brighten up! You'll be helping yourselves,

195

and the Republic too. Meanwhile, breed the mare to a trotter by all means. I'll give you a note to the Agricultural Department of the province, I'm going there myself on the way to Moscow. Ask for Comrade Goubaryeff. That's my name, don't forget—Gou-ba-ryeff. Nikolai Petrovitch Goubaryeff. Wait a minute, I'll write it down for you to show 'em."

He tore a clean sheet from his note-book and wrote in big block letters:

NIKOLAI PETROVITCH GOUBARYEFF,
PEOPLE'S COMMISSARY FOR AGRICULTURE.

CHAPTER · IX

To sire his foal, Nikita chose from the stallions shown him at the Agricultural Department the dark-bay Favourite, son of the famous Taglioni.

At the end of March 1921 Flattery threw a handsome colt. Having examined him, the old veterinary joined Nikita in his cottage, where they cracked a bottle of the strongest brew.

"Here's to our new horse-breeder, Nikita Loukitch!" said the veterinary as they finished the bottle. "That colt should be a stunner; he's got all the points of an Orloff. . . . Who knows but he'll turn out a second Champion!"

Syomka, sitting by his mother on the bench, nudged her gently with his elbow. "Hear that, Mamanka?"

Nastasya sighed. Penkoff's death had painfully strengthened her conviction that the mare brought no good.

"Fetch another bottle," said Nikita to his wife.

"What'll you call him?" asked the veterinary, as he

197

clinked glasses with Nikita. "We must register him, you know—all things decently and in order."

"Can't think of a name nohow!"

"Ataman!" whooped Syomka, leaning down from over the stove. "Call him Ataman, Daddy!"

He saw himself on Ataman, galloping off to night pasture, and again he pleaded, tugging at his father's sleeve:

"Ataman, Daddy!"

"He ain't a brigand! Dash'd fit him better. . . ."

"That's a name they never give 'em," rejoined Syomka peevishly; " 'Da-ash!' Poof! What a name!"

"Well, what sense is there in Ataman? Keep on squawking, like a magpie—'Ataman'!"

" 'Dash'! He ain't a dog!" persisted Syomka.

"How do you mean—'dog'?" snapped Nikita.

"That's what the Commissar calls his terrier—'Go it, Dash, fetch 'em, fetch 'em!' "

"Get out, you stinking brat!" Nikita blazed. "We're talking business, and you sit and— Off with you!"

Alexandr Egoritch smiled indulgently and clenched the argument: "We'll call him Grandson—his grandsire was a champion trotter—then they'll all know. 'Taglioni's Grandson'! Leave it at that, Nikita!"

The word Taglioni pleased Nikita by its rareness; words like that weren't met with in Shatnyevka. A real mouthful it was, though—mighty queer!

He scratched himself and looked shyly at Alexandr

Egoritch, then at Syomka: "Don't know, I'm sure. You say his grandsire was a good 'un, but . . ."

"Come, Nikita, settle it!" said the veterinary, poking him in the ribs, and filling their glasses to the brim.

"Eykh, I'm beat. . . . Have it your way, sir—Tall-yoney's Grandson."

Before leaving, Alexandr Egoritch once more accompanied Nikita to the stall. The grandson of the mighty champion, puny and pitiable, his matted coat fresh dried, snuggled timidly against his mother, feebly upheld by tottering, sprawling shanks. The bulging, dark-blue eyes with long, bright lashes darted from one strange object to another in this bewildering new world. Every movement of man, every breath of wind or rustle of straw, startled him. His legs, which seemed too long and thick for his short, lean body, kept slithering on the littered straw, till they straddled apart and he fell on his knees, more scared than ever.

Flattery turned towards the visitors and fixed her one eye pleadingly upon them, as if she would say: "Leave us!"

THEN came the great drought, all summer long.

In vain the peasants trudged the fields with icons and with banners, chanting propitiatory prayers. In vain the girls, by the old folks' counsel, sprinkled each other—and all strangers who passed by—with well-water, to lay the spirit of the drought. Small clouds appeared on the inexorable blue heavens, only to float past. And every day the white-hot sun blazed out, pouring his deadly glare on the parched earth.

By midsummer the fields were withered.

Instead of grass and yellowing ears, a dull-red growth bristled in tilth and meadow. The leaves hung sapless on the trees, curled like burnt paper spills, and with a crack fell crumbling to dust. The rigid earth gaped with broad rents, like the face of a stone monster marred by time. The cattle had no pasture. Over the village hovered the hungry lowing of the cows, the pitiful bleat of rams and ewes. The idle husbandmen slouched through the village, darkening the cottage doors with sullen, sighing groups.

Nearer and surer came the tread of that most ruthless of all conquerors, Famine. From north and south, from east and west, poured the black tidings of starvation. The ring of death closed on Shatnyevka. The knife was busy in field and cattle-shed, silencing the complaints of sheep and cattle. There was no salt. The uncured, reeking flesh was lowered into the cool, dark wells or stowed in barrels of fresh water, buried in pits lined with burnt stinging nettles, or sprinkled with gunpowder instead of salt; and when all shifts failed and the worm crawled in the rancid carcasses, the whole household fell upon the meat, breakfasted, dined, and supped on it, and, clogged by the rich, unwonted fare, sank into a dull, nightmare-haunted sleep. . . . And soon their looks were changed; ghoulish, carnivorous eyes peered from their faces.

At the end of October the first snow covered the bleak fields, and Shatnyevka cowered in its hollow, like a huge half-gnawed skeleton, with its thatchless roofs, and ravaged for fodder. Winter was at the doors, the deadly winter of 1921.

The first blow struck at Nikita by the drought was the sale of his yearling heifer. Nastasya wept when she set out for the miller's home with the fawn-coloured beauty. But Nikita was grimly reckoning how long the flour he got from the miller—and the chaff and sweepings for the mare—would last, and how soon he must sell the cow. . . . By winter nothing of his stock was left, neither cow, nor sow, nor sheep, nor poultry. His yard was bare as a bone, every straw, every grain picked out of it. Over it loomed the roofless barn, its gnarled black timbers streaking the wan twilight. On the ceiling of the shed, above the mare and her foal, Nikita had secretly stored bran and chaff—but the flour for the family's bread he mixed with husks of millet, and crushed acorns.

Towards Christmas Nikifor Petrovitch turned up at the hut. His visits were rare; once a year he would look in after market, cast his eyes over the yard, and be gone. But this time he came in, greeted his brother-in-law and sister silently, and sat down on the bench. After a while he shot a glance at Syomka. Then he drew from his pocket a match-box, wrapped in a sheet of paper. The box held little white grains, rather like pills.

"German sugar," he explained to his sister and Nikita. "We call it saccharin. You must take it with water."

He gave the box to Syomka and relapsed into long silence.

"I'm at my wits' end what to do," began Nikita. "Can't think how I can last out till spring. I'm hard put for it, Nikifor Petrovitch. . . ."

Nikifor nodded gravely.

"Time was when every man was victualled against the harvest, but this year . . . makes your heart sink! My kinsman Prokhor couldn't keep his gelding—had to make soup of him."

Nikifor waved his hand hopelessly and brooded.

"How's the mare?" asked Nikifor.

"Mighty poor. You wouldn't guess how bad she is! Tomorrow I was going to drive her to the forest for a bit of firewood, but I doubt if she'll do it."

"She'll do it," said Nikifor firmly. Nikita eyed him with amazement.

"She'll do it," he repeated, his stubborn black eyes glaring at the wall.

He rose to go. They stepped into the yard. "Let me see her," Nikifor grunted. He looked at Flattery.

"She'll do it," he pronounced conclusively.

"Pray God she may!" said Nikita, shaking his head

wistfully as he eyed the starveling mare and wondering how on earth he could feed her and the foal till spring came round.

"There's oats and flour for you. Come tonight," Nikifor whispered close against his ear. When Nikita turned towards him, the black, sullen eyes, motionless heretofore as stagnant water, stirred, and roved restlessly from side to side.

"Train full of flour, sugar, and oats—moves on tomorrow," muttered Nikifor. "When the church clock strikes three, I'll be at the crossing. The mare'll do it. We'll find oats. Just you come, I've reckoned up everything. You count on me. Oats! You can help yourself!"

Nikita staggered back. He looked at his brother-in-law aghast. His left arm rose and fell, as if he would, but could not, shield himself against this drum-fire of importunate mutterings.

"I'm thinking of my sister, thinking of the boy," Nikifor urged. "There's bread for them—cake if you like. If you don't come, Syomka will die. Nastasya will die. The mare will die. And the foal too. And without them, you'll die. Die of grief. Because you didn't listen to me. You'll all die."

At last Nikita found his tongue: "Don't bewilder me so, Nikifor Petrovitch, for the King of Heaven's sake! Don't talk to me of such things; since I was born I've had no truck with 'em. . . . Think no more of my

203

mare, she'll never start on such an errand. . . ."

"Your kinsman Prokhor cut his horse's throat, and yours'll starve," said Nikifor bluntly and aloud. With that he stumped out of the yard.

As the church clock on the hill struck three, Nikita drove up to the grade crossing.

Nikifor bundled into the sledge, crushing Nikita's leg. "Drive round by the back!" he whispered.

Nikita's hands trembled feverishly on the reins.

He and the mare were bound on shameful, perilous business. It seemed as if no living man went with him; the dead weight of Nikifor lay on his legs as though a rock were crushing them. To the left, the embankment sloped into the dark; who could say what was on it? Maybe a living man lurked there, watching them, ready to alarm his comrades. Flattery, poor beast, jogged painfully along beside the fearsome slope; you could just hear the runners brushing the soft snow. At a dark gap, a culvert built to drain off the flood water, they stopped. The burden of stone was lifted from the crushed leg. A freight-car loomed over them.

"Here!" said Nikifor softly. "Wait!"

Before leaving the sledge he leaned across to Nikita, waving his hands towards some region of the darkness. "That's where they settled Penkoff's hash. That's where he's buried, too!"

204

He plunged through the gap and vanished under the embankment.

Never had Nikita known such fear. The black night seemed alive. Alive too the dark freight-car looming over him. He had never seen a car so huge. Sometimes he fancied it was slowly moving. He held his breath and listened. His ear caught a crunching sound—steel biting its way through iron. . . .

Down the embankment, straight to the foot of the sledge, a sack came tumbling; a hurried whisper followed:

"Up with it, there's another coming!"

Nikita heaved the bulging sack onto the sledge.

"Oats?" he whispered in his turn.

Another sack rolled down, smaller and lighter.

Again Nikita whispered: "Oats?"

No answer came, but Nikifor himself pitched headlong down the slope.

Nikita, dazed and terror-stricken, lashed his horse. With her six-hundredweight load Flattery sped homeward.

"Faster!"

A shot rang out behind them. A second, and a third. At the crossing Nikifor trundled out of the sledge into the dark; Nikita flourished an arm towards the meadow, and still more frenziedly the faithful mare rushed on. . . . As she struck the rise, she panted hoarsely, but regained her breath and drew up presently at the famil-

205

iar gate. She staggered into the yard, exhausted.

One sack was full of potato-flour, the other of powdered sugar.

Nikifor arrived two days later. "Out of my sight!" said Nikita. "And take them sacks with you. I never want to see you or them sacks again!"

He strode out of the hut, slamming the door after him.

These two days Flattery had lain sick and still. For the foal's sake Nikita had doubled her feed of bran, but she ate little, and sometimes nothing. On the fifth day she struggled to her feet, but now she moped, and did not turn to Nikita when he came into her stall.

Soon after that night, which Nikita never forgot, Syomka's legs began to swell. At first Nastasya plied him with household remedies: lashed him with a hot broom, poulticed him with hot ashes. But when the swelling spread to his hands and face, she urged Nikita to take him to the railway hospital.

"I've no medicine that will help you," said the house surgeon to Nikita; "you must vary the boy's diet— change his food, man."

Nikita plodded homeward. As he walked beside the sledge, he remembered the doctor's words and looked wistfully at the pale, swollen face of Syomka, sitting in the sledge. Flattery could just lift her nerveless legs, and as often as she stopped, Nikita waited patiently to give her breath. At the hill the mare staggered abruptly and fell, rolling over on her side. Syomka crawled out of the sledge and tried to help his father raise her. Flattery did not rise. She lay with her legs stiff as poles, her neck thrust out over the snow. Nikita took her out of the shafts and tugged gently at the rein, coaxing her: "Get up, girl, get up!"

With a last effort the mare answered. She raised her outstretched neck, struck out with all four legs to find a foothold, heaved herself up on bent and quivering knees, and knelt thus for a moment, like a beaten gladiator before hushed spectators. . . . And again she sank down heavily. Nikita gazed long at the mare. She was breathing in short fitful sighs. Steam rose from her wet flank. From the crest of the hill came the whinnying welcome of the grey Grandson. He was the lustiest of them all. Every day the master had come in to see him, climbed up somewhere overhead, bustled about there for some time, making a great clatter with the pail, and then come down and called him. The pail sent up a sweet smell of hot corn, and in the thick mash floated crisp, luscious grains. . . .

When she heard his neigh, Flattery's head rose painfully and sank back in the snow.

"She's done for!" said Nikita hoarsely, looking ruefully at Syomka.

He searched under his coat-tails, drew a jack-knife from his pocket, and unclasped it. The Grandson ran up to his mother, just as Nikita, propped on one knee, thrust his cap over the mare's single eye and, plunging the knife into her gullet, struck it violently outwards.

Flattery's flesh was tough and smelt of sweat.

PART THREE

CHAPTER · I

NEAR THE OLD HORSE-MARKET, IN AN obscure thoroughfare on the south side of Moscow, the tea-house of Ivan Petrovitch Rakitin dragged out the evening of its day. Despite its homely face, modest blue sign, three wooden steps, and discreet little door, draped with oil cloth, it had been once the heart and brain of the whole horse-trafficking fraternity. On Thursdays and Sundays—market-days—the three low-ceilinged rooms were packed. Horse-dealers, cabmen, peasants from the outlying villages who had come to buy or sell a horse, livery-stable-keepers, drivers, jockeys, grooms forgathered at Rakitin's. And every evening in the back room, at his favourite corner table, sat Mikhal Mikhalitch Grouzdyeff, the famous horse-dealer; all Moscow knew him as the owner of a stable with eighty loose-boxes, who had settled in this street to be near the tea-house. Mikhal Mikhalitch was known to every dealer, not only in Moscow, but throughout Russia. They all dealt with him—bought from him, sold to him, touted for him on commission, or in some way depended on him. Therefore Mikhal Mikhalitch Grouzdyeff enjoyed vast respect and obsequious deference, and none dared seat himself unbidden at the corner table. Behind it a long spike was driven into the wall for Mikhal Mikhalitch's private use; in winter he hung on it his astrakhan cap and long cloak trimmed with fox fur—his silk muffler remained round his neck—and in the summer his alpaca skull-cap. His first glass of tea was always brought him by the host, Ivan Petrovitch. Beside him sat the farrier Semyon Andreyitch Kourotchkin and the horse-dealer Grishka Kortsoff, reputed one of the most accomplished scoundrels in the trade. At this table in 1914 Grouzdyeff had bought from the stud-owner Borschevsky a famous string of colts, on which he cleared a cool sixty thousand profit, and a year later, at the selfsame table, with the help of Grishka Kortsoff, Grouzdyeff persuaded the impoverished owner Zavyaloff to sell him his lame mare Swallow, who very soon afterwards showed such astonishing speed at the Moscow hippodrome that she was sold hot from the race to a prominent patron for the fabulous price of fifty thousand rubles.

That evening Zavyaloff rushed into the tea-house, drew a chair up to Grouzdyeff's table, and let fly at him: "What have you done? You've ruined me! Have you lost all shame? Pay me my due! At least half that money's mine!"

Grouzdyeff stroked his beard, cleared his throat, and observed blandly: "That's business. Didn't you sell her? If you took a sound view of the matter, you would feel grateful and indebted to me, because I appreciated your acute and, I may say, abject poverty at the time and, moved wholly by kindness and compassion, agreed to take the lame mare off your hands. Indeed . . ."

Having heard him out thus far, Zavyaloff sprang to his feet and glared at Grouzdyeff, his eyes flashing, his teeth chattering: "You've ruined me, and now you're laughing at me!"

Mikhal Mikhalitch stroked his beard, coughed, and proceeded: "This same kindness and compassion prompt me to offer you twenty-five rubles, knowing the necessity which . . ."

Zavyaloff dashed out of the tea-house, leaving his grey slouch hat behind him. This grey hat never left the house, for next day Zavyaloff blew out his brains with a shotgun.

How many shrewd and strange transactions, what buyings and sellings, gains and losses, might be recounted by that little table, covered with checked linoleum, in the corner of the back room of the tea-house near the old horse-market!

In 1925 all this was gone for ever. Traffic in horses was confined to the national syndicates and co-operative associations. The horse-dealers, thus left with empty hands and pockets, migrated northward to the Tverskaya, near the hippodrome, where they could get a straight tip on a certainty or pick up a small commission by scenting out some likely purchase for a horse-breeding association. Rakitin's tea-house was left desolate, like a corpse forgotten by the grave-diggers. The bulk of its old patrons spent their leisure north of the river at the Free Labour Tea-House, opened of late by Mitritch, formerly landlord of the eating-house in the Bashilovka.

Two only remained faithful to the old tea-house: Grouzdyeff and the aged farrier Semyon Andreyitch. The revolution had taken everything from Grouzdyeff: his stable with its eighty loose-boxes, his horses, carriages, and money; but the little table at Rakitin's was still left to him. Only once in the last year had it happened that Mikhal Mikhalitch, entering the tea-house as usual about seven, found his table occupied by strangers. He glanced at them and strode back to the counter, where Rakitin squatted, poring over a new income-tax decree.

Mikhal Mikhalitch cleared his throat, tapped the floor with his cherry-wood staff, and said: "Ivan Petrovitch, I must trouble you . . ."

Ivan Petrovitch bustled into the back room and returned promptly. "Forgive me, Mikhal Mikhalitch! . . . You know yourself, sir, times are changed, everything's topsyturvy nowadays."

This topsyturvydom was keenly felt by the old far-

214

rier, Semyon Andreyitch Kourotchkin. He came to the house every day, and always earlier than Mikhal Mikhalitch. He would sit down at the table next to Grouzdyeff's, waiting for him. When Grouzdyeff came, he would silently stretch out his hand to the farrier, take off his cap, and hang it up. Thereupon Kourotchkin shuffled over to his table. Often they would sit a whole evening without words, exchanging sighs or ejaculations.

When Grouzdyeff sighed, Kourotchkin followed on a wheezy, quavering note.

"A-a-ah!" intoned Mikhal Mikhalitch.

"Oi-oi-oi!" Semyon Andreyevitch responded.

One evening in September Kourotchkin entered the house late—Mikhal Mikhalitch was already seated. Wheezing and groaning, Semyon Andreyitch slumped into his chair and sat pensive, staring with filmy eyes at the glass of weak tea on Grouzdyeff's table. At seventy years Kourotchkin still kept his ruddy cheeks and a certain youthfulness. His sickle-shaped beard, broad but not long, and his bald head, framed at the back by a fringe of snow-white curls, recalled the icons of St. Nicholas. His left hand clutching a birch-bark snuff-box and an indigo handkerchief of startling proportions, he tottered up to Grouzdyeff, wiped the glistening sweat from his bald head, sighed, and gasped out: "My death's near!"

"Why do you say that?"

For a long while Semyon Andreyitch stared at the glass of tea in silence. Suddenly he raised his tearful eyes and fastened them on Grouzdyeff. "I've been dreaming."

"Well?"

"Dreaming of stallions. . . ."

"That's due to your occupation," Grouzdyeff said sententiously. "Every man to his trade. How many of them have you gelded in your time?—thousands!"

"Scores of thousands, that's true enough. . . . And yet I never dreamed of them till now."

Kourotchkin dropped his head on his chest; his beard spread out like a fan.

"Every night I dream of them. . . . And last night, towards dawn—I saw myself in the next world. What a strange sight it was! I walked and walked down a dark passage, so long there seemed no end to it. I was coming to the heart of hell, the throne of Beelzebub. And I found myself in a great square, like our horse-market. Yes indeed. . . . As I stumbled out of the passage, I was met by—stallions, droves of them, starting out of the ground, closing in right and left, and all coming straight at me—gaping, gnashing their teeth, pawing the air, flashing big eyes, like tigers'. And they roared at me, in some sort of human language: 'There, there! He's come! Now we'll settle with him!' And they all hurled themselves at me. . . . I recognized every one. They had all been through my hands. All—geldings now! And a great fear fell upon me, and I woke, streaming with sweat and cold as marble. . . ."

"Due to your occupation, Semyon Andreyitch," Grouzdyeff repeated, "and to your thoughts too. The best cure for dreams is salted cabbage-water."

"I've tried it, but I still keep dreaming!"

At this moment Grishka Kortsoff entered, a tall, insolent fellow, with a red, weather-beaten face. Like most of the horse-dealers, he was without work or money, but unlike the rest, did not complain; to the social formula: "How's business?" he replied, brusquely and almost aggressively: "A fool can live if he's got business; *I* don't starve without it!"

On the heels of Kortsoff came another visitor, clean-shaven, in a light-grey hat and check breeches. He walked jauntily to the table where Grouzdyeff, Kourotchkin, and Kortsoff were sitting, greeted them all, and drew up a chair.

"Glass of tea, Vassily Alexandrovitch?" inquired Grouzdyeff. "Where on earth have you been? I keep asking: 'Haven't you seen Vassily Alexandrovitch Sossounoff?'—nobody can tell me anything."

Sossounoff laughed noisily. His laugh was ventral, hoarse, and staccato—like the "chug, chug" of a tractor.

"Been potting at hares, Mikhal Mikhalitch—had a month's shooting."

Kourotchkin stared blankly at Sossounoff. He took

in the bow tie, the grey felt hat, the check breeches, and sighed. It was strange, incomprehensible to him that now, when all life was topsyturvy, pell-mell, and unrecognizable, a man should think of going shooting. . . . At last he ejaculated :

"Hares?—In these days?"

Kortsoff clapped Sossounoff on his chequered knee, guffawing: "Bravo-o-o, Vassily my boy! . . . Let 'em have their revivalooshun in China. We'll get along without it, thank you."

"Sure enough, Grisha, it ain't our affair!" roared Sossounoff. "Let's talk of something real. . . . There's a vegetable called a spongilla, makes very good eating. Serve it up with an omelet and a spice of onion—you know, grated and sprinkled over it—and a ham to follow. . . ."

He cocked his head on one side, screwed up his eyes, and rubbed his hands voluptuously together.

"Eykh, that's good!"

"Fond of your nose-bag, eh, Vassily!"

"Food's the one thing I live for, and I make no secret of it. Thirty-five years I've spent regretting that I wasn't born in the old serf-keeping days. . . . That was a natural life, my boy! All the four-and-twenty delights sat round you, at your beck and call; make your choice, wag your finger, and—'At your service, sir!' Ever read about Pyotr Petrovitch Petoukh? *There* was a man knew how to live!" Sossounoff jerked his head scornfully at the weak tea. "I was bored stiff sitting at home trying to drink that mouth-wash—there's no kick in it—just a belly-flusher!"

"Who was that Pyotr Petrovitch?" Kourotchkin asked warily.

"Ah, he was a great character, one in a million!" said Sossounoff rapturously. "Nikolai Vasilyevitch Gogol paints him to the life. A landowner, Semyon Andreyitch, a Russian landowner—never knew a dull moment, Semyon Andreyitch! He'd send for the cook, I remember, every evening, and discuss tomorrow's dinner. Fish pie, say, in four quarters. First quarter, with sturgeon's cheeks in it; second, with bruised buckwheat; third, mushrooms and onions; fourth, calves' brains and milk. . . . And iced rennet in the sturgeon!"

Sossounoff screwed up his eyes, smacked his lips, wobbled his head, let out a roar, sighed, sat upright, and with a rapt face, in a voice intense and vibrant, as if chanting a litany, he quoted: "Make me a pig's rennet, and lay a slab of ice in the middle, so that it stands up handsomely! . . . And dress the sturgeon well, season it richly! . . . Trim it with crabs and a morsel of fried roach, stuff it with a few smelt and chopped salad, horse-radish, and pepper-mushrooms, parsley and kidney-beans and carrots!"

Sossounoff threw his head back and looked round the company with tranced eyes, growing smaller and smaller as they gazed into the past. His cavernous horse-laugh rumbled and erupted: "There, Semyon Andreyitch, *that* was a life! . . . Eykh, you can't help sighing for those days!"

"They'll never come back!" said Grouzdyeff, sighing too.

"If only I'd lived a hundred years ago!" resumed Sossounoff. "And had nine or ten thousand acres of my own, well stocked with serfs! . . . Near the house, a trout-stream; beyond the river, a wood with plenty of hares in it. . . . Breakfast early, a mere snack, then off with the hounds and back for—lunch! Fish pies, wood-cock pies, cherry brandy—my own brew—and . . ."

"You're class-conscious, right enough, young man!" Kourotchkin interjected, snuff-box in hand, ramming a double charge into his ruby-coloured nose.

Here Grishka Kortsoff, with sudden spleen, as if the vials of his wrath were being poured out, railed against the Soviet Government: "Now, brother, we're under a Red-public! . . . They want to make us all equal, want to make us happy. . . ."

And as if someone had contradicted him, he began to dispute, with rising indignation: "Equal? Don't tell me they ain't fools! Take Mikhal Mikhalitch, he's got science, I tell you—ran a stable with eighty horses—and myself! How can you make us equal? Or take you, Vassily Alexandrevitch! You were a cashier in a dry-goods store, but I've been a horse-dealer all my life. We're different."

"You're off the track, Grisha," broke in Sossounoff, tapping his pocket; "*that's* where they want to level us."

"And they won't do that neither!" Kortsoff shouted, his eyes blazing, "they'll never do it! At my own game I can beat them still. Make rings round 'em. Only the other day, up comes a fellow looking for a horse—a big bug with a portfolio. I'd got a mare I was selling on commission. Outside price, five hundred; back like a knife, and had the ring-bone; but he, like a prize fool, 'Why does she keep wagging her tail?' says he. I nearly died of laughter; in the end he forked out fifteen hundred."

"What mare was that, Grigory Nikolaievitch?" interposed Grouzdyeff sharply.

"Why, the grey mare with the ring-bone!"

Kourotchkin wiped his bald head with his blue handkerchief and groaned.

"Everything's upside down," he said. "Even a dumb beast has sense and can tell one man from another. I never forgot what a very reliable man told me. His Majesty the Emperor Alexander the Blessèd once came on a visit to Count Orloff, to inspect his stables. The Count, of course, was himself 'His Excellency,' and the Premier Count of the Empire. But His Imperial Majesty was Autocrat of All the Russias. Well, as you'd suppose, the Count made his preparations, and—His Majesty arrived. As soon as he comes to the house, he steps out of his carriage and says: 'Take me to the stables, I want to see all your famous trotters and what sort of a life they live with you.' The Count escorted him to the stables. And no sooner had he crossed the threshold than all those thousands of horses started neighing with one voice; their dumb natures knew him and greeted him, like a loyal crowd that bursts into a thundering hurrah!"

Kourotchkin raised his head and surveyed them all with his glazed, watery eyes. Sossounoff's beardless lip was curling mischievously.

"Nothing to smile at, my dear sir! In those days beasts had more sense than many a man has now. Yes, sir!"

"I've heard another version of that story," said Sossounoff gaily. "The sense was not in the beasts, but in Count Orloff's steward, a certain Vassily Ivanovitch Shishkin, a rogue of the first water. He knew a trick or two! . . . Now listen!" he proceeded, turning away from Kourotchkin to the others. "When he heard that the Emperor was coming to inspect the stables in a month or so, Shishkin had shutters put on all the loose-boxes, and every day at the same moment the shutters opened and a shower of oats fell into the horses' mangers. Of course they came to know it; when the shutters opened, they expected oats, and when a horse gets wind of oats, he starts to neigh. Well, Shishkin had had a month's practice. When the Emperor came into the stable, Shishkin tipped somebody the wink, and they started neighing. Wasn't the Tsar delighted! He gave Shishkin a diamond ring. . . ."

Kortsoff, who had been listening open-mouthed, shook his head with ecstatic relish. "The dog! The sly dog! The crafty devil! Well, good luck to him! . . . What was his name—Vassily Ivanovitch Shishkin? . . . The sly dog!"

Kourotchkin looked sullenly at Sossounoff, sniffed, snorted, and pronounced: "You're over-educated, that's what you are! You know everything! Neither Tsar nor God for you—you and your check breeches. . . . You're asked to sit down with decent people, and you turn out a wolf in sheep's clothing!"

Sossounoff, not at all offended, leaned back and guffawed. He checked himself abruptly and said gravely to Kortsoff: "Might do a stroke of business with you."

Kortsoff was on his guard at once. His coarse, weather-stained face appeared suspicious, almost hostile.

"Got the goods all right," said Sossounoff in an undertone, using the horse-dealers' jargon. "A man has brought a horse here from the Ryazan Province. Saw him unloaded at the Paveletzky station. Four-year-old —just what we want—a colt!"

"For sale?" inquired Kortsoff.

"Deuce knows! Can't make head or tail of the man! Stabled him with Koultyapy. Come and look him over. He's a good horse."

"The swine!" said Kortsoff, referring to Koultyapy. "Never breathed a word to me."

"He'll be here in a minute," said Sossounoff, looking at his watch. "I've had a talk with him."

Grouzdyeff had been listening attentively. He looked uneasy.

When Koultyapy appeared, Kortsoff let fly at him: "Well, you son of a horse-thief! Want to be on your own, do you? Business booming?"

"Can't complain, Grigory Nikolaievitch? And how's yourself?" answered Koultyapy, conning their faces with his crafty eyes. "If it's the colt you want to talk about, you're wasting time. The man won't sell him. Brought him here for the races."

"We'll see about that," said Kortsoff significantly. "We weren't born yesterday! Races, says you! Last year there was a man came from Pyenza for the races. But his mare went lame!" he added, lowering his voice and winking at Koultyapy.

"I get you, Grigory Nikolaievitch!"

"Well, then! Where's the man from? What's he like?"

Koultyapy waved his hand scornfully.

"A clodhopper. . . . Brought a letter from Loutoshkin. Never seen Moscow before. But the horse is a good 'un. Four-year-old. Tell you what, Grigory Nikolaievitch, come round tomorrow morning early. The man'll be at the Bashilovka. You can see the colt."

224

"Any pedigree?"

"Won't show it; he's too scared."

"Right! We'll be round tomorrow!" said Kortsoff, and again he winked at Koultyapy.

Sossounoff gloated, rubbing his hands over the good things to come. "Then we'll get our teeth into an omelet. . . . Eykh, and a good one, Grisha!"

CHAPTER · II

THE MENTION OF THE GREY MARE FLAT-
tery in the veterinary's note brought back to Loutoshkin
long-forgotten visions of his sojourn on Bourmin's
estate, and sharpest of all stood out the shape of Aristarkh Bourmin. A nightmare shape, a monster, awe-
some and uncouth in his callous, imperturbable detachment from the living heart of man. His cheerless
den, where a live man would have stifled in a single day,
his arrogant, piping voice, descanting precepts, his rigid
rectilineal figure and Assyrian beard; his very lusts,
punctiliously dovetailed into his routine—all quick-
ened in Loutoshkin's memory, flashed up with appal-
ling vividness—and the whole life of that estate surged
back on him, unsouled, emasculated by one man's
caprice. . . .

"Revolution is the ruin of the nobility. Revolution
is the ruin of tradition. Revolution is the ruin of the
Orloff trotter, created by the inspired will of the ever
memorable Count Alexei Grigoryevitch Orloff Chesmensky. Revolution is chaos, most repugnant to the

will of God. And God will not allow it!" Thus Aristarkh Bourmin had spoken in a fit of overwhelming rage, not many days before he was shaken out of his stoutly built ancestral aerie.

Loutoshkin forced himself out of his day-dream, and looked at Nikita.

Nikita waited meekly, his arms hanging limp. His face, creased by a vexed and sleepless night, was gaunt and grey, his hair matted; and his khaki jacket shed a pungent smell of horse-sweat.

"Is the mare alive?" asked Loutoshkin.

"Dead," said Nikita dolefully. "Died in the famine year."

"How old's the colt? Three?"

"Three years last spring."

"Where is he now?"

Nikita pattered off the carefully conned address and in confirmation drew out a scrap of paper with directions scrawled on it.

"I know, I know," said Loutoshkin, without looking at it, "Koultyapy's. . . . Who sent you to him?"

Nikita told him how he had arrived in Moscow at the Paveletsky station, how he had begun taking the colt out of his box, when a man had come up to him, not an elderly man, nor yet young, like—just a plain man with nothing of the Moscow look about him— and then a gentleman had come up, with one of them soft hats, and long town trousers—might have been cut out of an old woman's shawl.

Loutoshkin's eyes sparkled; he wagged his head appreciatively.

"You see, we arrived yesterday—about five o'clock. Alexandr Egoritch, he says to be sure and see you, sir, as soon as I get here. . . . So you knew the mare, sir? Eykh, what a beauty! A good worker too, and that knowing! Well, though I say it myself, the colt's the spit of her, got her sly tricks and her sweet temper, and—skims along like a swallow! Alexandr Egoritch knows what's what! 'That colt's safe for the cup,' says he. Those were his very words!"

"Cups don't grow on every tree," said Loutoshkin staidly. "We must look him over first and try him out; then we can talk about the cup. . . . You go back to him now; after dinner I'll join you and we'll have a talk."

Nikita thrust his cap over his eyes and hurried out, to thread his way from the Bashilovka to the Mytnaya, a perilous passage, beside which the journey from Shatnyevka to Moscow had been child's play.

Loutoshkin watched him to the gate, reread the veterinary's note, and squatted down against the fence. His bent back and bowed head made him look like an old man.

". . . FROM my own observation I can vouch for the colt as a youngster of unusual promise. I can say with confidence that in your hands he will go far," wrote the veterinary.

But Loutoshkin cared little. The small of his back was aching. A month ago he had reached his fortieth year. After the grey Flattery's son, they would bring him some new colt "of unusual promise." Another, and another. . . . For the thousandth time the starter would brandish his red flag, the familiar bell would clang out from the judges' box above him, the yellow track streak out behind the sulky, the groaning stands and their Argus eyes flash past him; twice he would turn and twice launch out into the straight, back to the starting-place, the red flag, the bell, the stands again. . . . The grey would change into the roan, the roan into the black, the black into the grey again. Bourmin would give place to Nikita, Nikita to some new paymaster; but he, Loutoshkin, would still drive and drive, never relieved nor rested, like a traveller that has bought a ticket for life—weaned of comfort, banished from peace, broken on the wheel of change, pledged to the fleeting, feverish existence that had once beckoned so enticingly.

The stable where he was employed as manager had the best blood-stock in it. He schooled his horses well, and in more than one famous race he had driven them to the post victorious. What he had dreamed so fondly was now fact. Nine years ago such triumphs were fantastically remote. Now in three years he had won three cups. The Moscow racecourse ranked him as the best driver and trainer in the town. . . . But in these nine years a change had come. Loutoshkin had grown careless of success and failure; sometimes he felt keenly the futility of all his acts—futile and inept as a breakfast taken before execution.

Most poignantly he had felt this on the First of May, the festival of labour. He was trotting for high stakes with the best horse in his stable, the dark-bay stallion Upas-Tree, a self-willed dandy of a horse. His rivals were the six fastest trotters in the Republic. When he walked past before the race, thousands of eyes from the crowded grandstand were fixed on him. Loutoshkin did not look at the spectators; he did not single out one face, nor mark one pair of eyes. His whole being felt the immense, disquieting, and yet pleasing burden of that massed expectancy, and his nerves were shaken. High confidence gave place to doubt, officious memory jostled his brain with visions of untoward episodes, where a sudden chance had wrecked him. True, he was now more proof against such chances; his work under Bourmin had taught him much, tempered his will, and strengthened his endurance; in the heat of the fray he could consult his stop-watch, summing up the situation—the powers of his opponents, the speed of their horses, every idiosyncrasy of horse and man— and turn the most trifling slip to his advantage. But he had learned one thing more: besides skill, the winner needed "spunk," that "spunk" which he demanded of his horse, that "gameness" which distinguished a real "Trojan" from a spiritless hack, or a man like the dead champion Grisha from a perfunctory driver—which would prompt him at the crucial moment to some unpremeditated move, some quiver of the reins, some cry, some cluck of encouragement, some forward thrust of the body, seeming to transmute the driver's substance into a willed ecstasy—*that* was the force that hurled the trotter to the post and snatched the victory by half a head! . . .

None of this power did Loutoshkin feel on that glaring, sultry holiday. His nerves were shaken. As though his heart would not go with him to the fight. It was all one: victory or defeat. A chill ran through him. He would have liked to do as Philipp did when he gathered his hands into his coat-sleeves and sat huddled and shivering.

His cunning did not forsake him. He gauged the race to a nicety and won it.

But a hand's-breadth from the post the roar of a mighty engine smote his ear; a shadow loomed and overtook the trotter, whelming the bright track before him, and swung free as the plane climbed, and again the thunderous beat of that steel heart drowned the cries of the acclaiming multitude.

Loutoshkin staggered to the ground and gazed after the receding aeroplane; then he looked at the foaming, panting Upas-Tree and understood his own gloom, his emptiness of spirit. Horse and driver were entangled in the past. Present and future belonged to the engine, to the motor. His art could go a-begging now—no more acceptable to his fellows than bow and arrows to a rifleman.

A new life was in being.

Deaf to the clapping of the crowd, to the congratulations of the judges, who came down from their enclosure to the track, he drew his hand into his shirt-sleeves, shivering, like Philipp.

ON his way back from the Bashilovka to the Mytnaya, Nikita pondered the parting speech of the driver and sighed wistfully. He had brought the grey Grandson to Moscow in the firm conviction that as soon as he arrived, the colt would be started for the "cup"—and it had all turned out differently.

"What's he want to 'try him out' for?" reasoned Nikita. "If he weren't fast, why would I have come such a long road on such an errand? Just to be laughed at? But there's no call to try him; he ain't Mikishka's gelding; his name's registered as Taglioni's Grandson and his pedigree's drawn up. . . . I says to myself: 'You're a driver, ain't you? Well, clap him in the shafts, and God go with you!'—but it don't seem so simple."

Meanwhile in Koultyapy's yard Kortsoff, Grouzdyeff, and Sossounoff were examining the Grandson. Presently Kourotchkin joined them.

The colt was not at his best; ungroomed, unkempt, his mane and tail woefully matted. But at the first glance Grouzdyeff coughed importantly and knocked with his cherry-wood staff upon the ground.

His expert eye divined the breed of the animal under his rough soiled coat, observed the spare and sensitive head, the firm, faultless legs, the stoutly swelling ribs; and turning to Kortsoff, he piped in his squeaky tenor: "Fine piece of horseflesh!"

Sossounoff, trying to imbue his beardless actor's face with an air of competence and lifelong experience, hovered about the colt, paced the yard on one side of him, then on the other, squatted down to inspect his hoofs, cautiously felt his ribs and haunches, and shot back in alarm when the Grandson twitched under these probings.

"Hey, hey! None of your nonsense!" he shouted, whirling his arms in a frenzy of self-protection.

"So the fine gentleman's nervous!" commented Kourotchkin, as he sat on a big stone tapping his birch-wood snuff-box. "Every horse knows a nervous man—makes his hooks itch to be at him."

Nikita came into the yard just as Kortsoff, pinching the Grandson's nose with one hand, drew out his tongue with the other and was examining his teeth to verify his age.

233

Nikita rushed to the colt's head.

He snatched the halter from Koultyapy and pulled the Grandson free. His rolling eyes darted from face to face and fastened on the horse; his hands gripped the halter with such force that it would have been easier to cut them off than to wrest from them that strip of leather which bound them to the precious nursling they had fostered in the remote stillness of Shatnyevka.

"Why did you take out the horse?" said Nikita in a voice shaken with terror. "Who asked you to meddle? I'm his lawful master! What are you fiddling with his teeth for?"

Kortsoff wiped his hand on a wisp of straw, rubbed it on the tail of his coat, and, without looking at Nikita, remarked to Grouzdyeff: "All right, that colt—if it weren't for the ring-bone and . . ."

"That spoils him," cut in Sossounoff peremptorily. "Crumple up in his first race. Last spring there was a horse for sale just like him, a peach of a horse to look at . . ."

Nikita started. He stole a swift glance at the Grandson's feet.

"Where did you pick him up?" said Kortsoff truculently.

"I'm a Ryazan man," growled Nikita.

"Want to sell him?"

"The colt's not for sale," Nikita snapped.

Kortsoff laughed scornfully and turned his back on Nikita; before he could be observed, he whispered to Sossounoff:

"Play him up!"

"That mare looked splendid," said Sossounoff, loudly addressing Grouzdyeff, as if half-way through a conversation. "A feast for sore eyes, that mare was, and her pedigree right as rain. And what happened? She was just like that colt. The owner had bought her for the races. At first I thought she might just stay the course —but no! Did pretty well in the first half, but after that—fairly lay down and scratched herself. So the owner cut his losses—sold her for half-price to a cabman."

"Racing's out of the question, with the ring-bone," pronounced Grouzdyeff, stroking his beard sagaciously.

Kourotchkin squatted on his stone, aloof, his bleared eyes fixed in dismal meditation on Nikita. His hands were clasped, and the tip of his blue handkerchief dangled from them to the ground.

Sossounoff returned to the charge: "I say, Mikhal Mikhalitch, didn't you know Ivan Pavlovitch? Well, he was the man it happened to. . . ."

Kortsoff chimed in: "I can tell you of thousands of such cases! How many of them have I had in my stable!" He shook his head sadly at the colt. "Yes, I was green once. A mint of money that ring-bone cost me, till I learned my lesson. . . . Needs a practised

eye to spot it. Come for the races, eh?" he said, swinging round upon Nikita.

Nikita's face fell.

"The colt's racing for the cup," he answered.

"Racing? Well, maybe he is," said Kortsoff, smiling.
"But I doubt if he'll race far, with that ring-bone on
him! Won't see the cup through a telescope!"

"That colt's got ring-bone badly," said Sossounoff.
"*He's* not for the races, man! He'd break his legs in the
first quarter!"

"So they come to Moscow to catch fools nowadays;
none left in the country, I suppose!" Kortsoff flung
over his shoulder with feigned indignation. "Let's go
to the tea-house, Mikhal Mikhalitch. Won't you join
us? Come on!" he added to Koultyapy.

Kourotchkin remained seated on his stone. All this
while he had not breathed a word, but sniffed con-
tinuously, wiping his dimmed eyes. Nikita tethered
the colt and walked up to the old man. "What sort of
folks was they, gaffer?"

Kourotchkin picked up his blue handkerchief and
sat on, brooding. Bare-headed and forlorn he sat, a
hoary greybeard on a hoary stone fretted and stained
by wind and water.

All his long life Kourotchkin had spent with men
whose traffic was in horses. Thousands of mares and
stallions had been bought or sold under his eyes and
by his counsel. And with every sale or purchase he had

236

warped his conscience, "twisted his soul," as he now told himself. Time out of mind horse-dealing had meant fraud. Fraud was the stock-in-trade they worked on—petty jobbers, who seldom tasted a square meal, horse-dealers of moderate fortune, big dealers wallowing in wealth and respected by all Moscow. The fraud varied; with the small fry it was gross, as with the gypsies, not scrupling to smear tar on a cracked hoof, file an old horse's teeth to hide his age, drench him with stimulating drugs, and so forth; with the rich and respectable practitioners it was a more subtle and verbal trickery, like the chicane of a shrewd lawyer. The dealer himself kept in the background. A swarm of agents worked for him, buzzing about the victim, and when they had sucked his blood, it appeared as plain as daylight that he was no victim, as he fondly thought, but the recipient of a signal favour at the hands of some discreet philanthropist—such as Mikhal Mikhalitch Grouzdyeff. . . . Kourotchkin was deep-versed in all this knavery—the gypsy jockeyship and the financier's finesse—and often profited thereby; but never till now had it struck him that such dealings were unfair or sinful. . . . He had pondered his ways of late, since first he began to dream of stallions. A box under his pillow, and the pillow itself, were stuffed with imperial gold pieces, the savings of industrious years. He had been minded to bestow this hoard on the Don Monastery. But now his pious resolution wavered. The new Government had confiscated the treasures of the Church. The Orthodox Church herself, once whole and undivided, was now rent with schisms; everything was at sixes and sevens; his soul, which had dreamed of this last refuge, with the righteous fathers praying for his sins, lay suddenly stripped and houseless, tossed to the mercy of cold fate—and his sins hung like shackles on Semyon Andreyitch.

This is the reason why, for the first time in his life—as he sat on the bleak, time-worn stone in the stable-yard of the rogue Sashka Koultyapy—he had held aloof from the conversation of these men whom he had helped to drive a thousand bargains.

Looking down, earthward, at his dingy galoshes, which he wore next to his rheumatic feet, Kourotchkin answered with a sigh: "They're folks like other folks. we're all men, my son."

The old man brooded.

At last Nikita spoke again: "By their talk they should be in the horse trade."

"The man with the pointed beard was the greatest horse-dealer in Moscow," began Kourotchkin, looking up, "Grouzdyeff, Mikhal Mikhalitch—and the most respected too; he sold the Governor-General a pair of dapple-grey carriage-horses; and the tall man with Mikhal Mikhalitch was Kortsoff, Grigory, another horse-dealer. But the third, Vaska Sossounoff—well, he's just a—nincompoop; but for his check breeches

238

and his stylish hat, you'd never notice him!"

"But what did they come for, gaffer? I was scared to death. I thought—they'd take the colt away."

"They came on their own business, my son. And their business is buying here and selling there and bartering somewhere else. . . . That's what they came for, and they'll come again; your colt's tickled their fancy! That's what they came after—for the pleasure of seeing your colt, he's a splendid animal, sound as a bell, and worth good money. . . . That's what brought 'em."

Kourotchkin groaned, wriggled on his stone seat, sniffed into his birch-wood snuff-box, and was silent.

"And you, gaffer? What trade do you follow?" asked Nikita.

"Me? My business is with horses too, my son. We're all birds of a feather."

"Do you *deal* in horses?"

"Ah, dealing's done with now. . . . The times are changed. . . . I used to doctor stallions, fifty years I doctored 'em, my son."

"You'd be a farrier, I'm thinking."

Kourotchkin fell silent again; he shifted his snuff-box from one hand to the other and sighed deeply. "But now my day's done. . . . And my death's near! I've begun to dream of stallions!"

He told Nikita of his gruesome dreams. Nikita listened intently and gave judgment: "Your gelding's

239

quieter and more easy-tempered, sure enough, but he's got a grievance, and I'll not deny it! Only I tell you, gaffer, the master's the main thing. There's many a stallion would change places with a gelding."

Nikita pondered, smiled, and rolling his eyes, resumed: "If they were to use a man like that, they'd put a terrible great shame on him! Round Tamboff, in 1920, there was a gang of brigands—proper young limbs of Satan! Once they caught five police agents, and gave them the same medicine as you give the stallions. . . . Well, of course, that was their loss and no man's profit, but what you did was all to the good. Besides, horses and men are different."

"And yet I dream," said Kourotchkin, still uncomforted. . . . "For man's good, yes; but not for theirs. That's true, my son!"

He raised his rheumy, whey-coloured eyes to Nikita's face and, subduing the guile of half a century, talked freely of Kortsoff, Grouzdycff, and Koultyapy. . . .

"Never you mind their chatter. Your colt's as free of the ring-bone as I am. They're just trying to hoodwink you. . . . A man that's not in the know might be deceived, but don't you heed them. A simple man is lost if he once listens to such fellows. Here's my advice, and keep it to yourself; you take the colt away, he's a sore temptation—he might go lame in this place."

Kourotchkin spoke the last words in a whisper. He

clasped his handkerchief in his palm and stood up wearily. "Good-bye, my son. . . . Do as I say, and—mum's the word!"

Bowed to the waist and hobbling with red-stockinged feet in cumbrous, loose galoshes, the old farrier lurched out at the gate.

LOUTOSHKIN arrived at the Mytnaya after dinner as he had promised. Briefly and silently he overhauled the Grandson, not noticing Nikita, who watched his movements and expression with agonized suspense. After his examination he said dryly:

"Not a bad colt."

And again Nikita was disheartened. Loutoshkin spoke of *his* colt, the Grandson, as if he was an ordinary horse. He longed to tell Loutoshkin all he knew about the colt, his terrible speed, which made a man afraid to sit behind him, his uncommon staying power, and much else. . . .

"I must see him in the shafts," said Loutoshkin. "I'll send my groom for him today; you can both take the colt to my place in the Bashilovka. Tomorrow I'll try him out; then we can talk."

Loutoshkin looked at his wrist-watch and walked to the gate at a smart driver's pace. Nikita looked at his back resentfully.

At the gate Nikita crashed into the panting Koultyapy. With his eyes on Nikita, who stood in the middle of the yard, Koultyapy whispered to Loutoshkin:

"Kortsoff would like to see you in the tea-house."

"Who's with him?" asked Loutoshkin.

"Mikhal Mikhalitch is there, and Vaska Sossounoff."

As soon as the slightly stooping figure of Loutoshkin appeared at the tea-house door, Kortsoff rapped on his saucer with his spoon to call the waiter.

"Drop of the best?" he said, in lieu of greeting.

"All right."

"Milk the dun cow," he said, winking, to the waiter. "And bring sausages and omelets, make it snappy!"

Sossounoff screwed up his eyes and rubbed his hands together.

"Eykh, that's the stuff! . . . Not too well done, those sausages!" he shouted after the waiter. In his impatience he rushed out. "I'll be back in a minute."

And he disappeared into the kitchen.

"Well, have you seen him?" Kortsoff asked. "The nag's A1!"

"A good colt," said Loutoshkin soberly.

"We looked him over this morning. . . . We can find a buyer for him in two shakes—cash down. What do you think?"

"What are you hinting at?" Loutoshkin looked into Kortsoff's eyes.

Kortsoff laughed, a mirthless, rusty laugh.

"You don't know what? Drop it, Alim! You know

242

you can wind that man round your little finger! Your job's easy; just set the ball rolling, and we'll do the rest. You'll get your share of the boodle, right enough." Kortsoff lowered his voice. "We must teach these chawbacons a lesson or they'll rule the roost in Moscow! . . . Want to win the cup, do they? Just you tell him his colt's a non-starter, he's just wasting his time with him. We'll see that he don't start, eh?"

Koultyapy, who had been sitting at the next table, joined them. He smiled slimily. "In my opinion," said he, "we must lame him first; a turn or two with a whipcord under his fetlock, and the job's done! What can he do with a lame colt? . . . There was a man last year brought an Ardenne stallion from down Pyenza way. Fine bit of horseflesh, take my word for it! So we up and sent for Pashka Shishkoff. You know his turn-out—portfolio, zouave breeches, and revolver at his belt—like a big nob from the Cheka! I had the stallion in my stable. 'Yes, yes,' he said, 'he'll just do for the artillery—pay you the Government price for him.' . . . Takes down his particulars: owner, origin, and all the rest of it. The owner raced round the town, buttonholed the dealers, scoured the tea-houses —but of course wherever he went, he heard the same story. He got rid of the colt for half its value and made tracks."

The waiter came with a hissing frying-pan, and at his heels Sossounoff, smiling, winking, licking his chops. With a sensuous cluck he set down a dark bottle of home-brewed raisin brandy and thrust his feet under the table.

"We can talk afterwards. Better swig off that bottle, or some flatfoot'll catch us napping; don't want to get the landlord into trouble. . . . Eykh! That's the medicine!" He screwed up his eyes as he held his glass against the light. "Nothing to touch it! Beats your White Seal hollow!"

Loutoshkin had known these men for years. Formerly he had dealt often with them—bought from them, sold to them. . . . Once each of them had been full of business, working twenty hours a day, scouring the length and breadth of Russia for his merchandise. . . . How did they live now? Not one of them had learned a trade, or desired to learn anything useful. What had they to hope for?

"What say you, Alim? . . . We'll find a buyer for that colt as easy as spitting!" said Kortsoff.

"There's no business to be done, Grigory Nikolaievitch," declared Loutoshkin.

Kortsoff's bristly moustache twitched. "Why not?" he asked scornfully.

"It's no good, Grisha."

"Have you turned honest all of a sudden?" asked Kortsoff; his eyes sparkled with malice.

"I'm going to train the colt."

"For the cup, eh?" sneered Kortsoff.

"But what good will that do you, Alim Ivanitch?" Koultyapy pleaded in a slavering whine. "We're offering you a deal—money for jam."

Loutoshkin rose to his feet.

"Have you nothing more to say?" asked Kortsoff, his eyes flashing.

"Good-bye!" Loutoshkin held out his hand and, heedless of the protests of Sossounoff, who was finishing his omelet, walked, stooping, to the door.

CHAPTER · III

ALL HIS LIFE PHILIPP HAD BEEN A DRINKER; the smell of liquor drew him like a magnet. The shocks of the Revolution, bringing cataclysmic changes in the life about him, passed over his dull consciousness like clouds, leaving no trace. If the conversation turned on the early days of the Revolution or any event in the two years that followed, Philipp referred to this time as "when they drank lacquer and floor-polish." This was all that his memory could retain of it.

When he received from the management of the hippodrome expensive gifts after some victory of Loutoshkin's, whose horses he still groomed, Philipp would take his present on the same day to Mitritch. He never haggled over the price, but sat down promptly and drank for a whole day, or two, or three—till Mitritch, having computed the sum drunk, roused him abruptly: "Philipp!"

"Bit previous, ain't you?" Philipp would feebly demur, but Mitritch was inexorable.

"Well, that's the limit!" Philipp would sigh, and slouching off to another table, he "slowed into a trot" —that is, fell back on tea-drinking. . . .

When he was dispatched by Loutoshkin to the Mytnaya to fetch the colt, Philipp's first thought was of Rakitin's tea-house, where he had not set foot for years and where the landlord made a magnificent brew of raisin brandy. Kortsoff and Koultyapy greeted him with veiled hostility, guessing his errand to the Mytnaya.

"I suppose you and your master live like fighting-cocks under the Soviet," said Kortsoff, grinning at the groom's unshaven face. "Look how his mug's filled out! Do they feed you on pies and pastry?"

"The Soviet don't concern us," answered Philipp, in the most complete good faith.

His own life had changed little since the Revolution. Drivers remained, horses still ran, the "tote" was working—only the stakes were lower; formerly a ticket cost ten rubles; now you could chance your luck with three. Grooms remained grooms. Owners, to be sure, were ruined—melted like snow, as you might say. . . .

"We ain't owners. What's power to the likes of us!" Philipp added.

"Now you're in power yourselves, Red-public," snarled Kortsoff. " 'Proletarians of all nations, unite! ' Eykh," he sighed with implacable hatred, "there's a revolution in pickle for you scoundrels—then the sparks'll fly, I tell you. . . . Sure as my name's Kortsoff, I'll throttle a dozen of you with these hands!"

Philipp looked coolly at Kortsoff's fingers, furiously clenched upon his palms, and said: "I've come over for the colt. Won't you treat me to a drop of brandy, Grigory Nikolaievitch?"

"What are we celebrating, then? A deal? You've come for the colt, and I'm to treat you? Is the colt mine?" snapped Kortsoff.

Philipp's eyes wandered over the empty chairs. He sighed.

"Once they was all full," said he, addressing space; he cowered, as if from cold, drawing his hands deep into the frayed sleeves of his soiled buff jacket. His flabby, inflamed face was covered with brown bristles; from under his cap strayed hanks of hair, greasy and long unwashed; and his dull eyes, glazed and indifferent, seemed suddenly instinct with hate.

Koultyapy leaned forward against the table and touched him on the sleeve. "Like to fix up a deal? You'll get your drink, and a fistful of rubles with it."

Philipp eyed him stolidly and said nothing. His sloping womanish shoulders stirred irresolutely.

Koultyapy smiled his moist smile under his fair, stringy moustache. Shooting a glance at Kortsoff, he resumed: "Your part's easy—one, two, and it's all over! . . . Have you seen the colt?"

"Drop it, Nikolai!" broke in Kortsoff. "Don't you

see, he and his precious master have turned honest? Want to win the cup! . . ."

Philipp's lustreless eyes shifted from Koultyapy's face to Kortsoff's weather-stained countenance. And as if he had just heard Kortsoff's words, spoken at the outset of the conversation, he protested: "Why do you want to throttle me, Grigory Nikolaievitch? I never done you no harm. . . . You can't please nobody these days. . . . I came here on the street-car—regular rattletraps them cars are. I never let no man step on my toes, and I step on nobody's, not on purpose. Well, off starts the car, and down comes my foot on a gentleman's toe. He called me some pretty names, I tell you! 'Sorry!' says I, 'this car jolts.' But he wouldn't hear no reason, and he got me so upset that— plump, I trod on another man's toe. Then *he* started on me! So I jumped off before the stop. . . . Life's turned sour, Grigory Nikolaievitch."

"Did Alim tell you anything about the colt?" Kortsoff interrupted.

"Told me to take him to the Bashilovka, that's all."

"Will you be at Mitritch's tomorrow? Early in the evening Shishkin's coming. Then we'll have a gargle!"

Philipp looked glum.

"Even the drink don't comfort me now," he said moodily. "Alim Ivanitch keeps on dinging at me: 'Drop it, Philipp,' says he, 'or you'll get the sack one

249

of these days!' He won't believe that the drink means nothing to me. . . . Sometimes you'll buy a bottle, and a bite of food with it, and you take it home, and set it all out as neat as you please, and your sister brings you a nice mess of red cabbage. . . . And you just sit and stare at it. You sit and stare! Your throat's dry, and there's no taste in your mouth. Often as not you don't touch it, or you tip it into the jug and leave your food. Down goes the liquor—clop!—and you're none the better. . . . And you don't want to go nowhere, you're sick of everything, even horses! . . . Good-bye, Grigory Nikolaievitch, I'm off. You're mighty lonesome here," he said as he stood up. "There's more company at Mitritch's, though that's half empty. . . . Good-bye, Grigory Nikolaievitch."

Koultyapy followed Philipp out.

"Look here, Philipp," he said hurriedly, as soon as they were in the street, "Mikhal Mikhalitch has just offered two thousand for that colt; you'll get a good rake-off, and nobody'll be a pin the wiser. . . . Squirt in the juice, and the job's done. . . . What can the man do with a lame horse? He'll *have* to sell him! The colt's a winner, though; Mikhal Mikhalitch never wastes his breath. . . ."

Philipp listened mutely. Crouching and gathering his hands into his sleeves, he slunk along beside Koultyapy, looking down at his own feet.

Nikita, when he saw him, said to himself: "That man has lost his soul!"

And the sight of Philipp, arriving in Koultyapy's company, bred in him dark misgivings for the fate of the grey Grandson.

CHAPTER · IV

NIKITA LOOKED WITH IMMENSE AMAZE-
ment at the life of the trotting stable, which had opened
its gates to him. The long, bright passage, with doors
made of iron bars on either side of it, the large, clean
loose-boxes, and all the outlandish gear: toe-weights
and rubber boots for the horses' hoofs, cruppers as
soft as down, flannel and linen bandages, checks and
martingales. And the flimsy two-wheeled sulkies
seemed like toys, after the stout wagons of the country.

Nikita knew that yonder in Shatnyevka he took such
care of the colt as none of his neighbours gave his
horse; twice every week Nikita would clean out his
stall; and if another man cleaned his once a month perhaps, that was not for the horse's sake, but to shovel
up the rich manure and cart it to his field. In Shatnyevka the Grandson was a member of the family,
working as they all worked and enjoying equal rights
with all. Here every horse lived like a gentleman; ate,

drank, took the air in his toy carriage, and came home to rest.

"See what we've come to, you and I!" he said mentally to the Grandson. "How can I yoke you to the plough after these high doings? What'll become of us, I wonder."

"About once a year you groomed him, I suppose," Philipp snapped at Nikita as he plied his brush and currycomb. "Look at the scurf on him; might as well currycomb a flour-sack!"

"Please don't be angry," said Nikita guiltily. "I'll be glad to lend a hand any time you want me."

The Grandson had Flattery's trick of snatching playfully with her lips at her attendants, by the shoulder or sleeve or headgear—which after a gentle tug she would let go. When Philipp's head came within reach, the Grandson seized his cap and whisked it off.

"None of your tricks!" scolded Philipp, slightly alarmed and brandishing his currycomb.

"Never fear, never fear!" Nikita reassured him. "That's just his game, he's only a colt; he's as quiet as a lamb, though! The mare was just the same."

"Don't know nothing about his games," grunted Philipp. "I've had a few of 'em through my hands, real man-eaters; they'd have had the head off my shoulders if I hadn't watched it."

Nikita knew that Loutoshkin had given the Grandson a trial, but he had not seen the trainer since, and he was all agog to know what he thought of the colt's prospects. Timidly he broached the subject to Philipp: "This is what I had in mind to ask you, brother. . . . About the cup, like. . . ." He scratched his forehead. "That cup now, in a manner of speaking—I suppose any horse can win it. . . . It all goes by place, don't it—if one horse can outrun the rest? Suppose my colt, say. . ."

Philipp smiled scornfully and redoubled his efforts with the currycomb.

Nikita paused a moment and went on coaxingly: "We countryfolk live in the dark, you know—benighted, like. . . . What horses do we see in Shatnyevka? . . . But you know everything, all about the horses' places. . . . Just suppose my colt . . . Of course, he's a country colt and don't know these Moscow rules. But if they let him race and he beats them Moscow horses fair and above-board by all them rules, are they bound to give him the cup?"

"Cup!" Philipp mocked his country accent and added tauntingly: "There's many of you come to town for cups, but there's few that travel back with 'em."

Nikita sighed and stood pensive.

Loutoshkin entered the stable. His face beamed.

Nikita had never seen him in this mood. His spirits rose.

"Do you know that colt?" Loutoshkin asked Philipp, as he entered the loose-box.

Philipp knocked out the currycomb against the bars and raised his listless eyes. "What colt?"

"Remember Flattery?"

For some time Philipp looked at Loutoshkin with the same cold, stale expression; then he shifted his glance to Nikita. His bloated, stubbly face revealed perplexity. Muttering something unintelligible, he peered at the Grandson.

"Why, that's her foal!" exclaimed Loutoshkin. "Wipe the cobwebs out of your eyes and have a look!"

"Want to gammon me, eh?" Philipp growled, but his eyes, as he gazed at the grey colt, slowly lit up, and wrinkles seared his forehead, as with the memory of long-forgotten pain.

He turned and looked again at Loutoshkin. Loutoshkin smiled, an honest, open smile.

"Never doubt it," Nikita burst in. "He's her very own. It's truth I'm telling! And he's got a mark on his forehead, just the same as what the mare had."

Under the Grandson's forelock there was a little white half-moon.

Philipp moved his hand as if he were indeed brushing a cobweb from his eyes, and, still incredulous, he asked:

"Is he really her son, Alim Ivanitch—Flattery's?"

"Never doubt it, I tell you!" Nikita urged again. "His grandfather's name's Tallyoney, a famous stallion —won a lot of cups. . . ."

"He knows who Taglioni was!" Loutoshkin cut him short good-humouredly. "Come on, Nikita Loukitch, you and I must have a chat. I've been working your colt today."

In the yard Loutoshkin squatted down on some boards which had fallen from his fence, and remained long silent. Nikita gazed steadfastly at him, waiting eagerly. Loutoshkin was the all-powerful man on whom the Grandson's fate depended, and when he raised his head at last and said: "I'll win the cup with that colt!" the flood-gates of Nikita's joy burst, loosing a spate of incoherent praises of his wonderful grey nursling. . . . He squatted on the ground facing Loutoshkin, heels to haunches, peasant-fashion, and the trainer, hitherto strange and aloof, seemed suddenly near akin, companionable and friendly.

"But what will you do with him after the races?" asked Loutoshkin.

"Meaning what?" said Nikita.

"I want to know where you'll take him afterwards. Home to the country?"

"Where else should I take him?" said Nikita in amazement. "To Shatnyevka, sure enough! That's natural!"

Loutoshkin sighed. After a pause he said:

"But haven't you thought of selling him?"

"He ain't for sale, Alim Ivanitch!" answered Nikita grimly.

"Why not? You can get good money for him—two thousand five hundred any day."

A huge sum this—as huge as Moscow seemed beside Shatnyevka. A troop of household items filed into Nikita's brain: a new plough, tiles for the roof, a warm quilted jacket and stout breeches for Syomka, a horse-collar from the saddler Arsenty. . . . And he must certainly roof the barn with clay. . . ."

"That's a pile of money!" he said slowly.

"Judge for yourself," went on Loutoshkin; "if you take him back to that farm of yours, use him to plough and cart for you, he won't get the care he needs, nor the food either—you'll stuff him with chopped hay and bran. . . . He'll be spoiled for racing, though now he's a likely colt; we can make a trotter of him. You can't keep him in Moscow, just for the races. That needs money, which you peasants haven't got."

"Where should the likes of us find money!"

"There you are, then! . . . You could do with a good hardy brood mare on your farm, a half-blood, say, but a trotter's no use to you."

"Meat and drink to us peasants, a mare is," agreed Nikita.

"And what a mare you could get hold of for that money! You could just pick your fancy."

Nikita scratched the nape of his neck.

"Eykh, in the Settlement up our way there's a three-year-old, eight hundred they're asking for her.

. . . She ain't a mare, she's a steam-engine! You should see the back on her, and her chest!" he said with envious rapture.

"They'll pay two thousand five hundred like a shot, but we might get three thousand out of them," Loutoshkin urged.

Nikita sighed and ruminated.

Loutoshkin looked intently at him, bit through a straw with a snap, and raised himself. His lips parted in a smile: "Think it over, Nikita Loukitch.

"You're the owner," he resumed, in a tired, indifferent voice. "Think it over and decide. I'll find a buyer; he's a useful colt for racing purposes, but he's no use to you! . . ."

Nikita also rose. He pulled his greasy cap over his eyes, coachman-fashion, and as if turning over a heavy spadeful of earth, pronounced: "He ain't for sale!"

Loutoshkin winced. He shot a piercing glance at the face under the greasy cap and held his fire. Nikita sat down on a board. Like Loutoshkin at the outset of their interview, he stared at the ground and was long silent, while Loutoshkin faced him, in suspense.

" 'Tweren't for no sale that I gave him all that care, Alim Ivanitch. . . . Don't talk to me of selling him, for the love of Christ! I'll never do it!"

Solemnly, phrase by phrase, Nitika set forth all his days and doings, from that memorable moment when the bruised and weeping Syomka brought home the mangy nag, blind in one eye, pestered with galls and itches, and scarce able to stand up. . . . He told of the savage Penkoff and all his robberies, of the famine year, of Syomka's swollen legs, of the bran and rye sweepings which he had hidden over the ceiling of the stall. . . . His story ended, he sat brooding over that fearsome night, when he had been driven to seek food for Flattery and the colt by stealing. . . .

"That night I almost lost my manhood," he concluded grimly.

Loutoshkin drank in every word. His broad back bent in a driver's stoop, he paced along the boards, halting where Nikita sat, eying his half-moulted cap and his stained jacket of army shoddy, and beneath the words he sensed the speaker's life, so different from that of his forerunner, Flattery's late owner, Aristarkh Bourmin. . . . Bourmin was gone, with all his kind. His star had set, but a new light was kindling. With Nikita's words the quivering thread that bound Loutoshkin to the horse grew strong and taut again; from all the horses in his stable the grey Grandson sprang to mind, knocked at his heart like a human suppliant, claimed kinship with Nikita's life, and henceforth with the life of him, Loutoshkin. Suddenly he felt glad that Nikita had refused to sell the colt; his heart warmed to the man, he felt as if he had recovered something lost. . . .

Philipp came up to them, sat on a board beside

Nikita, and began talking of the colt. Loutoshkin was not surprised when the groom's voice betrayed excitement. He, too, was excited—keenly and wholesomely. . . .

"All roads lead home at last!" Philipp was saying. "Life's wiser than us all. . . . Nine years have passed, and everything's the same! I've looked him over well, he's the spit and image of his dam. . . . Eykh, the trouble I've had over her!—couldn't sleep o' nights and nearly fought the boys for her. You're always pitching into me, Alim Ivanovitch, but to my thinking, if a man ain't got no trouble—well, he's bound to drink, and once he starts . . .

"So the mare came into your hands?" he said to Nikita after a pause. "Life's strange. . . . Her old owner's here in Moscow. . . . And he's always writing. You go into the tea-house—there he is—he sits and sits, and writes and writes, as if Old Nick was at his elbow—looks up and glares at you sometimes, and you want to cross yourself. . . . With his black beard and his eyes like red-hot coals, he sits there writing; but what he writes and who he writes to—that's a mystery! . . ."

Philipp sat cramped and cowering, his hands drawn deep into his sleeves.

Loutoshkin seated himself beside Nikita and touched him by the arm.

"Look here, Nikita Loukitch," he said gently. "I

260

can win one race with that colt of yours. . . . But here's the point: if you don't want him to crack up after his first performance, you must leave him here for me to train. In three weeks I'll have him well tuned up; he's not in condition now, he's green. . . . You go home to Shatnyevka and wait till you hear from me. I won't enter him for the cup without your leave. But if you can't agree to that, take him away at once, to another trainer. Another man can drive him as well as I can; I won't drive him as you see him now. . . . That colt's worth something."

Nikita pondered.

NEXT evening, before leaving for the station, Nikita visited the Grandson in his box.

The Grandson snuffled with delight and stretched out his neck to his master's hand, which was feeling in his pocket. Closing his lips on the lump of sugar which Nikita had kept back from his tea, the Grandson munched it with voluptuous relish and pressed his shoulder against Nikita.

"Well, Grandson," sighed Nikita, "you must stay here. . . . I'm going. . . . But wait, wait! I'll come back to you in three weeks. I'm going to Shatnyevka, to our home. . . . He ain't a bad man, understand; he's a straight man, you can trust him. There's all sorts to be found in Moscow; there's good men, and there's bad men, that'll do you a mischief if they can. . . . But you stay here, boy, you'll be safe. . . . Good-bye, Grandson! . . ."

Nikita made the sign of the cross over the colt and hurried out, wiping his eyes.

CHAPTER · V

IN THE TEA-HOUSE WITH THE LEGEND "Free Labour" displayed over its blue sign, not far from the Tver Gate, Aristarkh Bourmin was filling pages of a tattered note-book with meticulous hand-writing. He wore an antiquated coat, once blue, now colourless and napless, bald, as it were, from age. Erect and angular as heretofore, through all the shocks of the Revolution he had preserved inviolate his sump-tuous, foursquare black beard. His trunk inclined like a leaning tower; he wrote, scratched out, and under-scored, his arrowy moustaches twitching. At the next table a party of horse-dealers pulled at flasks of vodka, hidden in their coat-tails. The smothered, husky voice of one was labouring to convince the others of the advantage of some deal; it called on God and all the saints, and the deceased Ivan Kousmitch, to witness, and after a pause for breath, resumed:

"Understand me, I wouldn't have let it slip—wouldn't have missed it for the world, I'd have clinched

263

the deal *myself*, see? It's money for jam, I tell you!
Well, I couldn't find the money. So I lost the deal—
for want of a few thousands! . . . Ah! Once there
was a man called Khokhryakoff. I was that man! . . .
Just look at this!"

The speaker drew from the inside pocket of his
threadbare velvet smoking-jacket a carefully-folded
program of a pre-Revolution race-meeting, spread it
out on the table, and pointed to one of the events:

"You see? Read it!" He snatched it up again.

" 'Chatterbox,' he read aloud, 'chestnut mare owned
by Stepan Fyodorovitch Khokhryakoff. . . .' You see
what an old stager I am! But look what a field she had
with her! Two Telyegin mares, Vyazemsky, Count
Lichtenberg's stallion, and—read it, man! . . .
Mitritch, come here!" he turned towards the counter.
"Remember my chestnut mare, by Nightingale out of
Gossip?"

The former landlord of the eating-house in the
Bashilovka, moon-faced and genial as of old, called out
from behind the counter:

"Did a mile in two thirty—early spring it was."

Aristarkh Bourmin looked at the owner of the chestnut mare and smiled disdainfully. On his own stud-
farm he had kept two hundred and fourteen horses.

He cleared his throat and went on writing:

". . . Diligent observation and study of the equine
material contending for the mastery in the contem-

264

porary arena entitles us to state with perfect confidence that the speed so vaunted by our ignorant rulers as the result of their own foresight represents the fruit of a rich garden, tended by our hands—a fruit now plucked by insolent marauders. The following table, which we commend to the notice of all those who have not yet lost all sense of rectitude and honour, attests the truth of our conclusion by incontrovertible statistics. . . ."

"Still writing, Aristarkh Sergyeevitch?" Loutoshkin hailed him somewhat quizzically as he entered. "There's more sense in a cup of tea! Mitritch, bring tea, and something solid with it!"

Some years ago, in this same tea-house, Loutoshkin had chanced to be present at a scene which stirred in him a contemptuous pity for his old employer. It was one Saturday night, on the eve of the races, when the poky little place was chock-full of dealers, drivers, touts, and turfmen. One of the guests, well primed with vodka, became noisy and backed his words with blows. Half the customers joined in the fray. Tables crashed, crockery smashed, omelets and pickled cabbage flattened themselves in greasy patches on the floor, round sausages bowled like hoops into the corners—and suddenly in the mêlée of arms and legs, close by his own table, Loutoshkin caught a glimpse of two precipitate hands scouring the filthy floor for sausages and scraps of bread. On the forefinger of one hand was the fa-

265

miliar broad signet-ring of Aristarkh Bourmin.

From that time forth Loutoshkin would often join him at his table and, without asking Bourmin's leave, order him a plate of cabbage, an omelet, or some more substantial dish. Once he offered him money. Bourmin thanked him, and refused, saying:

"In an era of legalized robbery and official prodigality the self-respecting citizen is distinguished by the incorruptibility and poverty of Diogenes."

But the omelets and the plates of cabbage Bourmin devoured with relish, and always availed himself of the free passes to the hippodrome which Loutoshkin gave him every race-day.

"They've brought me an interesting colt, Aristarkh Sergyeevitch!" began Loutoshkin, when Bourmin had finished eating. "He's a devilish smart youngster. . . ."

Bourmin made a two-pronged fork of his thumb and forefinger and raked his beard from throat to chin, smoothed it out from the top downward, looked sidelong at his right moustache, then at his left, tugging at them, and observed:

"Smart youngsters will get scarcer every year."

Loutoshkin smiled.

"You think so, Aristarkh Sergyeevitch? But look at our colts' performances! In the old days such speed was never dreamed of!"

"The breed of trotters is fast dying out, like the best

266

breed of men," Bourmin persisted; he scowled at the horse-breeding journal which Loutoshkin was extracting from his pocket.

"Look at this." Loutoshkin showed him a row of figures. "Were there so many colts in the old days that could step it in two twelve? But now they're as common as blackberries!"

"Humbug!" snorted Bourmin, pushing the paper from him.

"No, Aristarkh Sergyeevitch, it's not humbug," said Loutoshkin gravely. "The nationalization of our stud-farms has borne fruit. I'm quite convinced that we shall presently see trotters with such records as you private owners never dared to hope for!"

"The breed of trotters is dying out, as the nobility is dying out," said Bourmin doggedly. "Before 1917 the blood of the Orloff trotter was criminally polluted, and now they would mongrelize all Russia. Russia is doomed. Your colt is an offshoot from the parent tree, fostered by the nobility, fed from the roots of the Russia that has perished."

"You've guessed!" said Loutoshkin laughing.

Bourmin reflected moodily.

"Guessing is for quacks and fortune-tellers," he snapped.

"Haven't you guessed—really, Aristarkh Sergyeevitch? Why, it's your mare's colt. Remember Flattery?"

Bourmin shuddered.

"He's the very devil of a smart colt!" resumed Loutoshkin, smiling. "Showed a mile in two fifty at his first trial. Just like his dam. Sturdy, clever, and full of spirit. . . . Reared and broken in by a poor peasant from Ryazan!"

"I made that colt! I'm his rightful owner!" Bourmin shouted in Loutoshkin's teeth, as he stood up tall and menacing. With flaming eyes he glared at Loutoshkin. Then he stamped his foot and, tossing up his chin, strode out of the tea-house.

BESIDE the Leningrad Road Bourmin sat on a bench opposite the avenue leading to the hippodrome. He loved to gaze at the prancing steeds which flanked the entrance to the avenue. Indomitable, they champed and strained against the sinewy arms of the bronze charioteer. They had outbraved the Revolution. After eight years they were the same. Horses like these had ramped over the gate of the stable where Aristarkh Bourmin had once been master.

CHAPTER · VI

By one o'clock the long avenue lead-
ing from the Leningrad Road to the race-track looked
like some busy central street, but without shops or
houses. . . . On the left ran a grey wooden fence, an
asphalt path bordered by trees, and a road faced with a
thick layer of sand instead of paving. It stretched to the
grandstand, whose sculptured roof loomed in the distance. Awheel or afoot, the crowd streamed forward
in a ceaseless flood, as though a reservoir on the Leningrad Road were unsluiced and emptying to the dregs.
Some walked in haste, conning their race-cards; others
with the steady trudge of the seasoned race-goer; others
again with the sauntering gait of holiday-makers, who
cared little where they went. The foot of the avenue
was abuzz with program-sellers and cabmen, touting
for fares at a quarter of a ruble; street-cars were perpetu-
ally disgorging men and women, boys and greybeards,
rich and poor—and from the Bashilovka, which crossed
the road and car-lines, grooms led the trotters, draped

269

in flowered horse-cloths, to the stables of the hippodrome. And this pageant of proud horses, grey and
bay, sorrel and black, in hoods and blinkers, knee-boots
and white bandages, with blazing eyes and glistening
flanks, the muscles rippling on sleek arms and withers,
recalled a procession of gladiators marching to some
circus, hidden from view, but near at hand. . . .

When Nikita, on his return to Moscow, went to the
Bashilovka, Loutoshkin gave him such a welcome as
no man had ever yet bestowed on him; he asked him
to his house, into his dining-room, sat him down, with
Syomka, at his table, and began plying him with wine
and meat pies and all manner of toothsome things on
separate plates, with silver forks and knives. Then he
called to the other room, and out came a young woman.

"There, Saphir," he said jauntily, nodding at Nikita,
"that's the Grandson's owner, Nikita Loukitch."

Womanlike, smiling, she waited on him and Syomka and presently began talking of the Grandson. She
might have been born on the race-track. Her talk reminded Nikita of the old veterinary's—spiced with
the same queer lingo and outlandish tongue-twisters—
not at all like woman's prattle, when she touched on
the colt's points and manners.

"Your wife's just like our veterinary, Alexandr Egoritch," he exclaimed to Loutoshkin when they were
alone.

Loutoshkin answered with a laugh.

As soon as Nikita entered the stable, he dashed into the loose-box where he had left his precious charge three weeks before. Instead of the grey Grandson he found an ugly-tempered sorrel stallion. He turned to Loutoshkin in dismay.

"Why, don't you see?" said Loutoshkin laughing. "Come along, I've shifted him. This way, second box on the left!"

Nikita burst into the box, and halted spellbound on the threshold. He doffed his cap and stood scratching his head. It was not the rangy, tousle-coated Grandson that he saw, but a sleek, dapple-grey beauty, with a soft, bushy tail, a saucily clipped forelock, and a mane like silk.

Syomka whispered hurriedly: "It's not our colt, I'll take my oath, Papanka! It's not ours, they've changed him!"

"Grandson, is it you?" stammered Nikita, taking a pace forward.

The Grandson turned his head. The keen, glittering, blue-streaked eyes rested on him, the nostrils quivered, and the grey beauty, recognizing his master, snuffled, and nosed for Nikita's pocket. Hastily Nikita drew out a lump of sugar and in a quavering voice began to speak, at once addressing the horse and Syomka and Loutoshkin: "He knows me! . . . You see, he's trying to tell me. That's him, our Grandson! It's me, Grandson, me —Nikita! . . . I've come from Shatnyevka by the railway, in the express! . . . Syomka's here too—look at him, look! We've left Nastasya all alone. . . ."

The Grandson looked at Syomka, at Nikita, at Loutoshkin, glancing from time to time over their heads through the open door into the passage, and kept plying his ears, as if he followed the conversation of his visitors. Then he thrust out his lips to Syomka and finally dispelled his doubts; he pulled off his cap and tossed it to the ground. Syomka looked up at his father, beaming with delight.

"Well, whose colt is he now?" asked Loutoshkin from behind.

Nikita wagged his head smiling, in lieu of answer.

"We're trotting today, Nikita Loukitch," said Loutoshkin, drawing a race-card from his pocket—"in the fifth race. . . . Can you read? No? Can your son? Well, Semyon, here you are, read it!"

Sheepishly, syllable by syllable, the boy floundered through the printed lines under Nikita's forefinger. Nikita looked at him with eager pride.

"Tag-ly-o-ney's Grand-son. . . grey stall-ion."

"Quite right, grey stallion, that's quite right," burst in Nikita, afraid to breathe and fastening his eyes on Syomka.

"Born nine-teen . . . twenty-one."

"That's right too, the year of the famine!" cried Nikita.

"Own-er, Ni—Ni—Lou—Lou—"

"Nikita Loukitch Loukoff," prompted Loutoshkin.

Nikita bored his nose into the race-card. He wanted to see himself there with his own eyes, but Syomka edged away from him and went on boldly: "By Favourite out of Flattery. Driven by O. I. Loutoshkin, indigo jacket, white cap. . . ."

Syomka read on; Nikita wiped his streaming forehead.

"Take the card as a souvenir," said Loutoshkin. "It'll tell you all the other horses racing with your colt today. We'll have to step out, Nikita, the Grandson's in good company. We'll start for the track soon, then you'll see for yourself!"

Philipp stuck his head into the loose-box and reported: "Sinitsin's sent Mitka here again—keeps wanting to know how the colt's shaping."

"And what did you tell him?" asked Loutoshkin.

"Wha-at? 'Goes like the devil,' I told him. Because why? If I run him down, he'll smell a rat—'dark horse,' he'll say. But as it is, I'll keep him guessing!"

Nikita did not quite understand what the driver and the groom were saying, but he knew it was about his colt, and he drank in every word, watching the speakers' lips.

Loutoshkin clapped him gaily on the shoulder. "I saw to it that we should be trotting in good company. In the Grandson's race there's a mare running called Chicane. She's a holy terror—driven by my old friend

273

—we drivers do have friends, you know—Vaska Sinitsin. Now I'm going to show him a race! . . . It's a big
prize we're trotting for, Nikita!"

He fell silent. Nikita looked at him and said ar-
dently:

"Never you fear, Alim Ivanitch. Just give him his
head, and—hell for leather! But mind you don't take
the whip to him, he's touchy. At Shrovetide me and
my wife drove him to the Settlement; as we came out
on the meadow, I just flicked him with a twig—whish!
And up flew his heels—not meaning nothing. . . .
But believe me or believe me not, I thought we'd never
get home with a whole skin! It's by God's mercy I'm
here to say it! He's a whirlwind, I tell you, not a horse!"

"It'll be a hard race!" said Philipp grimly, as if answering Loutoshkin's thoughts.

AT two o'clock Philipp, Nikita, and Syomka took the
Grandson out to the Bashilovka and walked him slowly
to the race-track. On the Leningrad Road the holiday
crowds parted to give them passage, hailing Nikita's
horse with exclamations of delight. Whenever he heard
such praise, he wanted to stop and talk, to explain to all
those well-dressed Moscow strangers that the horse belonged to him, Nikita Loukoff of Shatnyevka; that he,
the owner, was taking him to the great race for the cup
—but Philipp frowned and kept shouting: "Don't

stare about you! Mind the street-cars or you'll get run over!"

Hastily Nikita would shorten the bridle and look round startled at the passing street-cars. When they came out on the track, Nikita and Syomka halted in amazement. The three-decked stand, like a huge open hive, throbbed and swarmed, ahum with a thousand voices. . . . Somewhere a bell clanged. Somewhere, out of sight, a band struck up. Over a round flat path smart horses trotted, drawing flimsy carriages. The metal spokes flashed as the wheels spun.

All this reminded Syomka of a fair, only that here he missed the merry-go-rounds. Nikita led the Grandson along the black path close behind the stands, gazing dizzily about him, and when he looked up at the teeming crowds, he held his breath—the Grandson, Syomka, and himself were in full view of all those peering faces.

At this thought Nikita puckered his brows, hunched his shoulders, tautened his muscles. Himself—Nikita Loukoff—the grey Grandson, and the lad stood for Shatnyevka; and all that bustling hive to the right of him, for Moscow.

Shatnyevka was racing, Moscow looking on.

He turned his head. A colt was stepping close behind them. Nikita whispered encouragement: "Never mind *him*, Grandson! Just you show 'em!"

Philipp nudged Nikita and pointed to a little bay

horse coming on at a smart trot, with a driver in a crimson jacket. "Chicane. . . . Trotting in your colt's race. . . . See her?"

Savagely Nikita eyed the Grandson's rival as she skimmed along the yellow track; but Syomka thought of this puny creature in the harvest-field, straining at a load of sheaves.

"Call that a horse!" he sneered.

Then he whispered to his father: "What's that red duster on the coachman's back? Did he cut it out of a flag, Papanka?"

UNLIKE the casual public in the second row, where stood the boxes, the great bulk of the spectators in the cheaper seats were regular race-goers; nearly all of them knew each other, they knew the drivers and their horses, remembered the events for dozens of years back, and chatted together in their horsy jargon, which was Greek to a newcomer, or rather a sort of thieves' Latin or conspirators' code. Indeed, besides his knowledge of horse and driver, each had his own secret code to inform him whether such and such a horse would win.

"Hey, watch his leg, that's the main thing!" they would whisper to some novice, mentioning a driver's name. "If he drops his left leg at the turn, he's tipping the wink to a friend of his to bet on him; mustn't bet themselves, you know—strictly forbidden. . . . Aha,

there's Yashka! Does all the talking with his whip!
Just you take notice—when his whip's behind him, he
won't win, but when it's up in the air, you can put your
shirt on him! . . ."

These men plunged freely, and reviled and hooted
the drivers if they lost. After a loss they would climb
down to the second row and, fixing a practised eye on
some prosperous greenhorn, stick to him like burs.
They would lead him slyly apart and whisper breath-
lessly:

"I know of a dead sure thing! Simply given away!
Safe as the bank!"

And if the victim were incredulous or doubtful, they
moved away with unfeigned sorrow on their faces, with
gait and gesture eloquent of regret. "Eykh," they
seemed to be saying, "there's the money under his nose,
and he won't take it!"

And again they would brush past him, breathing into
his ear:

"You risk nothing, man. . . . Nothing at all. He'll
walk home!"

If the horse won, they were sure of their commission;
if he lost—they vanished.

ON the lowest bench in the third row, right against
the railing, sat Aristarkh Bourmin. Never absent from
the races, he arrived punctually and always sat in the

277

same seat. The next was always occupied by a fat, clean-shaven fellow, with field-glasses round his neck. Time and again had the fat man sought to draw his neighbour into conversation, about horses, drivers, or the weather; but Aristarkh Bourmin had never deigned to bestow an answer on this garrulous stranger. Bolt upright he sat, like a wooden idol, propped on his walking-stick, and he seemed to heed and see nothing but the track itself and the horses moving up and down it. He ignored the greeting of Sossounoff, who stalked in front of the rails in his flashy beaver hat and loud check breeches, and since he knew by sight all the old horse-breeders and owners, though on speaking terms with none of them, deemed it his duty to salute them all, calling them by their Christian names and patronymics.

When Sinitsin drove out for the fifth race, on the bay mare Chicane, the fat man with the field-glasses began fidgeting and, longing to let off steam, strove to attract Bourmin's attention: "Just watch that mare's action! What splendid time she keeps! Superb! Her dam, Telyegin's Tina, never lost a race. Did the mile in two twenty—on a sticky track."

"Two eighteen it was!" a voice from above corrected him.

With astounding suppleness the fat man faced round on the speaker. "Two eighteen, eh? Well, there you are! Two eighteen, on the mud! . . . You know, when Nikolai Vasilyevitch Telyegin died, his hearse was drawn by Tina, that mare's dam."

"Such riffraff should be hounded off the course!" Bourmin hissed, addressing the earth in front of him.

"What—Chicane?" said the fat man vehemently. "Were you speaking of Chicane? Ought to be hounded off the course?"

Bourmin vouchsafed no answer. Laughter came from above him. Someone said: "Riffraff or no riffraff, all the betting's on her. The driver's sister-in-law's been backing her—to the tune of fifty rubles."

The fat man looked at the speaker, shot out of his seat, elbowed his way to the three-ruble window, fished out a crumpled note, and pushed it through. "Number one, please!"

Number one was Chicane.

Having received his ticket, he went back to his place and again plied Bourmin with praises of the mare. Bourmin was silent. He looked down at the race-track, sprinkled with yellow sand, and his lush black beard twitched ominously.

Sossounoff, lounging against the rails, turned to Bourmin and once more raised his hat.

Nikita and Syomka stood below, in the members' enclosure.

The mild sunny afternoon had drawn thousands to the hippodrome that Sunday.

Aeroplanes hummed in the cloudless blue; from the tops of the stands gay music floated; the crowd buzzed with eager chatter; in the inner circle of the hippodrome fountains played in lawns and flower-beds; the silken sheen of the drivers' jackets, the shrill strokes of the judges' bell, proclaiming that the races had begun, gave zest and sparkle to that sun-drenched festival.

Both Syomka and Nikita greedily devoured every detail of this glittering show, standing agape, like children at a toy-shop window. But when Sinitsin's crimson jacket flashed upon the course, Nikita's wandering eyes were fixed on him. His memory took stock of the round, red-jowled face and held it all his life. Of the horse too—a little bay mare, with the number 1 strapped to her saddle, she dashed past him, her ears laid back, her legs plying like a miraculous piece of clockwork. Though he had never seen a race, Nikita knew instinctively that here was his colt's rival. And every time the crimson jacket came abreast of them, his heart misgave him for the Grandson.

Loutoshkin drove out last of all. As he passed, close to the rails, he nodded gaily at Nikita. He wore a white cap and a blue silk jacket. The Grandson, gaitered in white linen, his head proudly tilted, seemed to Nikita strange and marvellous. At his saddle-strap hung a little board, with the number 6 on it.

Next to Nikita stood a man in goggles, marking his race-card as the trotters passed. Nikita plucked him by the sleeve and said, pointing at the Grandson:

"That's our colt! Mine! His name's Grandson!"

The man in the goggles looked at Nikita, then at Syomka, but said nothing.

"He's running for the cup. . . . We're from Shatnyevka," explained Nikita.

When the bell rang for the horses to line up, Loutoshkin drove back some distance and brought the Grandson forward at a sharp trot, to warm him up.

A hollow rumble issued from the stands. Overjoyed at this tribute to his nursling, Nikita swallowed his pride and tackled the man in the goggles once again: "That's our colt—mine! . . . I'm Nikita Loukoff from Shatnyevka!"

Just then the strokes of a bell shrilled out above them. A man with a red flag, hoisted beside the track on a wooden stand, like a speaker on a platform, shouldered his flag and bellowed:

"Ta-ake your pla-a-ces!"

The six horses, as if drilled to this manœuvre, broke into groups of three and trotted past Nikita at a lively pace, on the right and left of the track respectively. First of all came the Grandson, in the farther group. Loutoshkin's face was grimly set and—it seemed to Nikita—angry. When they reached the spot where a man stood with a paper in his hands, all six horses turned and dashed forward, Loutoshkin driving nearest to the rails, an arm's length from the crowd.

As he drew level with the platform where the man with the red flag was standing, the Grandson broke into a gallop. Promptly the bell clanged overhead, and again the six horses, in the same order as at first, swung past Nikita.

"Tur-urn!" boomed the man with the flag.

And again the Grandson, and he only, started to gallop. Again the bell rang out. The crowd murmured. Nikita saw Loutoshkin's lips move as he passed the man with the flag; the man gave no answer, but shouted up in the direction whence the bell had sounded:

"Number six, ba-ack! Ba-ack, six!"

After the Grandson other horses began to gallop before they reached the start. The crowd grew restive. A man hissed furiously. From the top seats came catcalls. For the fifth time the bell clanged.

Nikita noticed that the bay mare had not once broken her trot, and that each time the horses turned, she darted ahead of her companions. Syomka tugged at his father's coat-tail.

"Papanka, why do they keep whirling round? That's the sixth time they've done it!"

"Shut up! They know what they're about, stupid. Keep quiet!" said Nikita in a whisper, himself hopelessly at sea.

"Why don't they let 'em race?" muttered Syomka. "They ain't dancing a quadrille!"

"Tur-urn! . . . Steady, the field! Loutoshkin, steady—back!" thundered the man with the flag; the next moment he jerked it downwards and barked:

"Off!"

The bell clanged from above. Sinitsin's crimson jacket flashed to the front. The Grandson, outstripping the rest, promptly swallowed up the space between him and the mare Chicane, but, to Nikita's horror, lunged suddenly and galloped. Nikita caught sight of Loutoshkin's face—the mouth twisted, the bulging eyes fixed on the crimson jacket forging ahead close to the rails—noticed the convulsive jerk he gave the reins, and his back bent like a taut spring.

The Grandson checked himself, tossed up his head, and plunged.

Sinitsin's backers cheered and yelped: "He's well away!"

"That was a fine trick he showed Loutoshkin!"

"It's all over but the shouting now!"

"What can he do against that mare? Two fifteen!— he can't beat that!"

The fat man with the field-glasses, who had watched the start with unwonted agitation, turned in triumph to Bourmin. "Well, what do you say now? Hounded off the course, eh? Do you know what a pace that mare's trotting at? Hee-hee-hee! Just like her dam, Tina! No wonder they let her draw Telyegin's hearse!"

He took out the ticket with the number 1, flicked it up with his thumb, and added: "It's a dead sure thing, safe as the bank!"

Loutoshkin was quite unprepared for the Grandson's

break. When the colt galloped, the thought that he must lose the race unnerved him. In a flash he saw Nikita's face—and Syomka's. . . . He remembered Saphir, somewhere in that crowd. . . . Its uproar overwhelmed his reason.

"I'm beat!" he thought. "I'll never catch him!"

But the languid fit, the wave of despair, passed swiftly, and a moment later Loutoshkin mustered his faculties and launched his will like a stream of fire through the steel bit into the colt's body.

The Grandson shook his head, as if to free himself from the steel that fretted him, but the bit was speaking to him now, commanding him to throw his near foot forward. For a moment he jibbed, and shifted his feet awkwardly; then, striking his proper trot, he strung himself out in fierce pursuit of the horses far in front of him.

The stop-watch in the driver's left ticked out the seconds lost. Loutoshkin reckoned his own speed, appraised the powers of his opponents, and the distance between him and each of them. Swiftly the Grandson closed on them, rounded the bend on the inner side; and as he came into the straight, Loutoshkin swung him out boldly from the rails. It was touch and go.

THE Grandson's break had thrown out Loutoshkin's calculations. He must be careful how he urged him, or he would break again. But the Grandson responded so promptly and streaked forward so effortlessly that Loutoshkin was possessed with a sudden confidence, a triumphant ecstasy: that ecstasy which transmutes cool craftsmanship into creative force—when horse and driver mingle their essence, when the impossible is assured and they know only themselves and their exultant purpose. For a moment, ever memorable to Loutoshkin, time stood still. The path before him was illumined, the holiday brightness of the crowds enhanced —all was transfigured by the magic hue of passion; his heart leaped with the joy of battle, his eyes shone with the light of victory.

Cries burst from the rapt spectators: "Look, look! Loutoshkin's off! What a lick he's going at!"

Dozens of hostile voices answered: "Chicane's got the heels of him, all right!"

"Lost more than three seconds when he broke! Won't make that up in a hurry!"

"That break's settled his hash!"

"He can't possibly win against that mare," affirmed the experts. "Sinitsin's going easily, he's got the race in his pocket."

When Nikita saw that the Grandson had recovered and was catching up with the other horses, he plucked Syomka by the tail of his long shirt and panted: "Say your 'Angels and archangels,' for Grandson to get the cup! Say it, boy!"

"I don't know it!"

"Say it, you little stinkard! Now then, out with it!"

Nikita himself did not know the prayer, except for the first two words, which he kept whispering fervently, never taking his eyes off the horses, which had now turned into the straight.

In front came the little mare, a few lengths from the rest. But suddenly the field seemed spellbound. From the side it looked as if they had all stopped and only the grey colt were moving. The crimson jacket floated back, Loutoshkin's indigo pressed on, drew level, vanished behind it, and crept slowly to the front; farther he came, and faster, hugging the rails now. Chicane dropped back, yielding position and pre-eminence to the Grandson. Sinitsin's whip was going like a flail.

Nikita and Syomka climbed the barrier and, squatting down, slapping their ribs and thighs, cried to each other and the world at large: "See there! . . . See there! . . . Our colt's winning! Yes, it's our colt, the Grandson! . . . See how he's coming on!"

Higher and higher surged the tumult. The public swarmed on the benches, the railings of the boxes, the balustrades flanking the steps. Loutoshkin forged relentlessly ahead. The gap between the Grandson and Chicane rapidly lengthened. The Grandson was now near the post, but Loutoshkin still kept urging him.

"What's the man doing? He's won already!" shouted an onlooker.

"Must have gone crazy!" said another.

Nikita looked round at the great, bawling face of Moscow and in a frenzy of local patriotism tore off his cap, whirled it round his head, and smacked it on his knee. "Go it, Grandson! . . . Eykh, you're a beauty! . . . That's our Shatnyevka breed! Go it!"

"Is he trying to leave 'em all behind the flag?" said voices.

"Yes, and he'll do it!" others answered.

Aristarkh Bourmin turned to the fat man. "Where's your Chicane now?" he rasped.

"Well, what do you expect?" exploded the fat man. "Plain as a pike-staff! Loutoshkin was always a trickster; he's had this dark horse up his sleeve; backed him himself, of course, and . . ."

"Not a dark horse, my dear sir, an *Orloff!*" said Bourmin haughtily.

"Taglioni's Grandson an Orloff!" sneered the fat man. "How do you make that out? Grandsire three-quarters American—sired by Heubingen—granddam a cross-breed—sired by Baron Rogers—and you say his grandson's an Orloff!"

With that he pressed his bulk half over the barrier and howled at the oncoming Loutoshkin: "Swin-dler! Thief! Scoun-drel!"

And again he turned spitefully to Bourmin, whose face paled as he watched the colt, now nearly abreast of them: "May I point out once more that that colt owes his speed to the American Taglioni!"

"To his Orloff blood, you mean. . . . A fig for your Taglioni!" Bourmin shouted in the fat man's face. He rose, majestically erect. "His dam, the grey Flattery, was in my stable. In those days I owned her."

"Vanished like a dream, those days, Aristarkh Serg-yeevitch!" the fat man sighed, addressing Bourmin by name for the first time. He crushed his useless ticket in his palm. "You might care to know that I, too, owned a stud-farm once; it vanished."

Bourmin had not listened. He was already stalking out towards the gate, with upflung head and black beard bristling disdain.

As he came to the finish straight, Loutoshkin raised his whip. At its touch the Grandson shot forward like a bolt from a catapult, finishing in record time. The stands rocked and roared with jubilation. As the colt slowed up, the public saw two uncouth figures make a dash at him.

Having weighed in, Loutoshkin stepped down from the sulky and approached Nikita.

Never had he seen such joy on the face of man. And the knowledge that he, Loutoshkin, was the author of this joy in a humble peasant's heart rejoiced his own; the eternal, close-fenced circle of the hippodrome snapped—and a bright path streamed from it, far off, to the simple hearts, the smiling plains of human happiness. . . .

"Thank you, Nikita Loukitch, for the Grandson, and —for everything! Thank you!" he said as he embraced the peasant.

"Who am I? I'm nothing, Alim Ivanitch! . . . I did the best I could for him. I'll always owe you thanks —but what have I done? Who am I?"

Nikita turned his moist eyes on the Grandson, speechless, his heart bursting. Syomka nestled against the damp glistening colt and clung to his friend jealously.

From behind the rails of the members' enclosure a tall figure emerged and strode towards Nikita. "Well met, Loukoff! Congratulations!"

The amazed Nikita looked up and, recognizing Nikolai Petrovitch Goubaryeff, People's Commissary for Agriculture, who had once visited him at Shatnyevka, gripped the extended hand in a transport of unspoken gratitude.

"Congratulations to you too, Comrade Loutoshkin, congratulations!" said Goubaryeff. "Magnificent race! Well done, Loukoff! Come to the members' enclosure, Comrade Loukoff, and we'll talk. . . ."

CHAPTER · VII

Nine years had passed since the owner of the grey mare Flattery, Aristarkh Sergyeevitch Bourmin, had given sudden orders for the mare, already entered for the races, to be dispatched to his stud-farm; but Philipp remembered the occasion as if all this had happened yesterday. . . .

One Friday, it was. . . . When he went to see Bourmin at his hotel, Loutoshkin had promised to be back for the evening grooming. But Philipp had waited in vain. They began their work, and finished it, without Loutoshkin. Flattery waited too, in high fettle, sleek and happy. As usual at feeding-time, she waited, never hindering Philipp, like the other horses, but watching from her loose-box meekly, her eyes glistening, her ears twitching comically. When the feed had been served out, Philipp stood for a long while at the barred door of Flattery's box, listening as she crunched the crisp oats, flavoured with raw eggs. Then he would sit on the settle by the door with the stable-lads Vaska and Pavel. They talked always of the mare's prospects. Philipp knew all about the field; he feared none of

Flattery's rivals—"She'll have 'em pumped at the first quarter, sure as my name's Philipp Akimitch. . . ."

Darkness drew on, lamps burned in the Bashilovka; Loutoshkin did not come. Philipp looked in at Mitritch's; his master was not there. Philipp made up his bed in the stable, sure that Loutoshkin would return for early grooming. But he did not come. Philipp grew anxious. Loutoshkin's wife knew nothing. Philipp doubled back from her house to Mitritch's, thence to the Yar restaurant, and thence again to the famous Cross-roads Tavern. Nowhere had they seen him. Philipp took the bold step of ringing up Saphir. For a long time there came no answer, but over the wire he heard strange voices, the twang of a guitar, and laughter. He asked for Alim Ivanitch—'Philipp wants to speak to him on urgent business'; a woman's voice muttered inaudibly; a man's followed it, protesting that Loutoshkin had not been there that evening.

A second night Philipp spent in the stable. Every half-hour he woke up, hoping that Loutoshkin would arrive; for however late he came in, he always looked in at the stable before bed.

So the second night passed. The horses were groomed and fed. Pavel, who had gone out to draw water, was the first to see Loutoshkin.

"He's coming!" he bawled huskily.

Loutoshkin walked unsteadily. Pale, swollen-eyed, his back bowed like an old man's, heedless of their

greetings, he passed on to Flattery's box. At the threshold he staggered and, leaning against the partition,
eyed the mare as she stood feeding. His lips quivered,
hectic and inflamed. He looked like a madman. He
reeled back from the mare and rasped hoarsely: "Get
her ready to travel. . . . No racing for her!"

He ground his teeth awesomely. And then . . .

At the memory of what happened afterwards, Philipp
shivered and drew his hands into his greasy sleeves.

From that day forth he nursed a ferocious hatred
against Aristarkh Bourmin, and when he met him at
Mitritch's, made no secret of his joy at the great nobleman's ruin; if he blessed the Revolution, it was solely
because it had pitched that millionaire into such filth
and poverty as the lowest of the stable-lads had never
known.

But one thing mystified Philipp. While most of the
other owners, tossed on the scrap-heap, like Bourmin,
by the Revolution, greeted and shook hands with him,
groom as he was, and even sometimes made up to him,
begging him for a stable tip, Bourmin never so much as
nodded, or stepped aside to let him pass. He would
fling up his black beard and hold his course, as if Philipp
were so much air. . . .

ON the evening of the race, after grooming, Philipp
took a last look at the Grandson, who was munching

his oats peacefully. As Philipp came out into the passage, he uttered an astonished cry.

Straight at him along the dimly lighted passage marched the tall upright shape of Aristarkh Bourmin, cased in its blue cloak and belt of silver. With his black beard in the air he marched, as proudly as nine years ago. Philipp strode firmly on to meet him and, casting about for some weapon, snatched from the wall a stout piece of rubber tire with an iron bar thrust into it. One of its blows would quiet the most fractious horse.

Silently Bourmin approached. Philipp saw the small ferret-eyes, glinting like sparks as they searched the passage, and stopped his path, straddling across it, his body thrown back slightly, his right hand grasping the rubber truncheon. Bourmin came face to face with him and, still glaring over Philipp's head, asked in a curt, petulant voice: "Where's my colt?"

Torrents of laughter spouted from Philipp. He bent double, whooped with delight, till the tears came and he was almost choking; not a word could he find in answer to this side-splitting inquiry. Like a strangled snake, the tire dropped from his hand. But when he raised his head, he saw a square black beard looming above him, and under it, from throat to belt, a row of silver buttons on a nobleman's blue cloak. And there, stuck through the belt, was a hand with a broad gold signet-ring on the forefinger; that same hand which

293

nine years since had taken the lump of sugar from Philipp's open palm so squeamishly and offered it to the grey mare.

A foolish, fantastic thought unmanned Philipp; the thought that behind the stable walls, while he was busy with the currycomb, in the streets, the hippodrome, and all Moscow, *the day had come*, that day so often talked of over the tea at Mitritch's—which made Kortsoff gloat so bloodily, and Mikhal Mikhalitch Grouzdyeff sigh so deeply—*the old life had come back*. . . .

"Where's my colt?" the testy voice rasped over Philipp, and, getting no answer, shouted in his face:

"Out of my path, you lout!"

Philipp cowered against the wall. Bourmin's back, straight as a board, advanced along the passage to the box of Flattery's son.

From the stable-yard, by the gate, came muffled voices. The gate half-opened, a head in a grey hat peeped in, then two heads more: a leathery head, Kortsoff's; a giggling, slavering head, Koultyapy's.

"Olimp Ivanitch not here?" asked Sossounoff jauntily as he lounged into the stable.

Philipp looked at him, then at Kortsoff and at Koultyapy, and, making no answer, hurried into the Grandson's box, before which the tall figure of Aristarkh Sergyeevitch Bourmin stood haughtily. Before entering the box, Philipp took down the bridle from the wall and said in a strangled voice: "One moment, sir!"

Sossounoff stepped up to Bourmin and said as he swept off his grey hat: "Good evening, Aristarkh Sergyeevitch!"

Bourmin nodded.

It was long before Nikita, Syomka, and Loutoshkin, who arrived soon afterwards, could understand what now passed before their eyes.

In the middle of the passage stood the Grandson, with his best bridle on him. By his side, stiff as a ramrod, Philipp waited, cap in hand; before him towered the arrogant Bourmin, flanked by the plausible Sossounoff fussily probing the colt's legs, the sly Kortsoff, and, leering slimily under his hay-coloured moustache, Koultyapy.

As soon as he made out the familiar, never-to-be-forgotten faces of Kortsoff, Sossounoff, Koultyapy, the warning of the old farrier flashed upon Nikita. For a moment his heart sank, as he rushed forward to seize the Grandson. Then he looked round at Goubaryeff, close behind him, checked himself, and felt in the right pocket of his coat. There was his paper, signed and sealed; no one could meddle with the Grandson now.

Loutoshkin smiled. Goubaryeff smiled too, as he looked in Bourmin's face.

"Good evening, Aristarkh Sergyeevitch!" Loutoshkin said, leading Nikita forward. "Allow me to introduce you: Nikita Loukitch Loukoff, owner of Taglioni's Grandson, son of Flattery."

A NOTE ON THE TYPE IN WHICH
THIS BOOK IS SET

This book is set in Electra, a Linotype face designed by W. A. Dwiggins. This face cannot be classified readily as either "modern" or "old-style." It is not based on any historical model, nor does it echo any particular period or style. It avoids the extreme contrast between "thick" and "thin" elements that mark most "modern" faces, and attempts to give a feeling of fluidity, power, and speed. The book was composed, printed, and bound by H. Wolff, New York. The paper was manufactured by S. D. Warren Co., Boston.